Tales from the Clergy

Stories inspired by Ghost

A Nameless Editor

October Nights Press
Baton Rouge, LA
www.splattertheatre.com

Tales from the Clergy
Copyright © 2023 October Nights Press
Individual stories copyright by their author

All Rights Reserved

ISBN: 9798392018949

The story included in this publication is a work of fiction. Names, characters, places and incidents are products of the authors' imaginations or are used fictitiously. Any resemblance to actual events or locales or persons living or dead is entirely coincidental.

Without limiting the rights under copyright reserved above, no part of this publication may be reproduced, stored in or introduced into a retrieval system, or transmitted, in any form, or by any means (electronic, mechanical, photocopying, recording, or otherwise), without the prior written permission of both the copyright owner and the above publisher of this book.

Cover by Don Noble

Interior Layout by Lori Michelle
www.TheAuthorsAlley.com

Table of Contents

Introduction i
  Ash Briscoe aka "Fauxbias Forge"

To Dust You Shall Return 1
  Jo Kaplan (Mummy Dust)

The Lords Below 13
  Michael Paige (Rats)

Father Knows Best 21
  M. Wesley Corie II (Body and Blood)

The House of Laments 31
  Pedro Iniguez (Life Eternal)

A Pale Stranger 41
  Mackenzie Hurlbert (Witch Image)

A Sun Within the Fog 48
  Colt Skinner (Elizabeth)

On Hollow Pass 58
  Michael Balletti (Absolution)

Ghosted 68
  Everett Baudean (Dance Macabre)

Commendation of the Dying 81
  Lauren Bolger (Deus in Absentia)

Hallowed Ground 89
  David D. West (Death Knell)

Hello Darkness 99
  Brian J. Smith (Spillways)

Wrapped 107
  Robert Bagnall (Darkness at the Heart of my Love)

Her True Calling 115
    Doris V. Sutherland (Call Me Little Sunshine)

Peering Through the Blazing Gates 123
    David Costa (Depth of Satan's Eyes)

The Goat Priest 136
    Matthew Bartlett (He Is)

Figgy Pudding..148
    Vivian Kasley (Con Clavi Con Dio)

Creation 155
    Benjamin Kane Ethridge (Genesis)

Introduction

ASH BRISCOE AKA FAUXBIAS FORGE

My brother, Justin, handed me a burned CD and said, "You'll like this band. They sound like a Satanic Blue Oyster Cult."

The year was 2011, and the album was Ghost's *Opus Eponymous*. The first time I listened to the CD was on my car stereo—it wasn't exactly Hi-Def audio.

Still, I'll never forget the feeling as I heard the album intro *Deus Culpa*, which sent me into a wave of emotion, only to have my face melted off by the next track *Con Clavi Con Dio*. I then wondered, *WHO the hell are these guys?* as *Ritual* blasted on my car speakers, followed by what would become my favorite track from the album, *Elizabeth*.

Queue the relentless Google searches to find out more information about Ghost. To say that I was delightfully astonished by their mysteriously grotesque, evil imagery would be an understatement.

Since 2011, I've been witness to Ghost being a mere whisper within the underground metal community to winning a Grammy, numerous worldwide awards, a plethora of nominations, late-night TV show appearances, and going viral on TikTok. Ghost reaches into the souls of the masses with their delicately woven, playfully satanic lyrics, bombastic hooks, and dark look.

Over the years they've developed a storyline, otherwise known as "Lore," starring Papa Emeritus, Sister Imperator, Papa Nihil, Mr. Saltarian, Ghouls, and now Father Jim DeFroque. With their incredibly immersive lore, cosplayers, writers, makeup artists, photographers and the like have all found great inspiration in this band.

My interest in cosplay was ignited when I saw Tobias Forge (mastermind and frontman for Ghost) do his first unmasked USA interview. He appeared at his interview in what I can only describe as a Cardinal Copia meets Elton John costume. I lost my mind. I had to recreate this look.

Ash Briscoe

Fast forward to when I met Cardinal Copia and I was dressed like Tobias Forge from that iconic interview. He was complimentary; noticeably smiling behind his mask. As I walked away, he said, "You look great!"

With that encouragement I continued my desire to recreate. Since then, I've worked with various actors, models, and makeup artists to replicate what Ghost has already presented to the fans. I've also created numerous Ghost cosplays and become a bit of a Papa mask collector because of it.

I've always admired other cosplayers and writers within our fandom because they can take the existing lore and expand it into a never-ending universe of beautiful tales.

With this I introduce to you a wonderful collection of mastermind writers who've been inspired by Ghost's wicked lyrics and stylistic storyline!

To Dust You Shall Return

JO KAPLAN

Inspired by "Mummy Dust"

The big tent went up without so much as a howdy-do. Other traveling preachers had come before this one, but it still sent a buzz through town when they saw the yellowed canvas stretching over its frame like skin on bone. Famished, like the lot of them in this plot of Depression-gripped Indiana.

"You seen it yet?" said Jessie Farr as she walked with Henrietta Eastley, recently sixteen, in the falling light. Tongues of fire reached from the sun to the fields.

"What do I need to see it for? Another preacher? They're all the same."

"I heard this one's handsome." Jessie plucked a blade of grass and chewed it. "What d'you think the handsome ones go and pledge themselves to God for, anyhow? Does the Lord make 'em handsome on purpose, to test us?"

"I couldn't begin to imagine what the Lord has in mind about anything."

"Come with me, tonight?" Jessie tickled Henrietta with the grass, grabbed her when she tried to dodge, and they tumbled laughing through the dirt. After they parted, Etta fussed over the smears on her dress, knowing what her father would say about cleanliness and godliness. Her insides clenched as she went in. His ragged coughs clawed the bedroom door.

Over supper, her mother told her she ought to go to the revival. Her father, face like whey, spooned stew between hacking coughs. "Girl needs a chaperone."

"I'm going with Jessie." A burst of inspiration. "And her daddy."

Rheumy eyes latched onto her. "Got dirt on your dress."

"It's dirty out there."

"Don't you backtalk me." He raised his fist but fell into a fit of coughing instead. When it subsided, he said, "Go put on something decent."

Etta's cheeks reddened. As if they had anything decent. All her dresses were patched and worn ragged. She'd had to get rid of her favorite almost a year ago, when the bloodstains hadn't come out.

Before she left, her mother pulled her aside, spoke in low tones. She pressed a nickel into her hand. "You talk to that preacher, now. See if he might heal your father."

Etta met up with Jessie at the end of the road. They walked to the tent, lit up kerosene-gold in the falling dark. Outside the entrance stood a sign: *Holy Ghost Revival*. Inside, seats had already filled. Warmth bubbled from the lamps. Etta and Jessie found two seats near the back. Another sign announced the name *William Bolton!*

The chatter died when a tall, slim man in black stepped onto the stage, bloodless and fine-boned, eyes like dusty gems. "Brothers and sisters!"

Jessie leaned over. "He ain't that handsome."

Etta had been about to agree but stopped herself. There *was* something peculiarly charismatic about the man. She supposed that was the way of traveling preachers. To put it plain, no one would listen to a mouse; but say your piece loud and strong, and see if you don't find yourself with a few devotees. They didn't care what he said so much as *how* he said it.

Of course, Etta didn't think she was the best judge of handsomeness. She didn't favor the looks of men any more than those of women. She'd prayed on it, but was met only with silence.

"I have a story to tell. A miraculous story," William Bolton said. "I grew up in a town much like this one. A town covered in dust and disease. And the sky was all clouded over, everything gone brown and gray. I prayed to God every day for an end to the dust. And then—one day! Ash Wednesday! A mighty ray of sunshine broke the clouds and lit upon an old church which had fallen into disrepair. Brothers and sisters, I was *compelled* to that church, abandoned though it was; and when I stepped inside—*I beheld the Lord in all His glory.*"

He reveled in the way his words rang, the hush over the crowd. The nickel grew warm in Etta's palm.

"He stood there before me, radiant and shining, and He spoke unto me this commandment: 'My body and blood are yours; use them to be nourished and saved. My ashes and bones are yours; use them to heal

To Dust You Shall Return

thyself, and be well.' And a great flame came down from the Heavens, and set Him alight; and He stood like a beacon and burned without pain; and at last, when the flames had consumed Him, what was left behind were the very ashes He had commanded me to heal His children with."

The preacher held up a small pine box. "These are those very ashes. They will take away your pain and bring you peace, comfort, *prosperity*. Now, I know what you're thinking." He opened the box and held it so those in the first rows could see its contents. They craned their necks until he pulled it back and snapped the lid shut. "But let me ask you: have you ever heard of the Holy Communion?" When he was met with only a few nods, he raised his voice: "I *said*, have you ever *heard* of the *Holy Communion*?" The crowd nodded fervently, shouted *oh yes!* And now, caught up in the rapture of it all: "The Lord offers Himself to us, Hallelujah! The Lord has shown us the resurrection of the body, Hallelujah! He was placed in a tomb, but behold, on the third day that body was gone, and He was risen from the dead! And the Lord offers us His flesh for Holy Communion, but the Lord's body is more than merely flesh, my brothers and sisters!"

Shouts of joy swept the tent like a swell of wind in tall grass. An old woman Etta recognized as Mrs. Flint stood, leaning heavily on her cane, her left foot skewed at an angle. The preacher opened his box and took a handful of ash, which rained through his fingers; he held it in his fist and blew; a cloud of glittering dust enveloped Mrs. Flint, who breathed deeply, taking all of that Jesus dust into her lungs.

Astonishment washed over her face as she made a step without the cane. Her twisted foot came down smoothly, and she glided, almost like she walked upon a cloud.

The crowd rose with a cry.

All Etta could see now were backs. Jessie craned her neck. Hands went into the air, begging *please, heal my mother, my sister, my son*. The preacher reminded them of his finite supply. "There is only enough for the *truly* worthy. Those who live their lives in the glory of God's grace."

"He means those who live with God in their pockets," Etta muttered.

Sure enough, the collection started. Piles of money. More than Etta had ever seen at one time. More than this dirt-poor town should have been able to scrape together. She wondered who among this desperate lot would go hungry for the next week thanks to a moment of reckless hope. Would go barefoot. Would have their children chewing grass and potato peelings. When it came to them, she kept her nickel and passed the collection on.

"He has shown us the way. 'The Lord God formed man of dust from the ground and breathed into his nostrils the breath of life, and the man became a living being.' All you must do," said the preacher as a musician whose hands were gnarled with arthritis came forth, "is pledge yourself to

Him, the Bright Star, and accept Him as your Lord and Savior." He blew the cloud. "Remember that you are dust, and to dust you shall return."

Someone produced a banjo and passed it to the musician, who began to play.

"How does he do it?" Etta asked, looking around at Jessie. "What's the trick?"

"Maybe it really is the ashes of Christ!" Jessie shouted, clapping along with the music as a parade of dancing took up.

"Be sensible," said Etta. "Jesus wasn't cremated."

"I do believe Mr. Bolton has restored my faith. You think he'll talk to me?"

More donations flowed in. Hunger beat its wings in Etta's gut. "Let's find out."

The preacher closed his little box and backed away from the milling crowd to make his exit. Etta saw the flap at the back of the tent, grabbed Jessie, and pulled her to the entrance. They hurried around the side of the tent, the air biting cold and dark, until they saw the tall figure making for an aluminum Airstream trailer parked on the rutted dirt.

"Mr. Bolton!" Etta called. He turned, pale in the moonlight. "Please—"

"I'm sorry girls, but I'm finished for this evening. You might come back tomorrow and see if the Lord hears your cause."

"We just wanted to meet you," Jessie said breathlessly, color high in her cheeks. "Praise Jesus! If you want anyone to show you about town, I thought I'd let you know . . . I am available."

"How kind of you. Now, if you'll excuse me—"

"How'd you do it?"

He paused, turned back to Etta. "What was that?"

Jessie elbowed her, muttered not to be rude, but Etta ignored her. "You heard me. How'd you do it? If you expect me to believe you've really got the ashes of Christ in that box, you must think I'm as dumb as bread." She pulled away from Jessie. "Don't worry, I won't tell. There's plenty of folks around here who *are* dumb as bread."

"*Etta!*"

The preacher's eyes glimmered queerly. "Goodnight, ladies."

After he'd disappeared into his trailer, Etta and Jessie started their walk home. Shadows rippled and slithered from the tent's light behind them. "You didn't ask him to heal your pa," Jessie said as they came to the fork that would have them part ways. "What'll you say to your mama?"

Etta shook her head. The nickel was burning a hole in her pocket. "Maybe he doesn't deserve to be healed."

She watched Jessie retreat, hesitated—could almost hear that terrible coughing in the distance—then turned back the way they'd come. She

To Dust You Shall Return

knocked on the door of the trailer. After a moment, the preacher answered. "Where's your friend?"

"She went home." Etta chewed at her lip. "Look, I know you gotta keep up appearances and all, but I'm not here to sell you out. I just want to know how you do it."

"How I heal folks?"

"How you convince folks to give you their dough. If I could do that, I'd . . ." She turned toward the horizon, invisible in the darkness. "I'd get out of this place."

The preacher stepped aside to let her enter. A single lantern lit the trailer's sparse interior: a table with the pine box and an old book beside a basket of bills and coins, a trunk and a washbasin at the end of the narrow room.

He turned on her, looming. "What makes you think I'll tell you my secrets?"

"I could apprentice with you. Help out. Learn the trade."

"There's no *trade*, girl!" he hissed. She heard a thump from the back of the trailer which made her flinch. "What's your name?"

"Henrietta Eastley. Etta."

His lips twisted. "You ever heard of mummia, Etta?" She shook her head. "Mummies, my dear. Ground into a medicinal powder."

"Mummies? Like . . . dead folks from Egypt?"

Another thump. Etta flinched again, looking around for the source of the noise. It was only the two of them in the trailer. Her skin crawled.

"Yes. They mummified their dead, through embalming. Mummies can also be created naturally, through a process of desiccation. Mummia has been used as a medicine since ancient times. But the truth, Etta, is that nobody wants to consume powdered human remains. No, now they want God. So that's what I give them."

"And it works?"

A grin curled over his face. He nodded to the book on the table, and she discovered a thick tome with yellowing pages. The writing was in another language, but there were diagrams: a head opened with the brain showing, a long stick meeting it through the nostril; a body with jars around it. She reached forward, her fingertips brushing the old paper, but the preacher grabbed her by the wrist. The strength of his grip sent a flurry of panic through her. She looked up and for a moment saw an entirely difference face: leathery, bearded, one eye squinted, ready to bring a fist down on her ear until she was too dizzy to stand. She cringed away from him, prepared to fall, to kneel, the way *he* had always made her do. "On your knees, girl," he'd command, "and stay there until I say so." And then he would leave her there, for hours at a time, until her knees were bruised, until she could hardly stand without falling. Until she begged him for mercy. Until she wanted to die.

The preacher let her go. "Be careful with the book. It's delicate."

Etta returned to herself, embarrassed he could still do that to her, even though he'd been sick for so many months—too sick, these days, to hurt her. "My mama told me to ask you to heal my father. He's got the dust pneumonia."

"And would you like me to?"

When she opened her mouth, she wasn't sure what would come out. The words seemed to spill free of their own volition: "I wish he was dead."

"Hmm," said the preacher. "Perhaps I could teach you how to do it. Make your own mummia. Would you be interested?"

Her heart leapt. Etta nodded.

"We could even travel together. Folks would like that, wouldn't they? Billy Bolton and Etta Eastley. Oh, it has a ring to it, doesn't it?"

The thump came again. Etta almost thought it was a blow, that she'd been hit—then she realized it was coming from the trunk. "What's in there?"

Mr. Bolton's mouth twitched. "Would you like to see?"

Etta nodded. They approached the trunk, which was fastened shut with a lock. Mr. Bolton pulled a key from its hook on the wall and fitted it in. Etta's heart went into her throat; she had the sudden premonition that whatever was in that trunk, she did not want to see it.

The lid eased open with a creak. Despite herself, she peered inside.

At first, she hardly knew what she was looking at. Then the desiccated figure resolved in the low light, a shriveled sketch of a man, face a grinning skull. The stench made her sway, clamp a hand over her face. Just as she was able to wrap her mind around the fact Mr. Bolton was keeping a corpse in his trunk, the figure twitched, an emaciated arm flailed upward to knock at the lid that wasn't there, the jaw moved in silent agony. Etta reeled back.

"It's best to start the process when they're still alive. Makes the powder more potent." Mr. Bolton slammed the lid shut and turned the lock, pocketed the key.

Etta felt her gorge rise. She backed away from him.

"You'll want to begin the mummification slowly," said Mr. Bolton. "The process can take months to properly achieve. Then, you can grind him into powder—bit by bit." A grin crept over his face.

"You mean my daddy?"

Mr. Bolton nodded, and she saw it in her mind's eye: her father, enfeebled, curled up in the trunk, his flesh shriveling against his bones, his eyes filled with terror, with the realization that he, too, could be hurt, could be made to feel powerless, could be made to feel *wrong*—could clasp his

To Dust You Shall Return

hands together and pray and pray, those prayers unheeded, as Etta's always had been, for it wasn't *really* that benevolent idea of God he believed in, but the power. She imagined him looking up at her from out of that trunk with the full realization of what she had done to him, that *she* could have the power of God on her side, that *she* could deliver the pain of repentance unto *him*. The thought, so delicious, filled her with a swell of desire.

Religion had never done nothing for her. All it'd ever done was hurt.

"Show me."

Perhaps, by now, her mother had begun to fret. To wonder what evil had befallen poor Etta, why she had never come home. Perhaps Jessie was wringing her hands, sure, absolutely *sure*, she had left Etta not far from home when they'd walked back together. Perhaps her father was red with righteous anger, choking on the grit in his lungs.

None of it mattered anymore.

Etta read William's translations from the book, studied the diagrams, learned the process of mummification. Sun baked the trailer during the day. She wiped at her forehead, tried to ignore the feeble thumps from the trunk as the man inside slowly died. Tried to ignore the guilt clawing at the boundaries of her heart.

In the evening, William held his revivals, leaving her with a single kerosene lantern. Perhaps her folks had come calling, but he never said, and she never asked. Jessie's silly little crushes seemed so distant, now. School, all of it—what did it matter? When she was done with her studies here, she would command attention wherever she went. She would accumulate wealth like the southern warmth draws in the birds each winter.

She would never have to endure another hour upon her aching knees again, or a lash to the back.

"*Etta . . .*"

His voice seemed to whisper, sometimes, from the trunk. Even though she knew it wasn't him. It was some stranger William had found, nobody.

Yet sometimes she sat down, pressed her ear against the wood, and listened to her daddy talking to her, impossibly, from inside the trunk. No matter what she did, she could not escape him.

"*Don't you recognize when I'm trying to help you?*" It was something he'd said to her as he'd taken the switch to her back. And she could only wonder how the pain was to help her, how the nightmares that woke her in a sweat, how the blood she wrung out in the wash, how the God who wanted her on her knees, weeping, was to help her.

"*You think you can kill your own pa? You're more like me than you thought, girl.*" And he'd laugh, that rough, scraping sound, *ah-ah-ah*.

She pulled back, trying to squeeze the words from her brain. "I'm nothing like you." But something inside of her ached, knew the lie. She wanted to feel powerful, didn't she? Wanted people to kneel before her. That's what it really was, in the end: not money, but power. The kind of power Billy Bolton commanded in his tent.

One day, she asked: "Where'd you come up with that story about the abandoned church?"

William smiled. "What makes you think it's just a story?"

Etta didn't know what to think anymore—whatever he'd seen in that church, if he did after all, could it be the same Jesus she'd been taught to love? She could still hear, ringing in her ears, her daddy's voice: "You've sinned against Jesus! Repent!" while her back ripped open.

And that laugh, half a cough, haunting her from inside the trunk: *ah-ah-ah*.

She tried not to hear it, but it only grew louder the deeper she went in her studies, as if it knew what she wanted to do to him. That sadistic glee.

Ah-ah-ah.

After a fortnight, Etta had read the whole book, or at least William's translations. She closed it carefully, the binding creaking. The trunk was a solid, heavy presence in the lanternlight, filled with unnamable darkness, with death.

Then, as if it sensed her looking, it spoke:

"*You want to come inside here with me?*"

It wasn't quite her daddy's voice, not anymore, but rather like someone trying to imitate him. A good imitation, but unnatural. Something underneath the voice that wasn't actually a voice at all. She crept closer, heart reeling. Pressed her ear against the wood.

"*Open it up. You know you want to see.*"

Etta shivered, tried to remind herself there was nothing in that trunk but the dead man. The man whose death was slow and dark and endless.

"*Come on, Etta. Open it. Behold me in all my glory.*"

She felt *compelled*. Like William at the church. So she got the key and opened the trunk.

Below lay a vast cavern, a great black hole that might swallow her if

To Dust You Shall Return

she slipped over the edge. An awful, hypnotic nothing. But far in the distance was a light like a star, and it grew by degrees until it became a figure rising out of the darkness—a flaming figure, its face a burned-out hollow that seemed to tunnel into endless darkness—and its voice, no longer imitating her father, was deep enough to shake the earth.

"*Sicut erat in principio, et nunc, et semper, et in saecula saeculorum.*"

Then it was gone. Her ears rang. She looked down and saw not the cavern but simply the mummy in the trunk, staring vacantly with eyes shrunken and clouded over, jaw open in a scream, body shriveled to a raisin, one hand curled against the lid where long scratches wore grooves in the wood. The smell grabbed her throat.

She pulled his body free, rolled it on its side. A plume of dust rose, and she held her breath, refused to breathe it in. She pushed the body to the door, out onto the dirt.

When William returned from his latest revival, Etta told him she thought the man in the trunk was finally dead.

"Good," he said. "We can finish with him and begin work on your father."

He went to the trunk, opened the lid. Two hands pushed him, and he fell, landed in the empty trunk, dazed, cracking his head on the edge. He twisted his body, singing at the joints and the places which had knocked hard against the wood, and turned over just in time to see the lid slamming shut.

Billy Bolton, bolted inside the trunk, fed on nuts and seeds. He only had the darkness to contemplate, his knees bent against wood, the stink of his own body, the stale and dusty air that smelled of death. When pounding the walls of his tomb had skinned his palms and knuckles raw, when screaming had worn his throat raw, when swearing and cursing had left his ears filled with his own ragged breathing; when he felt the rumbling of the Airstream's engine beneath him, when the passing time had become an uncountable sludge—

He finally prayed.

Prayed to whatever might hear him. Prayed to whatever he'd seen in that abandoned church, that figure of flame with an empty face. To the God-thing which had told him strange prayers in strange tongues, and which had lurked behind him ever since, always watching over his shoulder, it seemed, though when he turned to look there was never anything there, just the empty space of its absence. His eyes, in the dark, tried to conjure the God-thing. But if it came to him now, or if it was only his imagination, all it did was laugh, and laugh, and laugh.

Ah-ah-ah.

The tent went up. It had been almost two years since anyone had come through here: long enough for Jessie Farr to get betrothed, long enough for Mrs. Flint to pass on, though she walked straight until the very end. Jessie convinced her fiancé, Alan Fletchley, to accompany her to the revival. She'd looked out for them as long as he'd known her, because they made her think of her old friend Henrietta. Alan obliged her, and they made their way to the tent that evening under a misty black sky.

The closer they drew, the harder Jessie breathed, recognizing all of this. And the sign they found inside stopped her cold: *Holy Ghost Revival with Etta Eastley!*

"You all right?" Alan asked, holding her elbow as she grew boneless.

Jessie shook her head. "It can't be. Ain't no one seen a trace of her since . . . " She backed out of the tent, shaking her head. "I gotta go." Before Alan could stop her, she ran off.

Torn between care for his betrothed and a curious inertia, Alan stood at the back, watching the woman on stage, whose voice burned, whose eyes were like bottomless pits. She spoke of a holy rapture, of a preacher who sacrificed himself in the name of the Blessed Virgin, and of a miraculous dust which she clutched in her fist. When she blew it over the crowd, it moved like a cloud, and a wretched coughing took up the congregation. One by one, they fell, clawing their throats, hacking; blood spattered the dirt, the lanterns flared, and the woman on stage laughed as she stepped down to move among the seats, blowing more dust from her fist.

Before he could push through the tent's flap into the cool night air, Alan felt a tickle in the back of his throat.

Jessie ran the familiar path until she arrived at the Eastley house. Her frantic knocking was met by Mrs. Eastley throwing open the door, hair gone gray since she'd seen her last, eyes like two wet bulbs. "My lands!" she cried.

"Etta—she's back—" Jessie tried to speak around the stitch in her side. She stumbled into the house, heard the wooden creak of wheels before she

To Dust You Shall Return

noticed an emaciated figure roll into the light. When she saw Mr. Eastley, her back went straight. His skin had mottled, hair a thin wisp over a pronounced skull. His chair shrilled as it rolled, and the sound made the hair stand up on Jessie's neck.

"Don't you . . . speak her name."

His lungs had never fully recovered from the dust pneumonia, and he'd aged beyond his years. Every move made him wheeze. Seeing him brought on a secondhand fear in Jessie, who knew enough of Etta's life to still her tongue. For a moment, she regretted coming here, knowing how desperate Etta had been to get away. And though she loved Alan Fletchley, she wished she were tumbling with Etta down in the dirt.

Then the door behind her creaked open again.

She turned, and there was Etta: red hair pulled back in braids, severe chin standing at an angle, dressed sharp and smart in black slacks. But her heart sank when she realized Etta's eyes had only sights for her parents. Jessie pressed herself against the wall, trying, for once in her life, to become invisible.

Mrs. Eastley gasped, but Etta pushed her aside, approached her father, whose face twisted in disgust.

"Come now, Daddy. Don't you want me to heal you?" Etta said. "Ain't that what Mama asked me to do, when Billy Bolton came to town?" Etta raised her fist. "Don't you recognize when I'm trying to help you?"

She blew a fistful of dust at him, and Jessie watched as Mr. Eastley's skin stretched back, turning his face to a rictus, his arms to knobby sticks, shriveling gray flesh over bones like dried leather; his eyes bulged out of the wasted shape, gummy and bloodshot; yellowed teeth stood out like a dilapidated fence. His hands gnarled on the armrests of his chair, twisted into useless claws.

"Don't worry, Daddy. I didn't kill you," said Etta as she took him by the hand. She bent him by the wrist. "Killing ain't worth nothing, after all. Killing is a kindness. Living, and wishing you were dead—now, that's the real punishment." His eyes bulged, his wrist bent to its extreme, and something snapped. His hand came off in a plume of dust.

Without bothering to grind it, Etta bit off her father's middle finger at the knuckle, chewed it to a powder while he watched. She held out the desiccated hand to Jessie and her mother, who stood frozen. "Take this and eat it, for this is my body, which is broken for you." When neither reached out, Etta laughed. "Haven't you ever heard of the Holy Communion?" Tears spilled from her mother's eyes, and she fell to her knees. Jessie backed up to the door.

"I *said*, have you ever *heard* of the *Holy Communion*?"

She licked her lips, and Jessie saw the forks of her split tongue dance over the edges of her mouth. And she saw something else, too—just behind Etta's shoulder, the suggestion of another shape, like a shadow that blistered the world.

Mrs. Eastley began to cough.

"Now, pray, Daddy." Mr. Eastley wheezed, still alive, somehow, eyes rolling. But they were clouded over, blind. All he could see was darkness. "Pray," said Etta. Jessie saw the figure behind her begin to rise, to unfurl two flaming wings, and she screamed—

But Etta? She'd gotten what she'd always wanted. And now she laughed, and laughed, and laughed.

Ah-ah-ah.

The Lords Below

MICHAEL PAIGE

Inspired by "Rats"

Shadows reigned thick in the sewers of Hampstead, and within its wetness, slogged the heavily coated figure of Harper Crowe—a tosher.

Taut around his frame a canvas apron clutched, brimming with pockets, and strapped to his breast swayed an old lantern. By candlelight, his shadow crawled up the tarnished walls, a primitive hunch to its stride.

Wading further down the tunnel, he eyed a grating above him and quickly closed the shade over the lantern. Best to be left unseen.

Beyond the grating, the streets would eventually rouse with activity. First by the early sweeps, then the dustman's bell, and eventually the frantic cries of grocers as the day market commenced.

But while they all still slept, Harper would toil below, disturbing the darkness with sloshing boots. Sounds of his presence were much less bothersome here, as they were cloaked by the soft yet consistent murmurs of the river fleet. The fleet coursed beneath the city, carrying all matter of waste and blight through its bowels.

Iron hoe in hand, he hacked through a heap of muck in the corner, turning over all matter of scat and rotting vegetables in search of tosh. Bits of rope, bones, scrap metal: anything able to be cleaned and sold. He peered into the mess, and when there was nothing, moved onto the next heap.

Wages were low on the surface, and opportunities even more scarce. But here, within the halls of putrid stench, hid the crumbs of rich pickings. Silver handed utensils, copper coins, jewellery, all lost to the sewer's flow and caught somewhere in its cavities, where Harper assumed ownership.

The labyrinth of porous brick could distort even the best of toshers' minds if they strayed from its main branches, but not Harper's. Like a leech thirsty for a vein, he'd grown friendly with the deep pockets, the ruddy junctions, and wherever else the best loot could be salvaged.

Though the dark was not without its dangers.

Any poor soul could meet their end to the crumbling walls, the sinking quagmires, or the hordes of diseased vermin. On the streets, rats fled to their crevices; in the sewers, they stood their ground like sentinels, primed for attack.

Harper would never forget the first corpse he'd seen, swollen and blued by the fleet. A tosher by the garbs of him, most likely swept up in the sluices—raised by the flushers at low tide as a torrent of water ripped through the sewer and yanked everything along with it.

What Harper could make out of his sagged features was indicative of a slow, prolonged agony; his skin gleaming with fatty dew from the curdled river and only gnarled stumps where his fingers had once been.

The rats had gotten to him.

Though some bites looked much too large for a rat's teeth.

"Clean your boots, sir?" A shoeblack asked him once outside the dolly shop, brush in hand, ready and waiting.

Harper, who'd just sold off some findings to the merchant, eyed the mild scuffs on his boots and rested one on the boy's box. Unlike the pair of old slops that joined him in the culvert, these boots were ones of high regard. They, as well as the fetching clothes he wore throughout the day, paid homage to his hidden labour.

When hauls were particularly kind, this Harper (his other half, he called him), indulged in life's more decent qualities— a brightly patterned waistcoat with kerseymere trousers, bread and meat washed down with mild beer, and a cramped but warm tenement to sleep in.

The boy went to work, his head and shoulders pocketed in a black cap and patched jacket. A bruise marked his cheek, where he had no doubt been flogged. He brushed the mud away tirelessly and rubbed the blacking in. Such polish!

Around them, thousands of different, desperate cries shook the air.

"Half-a-quire of paper for a penny. Buy, buy, b-u-uy!" brayed the butcher, carcasses strung at his stall and gutters teeming with blood.

"A cock linnet for tuppence," piped the bird-catcher at his stand, birds fluttering in their cages. "Who will buy a new love song? Only a ha'-penny a piece . . . Jest hear'em sing!"

"Ripe strawberries ripe, ripe strawberries ripe . . . only six-pence a pottle!"

The Lords Below

"Penny a bunch a turnips and carrots!"

Then, a new voice sounded over the turmoil, like the screech of an owl faced with a predator. "Coppers! Come and look! There's toshers down 'ere." The cry came from a beggar girl on her knees, hunched over a sewer grate, spying something beyond the bars. "Come and look!" she shrieked again with great indulgence.

Around her, other snitches joined in an attempt to grab the credit, tossing their own shouts into the air.

The peelers had closed off the sewers and since then, offered a reward of five pounds to anyone who caught the toshers at their work. Honest working men turned criminals. A dying breed restricted from their rights to fair pickings.

Even the mudlarks, with their knees buried in coast slime and sticks prodding through the silt, were now being hauled off the shore by police galleys. Cut off from their riverside takings and left to starve in the streets.

But he would be damned—damned to hell—to end up like their lot. And unlike his predecessors, who he'd seen whisked out of the grate and arrested in the street, Harper Crowe could never be caught.

"They're after someone," the shoeblack spoke toward the commotion, "more shore-finders. Pa calls 'em lurkers. You'd think they be too afeared of the sewers, what with the wild pigs down there."

Pigs? Harper thought, swallowing the words gathering in his throat. He'd heard the tale before from shoremen in the pubs, about a pregnant sow who'd dodged a butcher's blade and tumbled into the sewers, bearing her litter there to root and feed in the darkness. In drunken rambles, they told of the horrors they'd seen. Distant squeals louder than any rats. Roaming shadows amassing into a herd of great beasts.

Harper scoffed at the claims.

'T'aint no such thing as them down there, he wanted to tell the shoeblack, *'Not'ing but tall tales from scared willies. And we ain't lurkers my boy, but treasure hunters. Chaps workin' to make a livin' for ourselves, while up here, you shine the shoes of lords and ladies alike. Open your eyes lad, the real lords ain't up here, but right below you.'*

Instead of speaking any of this, he merely paid his pence and left before the shoeblack could tilt his cap.

Harper continued further down the tunnel, enclosed by caked ornate walls.

The low tide had risen and buried his knees in its roll. To his right, an outflow pipe belched and dribbled.

Michael Paige

Taking out his circular sieve to sift for coins, Harper stopped as something caught his eye.

Within a chink in the wall where the mortar had worn away, his lantern light revealed a glint—the glint of something valuable.

Harper's mouth widened into a grin short of a few teeth.

A handbag, teeming with jewels, had been lodged in its confines. It must've been a great misfortune for the missus to reach for her bag of jewels only to find they'd fallen from her side.

But now they were in the below, and all that was below was his.

He dug his arm into the crack, but even up to the shoulder, his fingers could not reach.

He wiggled the iron hoe through the crevice with no luck. It was too wide for any use.

The jewels mocked him, so close but ever so far.

From one of his pockets, he produced a slim crowbar and fished it further into the burrow, practically kissing the mildewy walls.

Further down the tunnel, the fleet had begun to growl. Harper did not hear it; he was too focused on the claw of the crowbar scraping at the slippery velvet and inching it closer to the jewels. Tension tightened his already craggy features. Around his knees, the tide had begun to kick.

His neck suddenly arched, cocked with alert as the sinister mumbles of the tunnel rose to a deafening scream.

The sluices. They've lifted the damned sluices!

He looked once more at the bag, praying it not to be snatched or whisked off to God-knows-where and then raced back the way he'd come.

Behind him, the fleet kicked into a torrent of angry, rushing water.

He stumbled a few faltering paces forward, hoping to catch a branch sewer to escape into.

It was on him within seconds, first smacking against his frame and then seizing his legs.

His feet slipped from beneath him.

Grey water washed over his face and up his nostrils.

Harper—now horizontal with the water—clawed desperately at the walls, scanning for any crack or shallow depression he could cling to. Given the force of the current, holding his ground wasn't feasible.

The current tossed him around like a cigar end, smacking his shoulder hard against the brickwork.

The iron hoe left his grip and disappeared in the flurry.

And through a rushing, watery film, Harper could only watch as he was pulled into the maw of a different passage.

The Lords Below

How long he was out, Harper was not sure, but it was the drops from the ceiling that finally stirred him.

In half wakefulness, he rolled and then heaved the vile water from his throat.

He felt around and touched the ball of pain living in his shoulder. Badly bruised, but at least not broken.

His hoe was gone and the lantern, though still attached to his person, was terribly shattered. A single crowbar was the only survivor.

The sluiceway had spat him out into an outfall chamber where it then calmed and dispersed into several more offshoots.

Bobbing from the scrim closest to him, a grey cat's corpse floated by, its fur matted and slimed. They'd both ridden the wave together—one less fortunate than the other.

With vigour, Harper swallowed back the distress in his chest. He'd survived through worse, feeding off the give-and-take of the tides for years. 'Twas not always suicide for the tosher who was lost—and he was the best there was. He strode forward into the new gloom he'd been whisked to.

As he took his first step, something else joined the sullen drippings. A sound he did not expect to hear. The sound of a hoarse, heavy grunting.

A lump grew inside his throat, defying his chest another breath.

The sound grew louder, wallowing ever closer.

He could no longer hear the trickle of the drains or the distant gurgle of the pipes, only the *huf-huf-huf* of the bestial breath approaching.

Sounded by a sharp twitch in his ear, his eyes peered to the side and pulled something from the black—a form that gave body to the horror shaping his thoughts.

A great mass pushing through the stream, hulking from the swell like an island over a tainted ocean.

He was close enough to see the furry bristles of its humped back, the leathery snout protruding from two large tusks, and the sack-like belly dipped into the froth. A swine—the largest he'd ever seen. Larger than any hanging in the butcher shop.

His sewer-licked face went pale.

It passed him by and approached the cat, perhaps not whiffing his own scent within the sopping wet clothes.

From its bulk rumbled a mighty bellow as the mass fell upon the corpse.

A noisy splash could be heard as teeth found and ripped into furry flesh. Small, delicate bones crushed and chewed between hearty grunts.

Michael Paige

The sound rustled further activity in the shadows—cloven toes scraping like bone over the floor, shadowy shapes scrounging around lazily through the water, letting out nasally snorts. Pieces of the dark made solid.

They trudged around, digging wrinkled heads into the refuse, their robust bodies lubricated with the slop of their dwellings.

His eyes traced back to the stream, following it to the vague squarish shaft ahead of him, just large enough to fit through. Where it led, he hadn't the slightest clue, but anywhere was better than here.

Behind him, a scuffle over the cat's corpse resounded with squeals and vexed whines.

No such thing as them, he almost told the shoeblack, *just tall tales for scared willies.*

But here they were. Real as the ash and cinders between the bricks, from the black, muddy scent of their hides to the braying squeals of their young.

The sewer had spawned them, its chasmic halls their territory, its sluiceway their feeding trough.

And a lone, lost tosher, Harper thought, *was the greatest meal of them all.*

Increasingly worried, Harper moved slowly forward, trying to find what stable footing he could over the greasy ground.

A sound reached him from dangerously close by—a puff of air firing out of a wet snout. One of the beasts waded its way closer, its head arched and tasting the air. A swinish bleat broke through the soft snorts of the others.

As though sensing a disruption in their ranks, the swollen silhouettes around him began to shift. The quarrel over the carcass ceased. The stream flowing through the chamber became jostled, disrupted.

The swine knew something was amiss, and soon enough, their light-starved eyes would find him.

He bolted, plodding forward in a mad rush toward the passage.

A squeal—joined by an ungodly choir of others—promptly sounded. Water churned and splashed as large bodies crashed through it.

He clambered down the dark tunnel, smacking at the walls to probe his way forward.

A gap, impossible to see in the muck, clutched his foot and sent him slipping forward, stumbling like a drunk in the street.

He recovered, barely.

All around him, the rugged walls screamed, as though the gates of hell had suddenly been opened.

And perhaps they had.

The tunnel he'd chosen crossed and recrossed ahead of him, branching left, then right, then left again.

The Lords Below

The shattered lantern swung and bobbed beneath him.

By mere chance, he practically fell into a new opening at his side—an incline linking back to the upper level.

The swine were close behind, piping their hungry call, hoggish screams wanting so desperately to catch him.

He ascended the slope, heaving himself up the narrow chute and against the flowing stream.

Water pushed at his knees as he braced against it, gaining a foothold in the cornering and pinning both hands on the tight walls around him.

The pressure was heavy, and despite the slippery masonry, Harper's grip held firm as he worked his way up the shaft.

At the base of the small tunnel, the scrabble of swine shrieked and shoved at one another in a desperate attempt at pursuit, only managing a few ravenous mouths through the hole, their grimy hooves too slick for traction.

Like a terrible heat, pain grappled at his shoulder, attempting to seize it with shock.

Then, as he was halfway to the top, his left foot slipped out from under him, sending Harper in a mad slide toward the bottom.

His own scream matched the ones waiting for him below. A dying note.

He clawed wildly at the walls, shoving his legs out to regain any form of footing.

Porcine squeals welcomed him, echoing out of bent snouts and great black bellies.

Ragged tusks snapped at the meat of his leg, just out of reach as he managed to come to a halt.

A split in the brickwork, barely wide enough for one of his heels, had anchored him for dear life.

His bearings returned—he made his way back up the shaft, clenching the marred walls, boots one after the other.

Through the sweating passage, he hurled himself out and onto the floor of the main sewer, crawling as far from the chute as he could. His strength had been sapped like a spent match; his tongue coated with filthy water.

As before, he staggered down the tunnel, unsure of what else waited for him in the forlorn, sooty depths.

Through the darksome cavern, he'd managed to come to one of the sewer outlets, blocked by an iron flap hinged at the top, designed to ward off seasonal floods and perhaps, also, unwelcomed guests.

Michael Paige

With stiffness, he took the crowbar and went to work to lift the corroded flap.

Inch by inch he raised it, even as the pain in his shoulder awoke worse than before and forced a gasp out of him.

As it opened, bundles of muck poured out through the gap with him, spewing forth to the long-awaited outside.

Iron chains from the penstock dangled gently overhead while a tall iron ladder led up the large wall and to the pier.

He climbed it with caution, carefully peering out at the top to make sure nobody was showing among the warehouses.

The wharf lay quiet.

Then, the shabby wretch that he was, Harper fled the docks and into the night until he reached the backstreets where no peeler would find him.

The fog had drifted down, swathing over London and its gaslights in a vague sheet.

He collapsed in an alley.

Sick, reeling, and all manners of fatigued, Harper could only sit and shake along the cobbles.

His vision swayed like a boat in the swell.

Could he ever stand again? Yes, he did not have a choice. He needed a place to rest. Shillings to fill his empty stomach. A good brandy to moisten his lips.

Out of sight, he'd survived off the cold, wretched corridors beneath him, scrounging all matter of spoils. But now things had changed. He'd seen the same horrors the fuddled shoremen prattled on about. An awful and new truth now flooded his thoughts.

Even as the sun rose and Hampstead erupted once again with all its sights and sounds, he would surely see them in his dreams again: Lumbering mounds lurching about. Brittle bones snapping apart. Craving eyes searching for more. Yellowed teeth longing to pull him apart until his cries were forever silenced.

He'd sooner try his luck back at the shorelines before ever returning to the sewers, mudlarking like his younger years.

And yet, for brief moments, he would still feel an inkling to go back and seek those jewels out, that maybe they'd survived the sluices' fury.

But the urges were choked back, stifled by the fear and cold realisation that the sewers and all its curiosities were never his to begin with.

They belonged to the real lords, the ones below him.

Father Knows Best

M. WESLEY CORIE II

Inspired by "Body and Blood"

Father Gareth Souiller moved around the sacristy preparing the elements of the Mass. His hands went through the familiar motions, arranging the Host and sacramental wine, ensuring everything was as it should be. He blindly grabbed a bottle of wine from the storage cabinet, removed the cork, and put the bottle to his lips for a gulp. A queer expression crossed his face, equal parts amusement and disgust. Father Souiller vividly recalled the warning he had told his acolytes on many a Sunday morning, "The bottles in the back are for fun, the ones in front are for the Mass." The lingering funk of teenage asshole ringing the neck of the bottle did not pair well with the Merlot.

The priest swallowed the musky wine and re-corked the bottle. *Best not serve this at Mass-Querade*, he mused as he put the bottle into the back of the cabinet. He carefully selected another bottle from the front. He sniffed the bottle, smiled, and pulled out the cork. Another swig straight from the bottle, and its flavor met his approval. "Thirty-three A.D. must have been a good year," he proclaimed. He took another mouthful, gargled, and spit the wine into the open cruet. He topped off the cruet with a long pour from the bottle and swirled the mixture within the sacred container before putting the corks on both vessels. *Everyone would enjoy a little taste of Father tonight.*

He subtly smirked as he told himself, *I hope those kids enjoy their night off. They earned it.* Yes, the acolytes were off duty, making the whole preparatory process tedious, and there was no one to laugh at his "Father jokes." The priest would have to perform the entire Mass himself, but they had been such good boys this year, so eager to perform their duties with open hearts and open mouths. As Father Souiller finished the preparations, he frowned. There was a visible yellow stain across the linens used to cover the Host. "I swear I told them to never finish on the linens! Goddammit!"

At St. Agnes Catholic Church, Sunday evening mass was typically a casual service. This was a special day, as Halloween fell on a Sunday this year. Father Souiller coined the phrase "Mass-Querade" and imagined himself clever for it. On this unseasonably warm night in south Louisiana, he would set the sanctuary lights a bit dimmer and would keep the Mass "short and sweet." After Mass was over, the parishioners would enjoy Halloween food and fun in the safety of the fellowship hall. Tonight would be for the children. Tomorrow's All Saints Day Mass would be a more somber service of remembrance, and the priest dreaded it.

Father Souiller carried the ciborium, filled with the Host, and the cruet of crimson communion wine to their places around the altar, and gave everything a quick once-over. He used the cruet to fill the ornate chalice with the wine he had already sullied. Father Souiller smirked, yet he was slightly annoyed to be performing all these steps himself and told himself he would not be so generous in the future. "If I spoil those boys, they won't respect their Father," he mumbled while placing the coverings over the elements of Communion.

The priest flipped the ornate altar Bible to the prescribed scripture for the Mass—First Corinthians, chapter eleven. The priest quickly skimmed through the scripture and rolled his eyes, *What a mood killer! We'll skip it. Plenty of Bible time tomorrow.* Father Souiller looked at the life-size wooden crucifix suspended from the ceiling behind the altar and met the gaze of his Lord. He whispered, "You know, it wouldn't hurt to smile once in a while," and chuckled. The Lord maintained his mournful expression.

He glanced at his diamond-encrusted watch and checked the time—nearly seven o'clock. The sanctuary was empty save for him, but that would change soon. *Almost showtime!* Father Souiller glided towards the foyer at the front of the sanctuary. He smoothed his vestments and inspected the processional cross, waiting for the automated church bell to ring on the hour.

BONG! BONG! BONG! BONG! BONG! BONG! BONG!

With a smooth motion he'd performed a hundred times before, he lifted the processional cross and started his stately march to the altar. He sang the traditional processional song *a capella*, as he had generously let the organist off tonight too. Ten paces down the aisle, Father Souiller heard the sanctuary doors swing open, creaking loudly as they always did. Behind

Father Knows Best

him, the sounds of shuffling feet and muffled voices slowly spread into the sanctuary. Father smiled to himself.

Father Souiller approached the altar and turned to the right, carrying the cross to its assigned place on the platform. He positioned it carefully and looked to the giant crucifix, giving Christ a wink. He turned around, quickly kissed the altar, and stood to face the congregation. The priest gasped as he took in the full panorama. Every man, woman, and child arrived in elaborate costumes, and almost every pew was filled. Costumes ranged from the classic Halloween monsters to the creepy—the priest was not fond of clowns, scary or otherwise—to the demonic. Father Souiller could not make out a single familiar face, as the faithful parishioners had taken his suggestion to heart. This was the "Mass-Querade" Father had hoped for, and he was almost giddy.

The priest walked around to the front of the altar and made the sign of the cross. The congregation gestured as prompted in an awkward unison. Father Souiller held back a laugh; he never considered how ridiculous it would be for a congregation of zombies, witches, mummies, and vampires to go through the sacred motions. He gestured for them to be seated. Father Souiller smiled and addressed the congregation, "Welcome all to this Holy Halloween Mass! This is our first Mass-Querade at St. Agnes; a chance for us to gather here for Communion, and afterwards enjoy Halloween fun in the fellowship hall. We will be skipping the Liturgy of the Word tonight and proceeding directly to the Liturgy of the Eucharist. I'm sure you all won't mind if we speed things up a bit?" The masks made the congregation's laughter sound strange, but Father was glad to hear it.

The priest made his way around the back of the altar in preparation for the Communion rite. He offered up the Eucharistic prayer and exhorted the congregation to join him in the Lord's Prayer.

> *"Our Father who art in heaven,*
> *hallowed be thy name."*

BANG! BANG!

The priest jerked his head towards the foyer. The sanctuary doors were closed, and someone was knocking loudly on them. He continued the prayer with eyebrows furrowed.

> *"Thy kingdom come,*
> *Thy will be done*
> *on earth, as it is in heaven."*

BANG! BANG! BANG!

M. Wesley Corie JJ

The priest looked again and scowled. The congregation didn't seem to notice or care about the distraction, so he finished.

> *"Give us this day our daily bread,*
> *and forgive us our trespasses,*
> *as we forgive those who trespass against us,"*

BANG!

Father Souiller lost his concentration and stopped. He angrily gestured towards the foyer, "Someone go check the doors, please?" A large mummy sitting close to the center aisle awkwardly jerked up and stumbled towards the sanctuary entrance. Father Souiller prayed.

> *"And lead us not into temptation,*
> *but deliver us from evil.*
> *Amen."*

The mummy made it to the doors and swung both wide open, the hinges squealing in protest. From the platform, the priest could see nothing but the black night outside. The mummy shrugged, closed the doors, and shambled back to his seat where the Bride of Frankenstein awaited him. Hesitantly the priest proclaimed, "This is, after all, the night for tricks . . . and so now we will celebrate a treat from our Lord!" The congregation's distorted cheers filled the sanctuary.

An unexpected mixture of emotions rocked him as he started the Litany of the Eucharist. It was bewildering—Father Souiller did not anticipate the parishioners to be this enthusiastic tonight. Some of the members put in a lot of time and effort, as hungry-looking abominations stared at him from the pews, some of them looking a little too real, almost glistening in the dim light of the sanctuary. Sweat beaded on the priest's forehead, and he had to consciously stop himself from using the sanctified cloths on the altar as a handkerchief. Father knew better than to do something crass in front of the faithful.

The words of the Liturgy flowed from Father Souiller's lips without much conscious effort. The motions and signs he had made many times before, and he found the ritual centering. The congregation responded as they should, although their words were distorted by their elaborate masks. For a moment, it sounded like they were mocking him, instead of responding with the proper due reverence.

A drop of something cold dripped onto Father Souiller's neck and he froze mid-sentence. He wiped the back of his neck, inspected damp fingers, and quickly sniffed them. *Water?* He gazed towards the ceiling. The

Father Knows Best

impaled feet of Christ were suspended above him, and as he watched, another bead dripped off His big toe and landed in the priest's confused, gaping mouth. He tasted salt and sputtered, "Okay, okay! You got me! Deacon Aveugler? That's a good trick!" The congregation erupted in raucous laughter and the priest's face flashed red with anger and embarrassment. He gestured for the faithful to be quiet—Father did not enjoy being laughed at.

He took several deep, slow breaths to calm his racing heart, and the priest found himself mechanically genuflecting behind the altar. Father Souiller reached for the Host. He took it, held it over the chalice brimming with dark red wine, and faced the congregation.

"Behold the Lamb of God,
Behold him who takes away the sins of the world.
Blessed are those called to the supper of the Lamb.
Lord, I am not worthy"
A voice from the congregation murmured, "That's the truth".
"That you should enter under my roof,
But only say the word
And my soul shall be healed."
"Too late for that."
"May the Body of Christ
Keep me safe for eternal life."

"You'll choke on it!"

Father Souiller's eyes went wide as he wondered if he truly heard someone say such a cruel thing, or if he had only imagined it. The voice in his mind screamed, *This is not the time!* and so he determinedly maintained his professional, priestly demeanor. He opened his mouth and placed the Host on his tongue, and waited a moment for it to dissolve before swallowing.

The Host did not dissolve, and it was so bitter the priest had to fight his gag reflex. Accusations streamed through his mind, *Did the boys do this? This is disgusting!* As he forced himself to swallow the Host, he could swear the thing twitched on his tongue. The insolent Host was a mass of raw gristle as it slid down his throat. The priest's face contorted with pain and confusion as the bitterness he had endured turned into searing heat as if he had swallowed a bite of ghost pepper.

Father Souiller sweated profusely, his face and neck both turning an uncomfortable shade of crimson. He frantically grasped the holy chalice and held it aloft, hoarsely stammering out the words,

M. Wesley Corie II

*"May the Blood of Christ
Keep me safe for eternal life."*

    Without hesitation, he brought the chalice to his lips and drank deeply. There was no pretense of reverence here; he greedily gulped the wine to put out the fire burning inside him. As he drained the chalice nearly dry, the fire within was extinguished, but something else was amiss. He knew this wine, had tasted it so many times before, and this new coppery, salty flavor was entirely wrong. The wine snaked its way into him and mixed with the Host. Father Souiller's stomach spasmed with intense force as if someone had kicked him straight in the gut.

    He dropped the chalice—it bounced on the altar and splashed bloody red wine all over its surface, a spurt of crimson crossed the open Bible and dribbled on the floor. Father Souiller grabbed the side of the altar with both hands to steady himself. His body was violently rejecting what he had consumed, or the priest considered, *Was it rejecting me?* His abdomen audibly gurgled and bubbled, all while the congregation looked on with macabre anticipation.

    The priest could no longer contain the virulent sacrament writhing in his belly. Violent cramps deep within spurted a burning, watery stream of feces out of his clenched sphincter. Sulfurous gas trumpeted out of his intestines like a perverse Gabriel blowing his horn. Everyone could hear it. Everyone would smell it. As he held hold of the altar, the sudden sensation of vertigo overpowered him. His face burned with embarrassment, total humiliation. A final demonic birth pang expelled all the remaining contents of his bowels, his trousers overflowing, and his rectum at the point of prolapse. A stinking fecal trail spread down his vestments and pooled around his feet. "Christ forgive me!" he mewled, but his Lord did not respond from his position nailed to the cross.

    They all laughed at him. Every faithful mouth howled such cruel laughter—filling the sanctuary, a barnyard cacophony of braying asses. "I don't deserve this!", but Souiller's contrition was fruitless.

    The malodorous mélange of his vile secretions combined with the intense dizziness was more than Father Souiller could handle. He feared what would come next, and he fought hard to keep down the burning liquid. His vision blurred, and his trembling, sweaty hands could no longer hold firm to the altar. The priest forcefully regurgitated the communion wine along with what looked like a ragged chunk of pale white flesh with a single monstrous heave. It poured out all over the altar, the vomitus brown and polluted. He was utterly drained; there was no more to expel. His sweaty, vomit-slicked hands slipped from the altar and he collapsed to the

Father Knows Best

ground into a vile puddle of his own reeking filth. He fought to remain conscious while terror and confusion smothered him.

"Please help Father?" he moaned, and everything faded to black.

Father Souiller gasped for air, opened his eyes, and stared at the ceiling. He was still lying flat on his back behind the altar. Fractured thoughts ran frantically through his mind as he tried to make sense of what happened. *Did I faint? I must have hit my head. The little shits drugged the wine!* Something dripped from the crucifix hanging high above him and onto his forehead. Those cool splashes must have roused him—*"Jesus . . . wept?"* He opened his mouth to shout for help but only a pathetic groan came out. From the fringes of his vision, the shapes of the costumed congregants became closer and clearer. *Oh, thank God!*

They were not men in costumes—they were not men at all, and never were. Father Souiller saw the truth as they leered over him, every face a demonic mockery of man or beast, their hot, fetid breath reeking of sulfur or rotten meat. The delirious man groaned in agony as six hulking things seized him—lifting his blood, vomit, and shit-smeared body off the ground. Their claws and talons dug into him, piercing through the filthy vestments. *But this . . . this is a Holy place!* his failing ego protested. The priest was too exhausted to offer any resistance, and the terrible reality of the situation paralyzed his mind.

They hauled him away from the altar platform like pallbearers. The grotesque congregation erupted into laughter, applause, whooping, whistling, cat calls, and hisses—the pandemonium overwhelming. Those shapes he thought were children, now revealed as giant misshapen toads, viciously mocked him as he was paraded down the aisle, their wretched high-pitched voices cheering.

> *Body of shit!*
> *Blood of shit!*
> *All is shit!*
> *All of it!*
> *Up your ass!*
> *Down to Hell!*

Father Souiller was hollow, impotent—nothing remained to fuel an indignant rage against the taunting. The parade slowed to a stop in the foyer as the sanctuary doors creaked open. A hot, swampy miasma poured in. Sulfur. Sounds of crackling flames and tortured screams echoed far in the distance. *This has gone too far!* With all his remaining vitality, he managed to cry "Enough!"

The deafening silence was not what Father Souiller expected. The only sound in the priest's ears was his own pounding heartbeat. He whispered hoarsely, tears streaming from his bloodshot eyes, "Please put me down. Please!" After a silent eternity, the entire fallen assembly roared in terrible unison, "Amen!" With one graceful motion, they hurled Father Souiller out the sanctuary doors into the black abyss beyond.

Outside the sanctuary, the members of the congregation were annoyed and confused. The many families of St. Agnes had arrived in costume to celebrate the Halloween Mass and enjoy the Mass-Querade party. Some families went for group themes—there was a Wizard of Oz and an Addams Family ensemble, but most of the parents were wearing their typical casual Mass attire, with their younger children dressed as their favorite superheroes or princesses, and some of the older ones looking like 80's horror movie villains.

The church bells had summoned them, but their imploring knocks on the great doors were unheeded. Faint lights shone through the stained glass, and some swore they could make out movement as shadows danced across the elaborate colored panes. Deacon Martin Aveugler tried to open the sanctuary doors with his keys, but they would not turn the locks. He pounded on the doors and leaned his ear against it, straining to hear any indication of activity inside. Silence.

"Is Father Souiller in there? What's going on?"

"Someone is in there—I can see them. Is this a prank?"

"What do you mean your keys aren't working?"

"It's almost half past seven, why hasn't he opened the doors?"

"If this is a trick, it isn't funny!"

"I don't know! Just stay calm. I'm going to go check the side door!" the deacon shouted to the parishioners. His keys would work on the side door, he hoped, but he never had to unlock it before tonight. How could Father Souiller pull a trick like this on the congregation, especially after explaining how his "Mass-Querade" was a family event? The deacon muttered to himself, "It's tacky, but 'Father knows best!'"

As he turned away from the distraught parishioners, a small hand grabbed his arm. He looked round to see the stern wrinkled face of Sister Lydia, one of the few nuns left in the parish, staring intently at him.

Father Knows Best

"I don't like this one bit, Martin!"

"I don't either!"

"Well, I've got my flashlight and my phone. Going to check the graveyard for any shenanigans."

"That is not a good idea, Sister; please just wait for me to open the sanctuary."

"I'm not an invalid, Deacon. I have Sheriff Sanglier on speed dial!"

And with those words, Sister Lydia left the deacon and stomped towards the cemetery, shining her flashlight at the ground ahead of her. Martin made his way to the side door and fumbled through the keys. His hands shook as he moved the key into the lock. Screams echoed from the front of the sanctuary, and the sound startled him so much he dropped them. He ran as fast as he could back around to the congregation.

The sanctuary doors were standing wide open, but no one had yet dared to enter the foyer. Parents covered the eyes of their children, slowly backing them away from the church. So many faces expressed shock and disgust. They were a shouting, confusing discord,

"Who opened the doors?!"

"They just swung open!"

"Where is Father Souiller?"

"Deacon, this isn't right!"

"Someone call the sheriff!"

Deacon Aveugler pushed through the crowd and turned to move through the gaping sanctuary doors. He understood the screams now. His heart pounded in his throat, and he shouted, the pitch of his voice growing higher with each word, "Take the kids home now! My. God. My God!".

The deacon ran through the foyer, up the main aisle of the sanctuary to the altar platform and grabbed the railing in front of the altar to steady himself. He heaved and vomited. He gasped "Lord forgive me," as he spat on the floor. He heard footsteps running behind him, and shouted "Stay back! I'm . . . I'm okay." A middle-aged man from the congregation called out to him, "Martin, what's going on? I called the sheriff, and they are on their way. Everyone else is going home!" The deacon moaned, "Thank you, Jonathan . . . I . . . Oh God, Jon, it's awful. Who would do this?"

Before him, the altar lay desecrated, covered in vomit and filth. The Communion chalice was knocked over, and what looked like brown congealing blood was poured out and pooled on the floor. Ugly black flies buzzed loudly around the Host. The altar Bible looked to be splattered with blood, the whole sight a disheartening disgrace.

The worst part—that unholy bouquet wafting from the altar—rotting flesh, the metallic smell of blood, and the pungent scent of bile and feces nearly caused Deacon Aveugler to faint. He clung to the altar railing and inched his way around. He could see a puddle of liquefied human waste on the ground, and after a second look, fecal streaks leading away from the altar, like something, or someone, were dragged away. Martin anxiously called out, "Father Souiller? Father Souiller!? Are you here?"

The deacon inched closer to the altar from the side, trying to ascertain the nature of this desecration. He was careful to not touch anything, as he knew this was now a crime scene. But he wanted to know, he must know what they had done to his poor church. His eyes landed on the open Bible, a bloody circle traced around lines of scripture. The deacon gasped loudly, "Oh my sweet Lord, have mercy!"

Jonathan called out to him, "Martin? What happened to the altar? Any sign of Father Souiller?" The deacon looked away from the vile mess and over to the man standing at the back of the sanctuary. His eyes moved back to the defiled Bible, and as if forced by an unseen hand, Deacon Aveugler leaned over the book and recited the blood-marked scripture.

"Wherefore whosoever shall eat this bread, and drink this cup of the Lord, unworthily, shall be guilty of the body and blood of the Lord. But let a man examine himself, and so let him eat of that bread, and drink of that cup. For he that eateth and drinketh unworthily, eateth and drinketh damnation to himself . . ."

The gut-wrenching cry of an elderly woman knocked the deacon out of his trance-like state. "Sister Lydia?!" the two men shouted in near unison. Jonathan ran out of the sanctuary around to the graveyard, while Martin made his way down the platform fast behind him. Jonathan crossed the yard and made it to the cemetery gates, a few heaving breaths before the deacon caught up to him. Her flashlight flickered in the darkness a few yards in, and they could make out the small shape of the woman kneeling on the ground.

Whatever sound Sister Lydia was making, it was not intelligible speech—it was a coughing, sobbing cry, instilling dread into the men. Jonathan ran to her aide, while Deacon Aveugler struggled to match his pace. Her flashlight was laying on the ground beside her, shining an accusatory beam in the pitch-black night, illuminating a patch of freshly upturned soil crowned with what looked like a crude headstone.

Wheezing and sweating, Martin stumbled over the disturbed soil to inspect the stone. There was writing on it—he wished he had not read it; sometimes ignorance was a blessing. The words elicited a mournful wail as the Deacon fell to his knees next to Sister Lydia; his spirit crushed. Crudely scratched onto the filth-smeared stone were the words:

HERE LIES SOUILLER
IN BODY AND BLOOD

The House of Laments

PEDRO INIGUEZ

Inspired by "Life Eternal"

Rodrigo pulled off the highway and turned onto a narrow country lane just as snow began to pelt the windshield. The sedan bounced over a stretch of uneven road. Julia felt the baby kick and placed a hand over her belly.

"Sorry," Rodrigo said, "I'll drive slow."

Julia looked at her baby bump. They hadn't gotten this far and not for lack of trying.

"Don't worry," he said. "Things will be different. The doctor said so. The baby—Alma—is looking healthy."

"Yeah," she said, glancing out the window. The snow started to come down, dusting the countryside. The clouds had blotted out the sun, leaving the sky a mottled watercolor painting. It was a far cry from California.

Off the road, a hand-painted sign jutted crookedly from a patch of dead earth.

Estate Sale. End of the Road.

"There it is," Rodrigo said. "We're heading the right way."

After a mile they pulled up on a run-down homestead nestled on a vacant farm, its soil under an inch of fresh powder. The broken stems of dead corn stalks pierced the snow for miles in every direction.

There wasn't much to look at besides a rusted silo, a decrepit house, and a thicket of spruce and elm trees stretching a-ways back.

There were already trucks lined up on either side of the road, their flatbeds loaded with boxes and roped-down furniture. Rodrigo found parking alongside a fencepost near an old mailbox with a weathervane poking out the top.

Julia peered through the windshield. She wasn't used to houses like this in Los Angeles. Her whole life she'd yearned for a taste of the rural, the quiet that couldn't be found anywhere else but middle America. After the miscarriages, she knew the move to South Dakota would do them both good. And since they both worked from home, it wouldn't be a hindrance to their careers.

"Something sad about this place," Julia said, her gaze fixed on the farmhouse.

"Write about it in another one of your books," Rodrigo said looking out with her. "Maybe it's haunted."

She nodded blankly. The house, though charming in its own way, was in shambles. Even from inside the car, Julia could see the effects time and the elements had inflicted on its bones; the rotting clapboards and peeling paint left the house with a dirty, grey façade. Even the black curtains hanging over the windows were ragged and woeful. It stood as a corpse long picked clean by prairie scavengers.

Rodrigo helped Julia trudge up a creaky set of stairs and past the porch. A woman in a peacoat stood at the door. She waved her clipboard and smiled.

"Hello," she said, "and welcome to the Martin estate sale. Feel free to look around. Everything is marked and priced to sell."

"What happened to the previous owner?" Rodrigo said, bluntly, as he removed his gloves.

The woman lowered her clipboard, the cheer wiped from her face. "Well, Mr. Phineas Martin vanished a few years ago and was recently declared dead. Having no next of kin, the county possessed his property and is selling off his belongings before the place is condemned."

"Condemned?" Julia asked.

"Yup. The house is in disarray and the terrain isn't good for growing anymore. The county thinks it'll be easier to vacate the land and fence it off rather than try selling it. Now, please, go and have a look." She half-shooed them into the house as more people began to make their way up the porch.

As Julia shuffled inside the living room, the floorboards creaked and bowed slightly under her shoes. The room was almost bare, save for a few rickety-looking chairs and the fireplace mantle full of assorted trophies and porcelain figurines.

She crinkled her nose. The house smelled of old newspapers, coffee, and stale cigarettes. And rot. A wet, foul stench she couldn't pinpoint.

She did her best to ignore the smell as Rodrigo reached out and squeezed her hand. He'd been doing his best to comfort her these last few months, she knew, in case *it* happened again. She shook the thought and buried it deep inside as they came upon an office. A cherrywood desk sat toward the back of the room, almanacs and encyclopedias spread on its surface. Behind the desk, a lone window draped in thick, black cloth, most of which was covered in a thin layer of dust and cobwebs. A sliver of daylight pierced the curtains and caught on a large corkboard hanging on the wall. It was pinned with faded pictures of missing children clipped from the backs of junk mail letters and newspapers. The most recent was from ten years prior, a missing four-year old girl from just outside town.

"Breaks my heart," a gruff voice said behind them, giving Julia's heart a jolt. An old man dressed in jeans and a plaided long-sleeve shirt leaned against the doorframe. His tired eyes scanned the corkboard with what Julia regarded as pity. "Mabel never could have kids and after she was killed, Phineas took to searching for missing children as a way to cope. Lord knows we have our share of runaways 'round these parts. I'm sorry," he said, reaching a hand out, "My name's Frank Hess. I was their neighbor for forty years. I live on the next farm over."

"Rodrigo and Julia Ortega," Rodrigo said shaking Frank's hand. "Frank, you said Mabel was killed. Mind if I ask?"

Julia elbowed Rodrigo in the ribs.

Frank bit his lip and his eyes rolled upwards as if plumbing the depths of his mind. "Well, it's been about twenty years now. They were on vacation in the Yucatan Peninsula, and, well, Phineas thinks she was mauled by a jaguar." Frank curled his fingers around his neck. "Poor Mabel's throat was ripped out and Phineas barely survived himself. Says he was blindsided by the thing, so no one quite knows what killed her, truth be told."

"Jesus," Julia said. She ran two fingers along her throat. A shiver ran up her spine.

"Yup," Frank said, crossing his arms. "The poor man was never the same after that. He'd already been suffering from dementia, but that just put the nail in the coffin. Phineas rarely left the house after he got back. Just kept to himself until he vanished. I think the poor bastard lost his senses one night, wandered off, and got himself dead. Probably exposure. Lots of prairie out there."

"I hear that," Rodrigo said.

"Well, I'll let you folks rummage around." Frank eyed Julia's belly and winked. "Nice meeting you three."

"Fucking terrible," Rodrigo said. "Maybe this house *is* haunted."

Julia nodded and left the office. They turned into a narrow hallway, and she ran a hand along the brittle wallpaper, her fingers collecting dust and flakes of paper. There was grief within the walls as if a lingering soul weeping within. "I feel sorry for the both of them. Just tragedy after tragedy."

Rodrigo agreed, somberly.

Pedro Iniguez

They stepped into the master bedroom and Julia flicked on the light. The window toward the opposite end of the room had been boarded up. Fine shards of broken glass twinkled like diamonds beneath the windowsill. The mattress had already been stripped off the frame, leaving a thin metal skeleton in the center of the room. Something about the sight filled Julia with sorrow. How many nighttime conversations were had in this room? How many dreams birthed? Now it had all been dismantled, sold off to strangers.

Rodrigo had told her she suffered from an *abundance of empathy*. Right or wrong, she tried not to let the thought get to her. Only two nightstands remained on either side of the frame. Julia walked over to the nearest one and opened a drawer. Her hands pawed around in darkness until she touched something slim and solid. She pulled out a vintage Kodak disposable camera. The kind her parents had used in the 90s on summer vacations when she was a little girl.

"What you got there?" Rodrigo said.

"It's an old-school camera," she said, flipping it over. "There's no tag on it."

"Does it work?"

"Let's see," she said, peering through the viewfinder. She centered Rodrigo's face and pressed the shutter release. The camera snapped and flashed.

"Hey!" Rodrigo said, rubbing his eyes. "Little warning next time?"

"Still good," she said spinning a small dial on the camera. "Let's get a selfie."

"Sure, babe." Rodrigo squeezed beside her and made himself small as she raised the camera above their heads. They pressed their cheeks together and smiled. Julia pressed the release again. The camera clicked and flashed.

"That was it. Last one."

"That takes me back," Rodrigo said. "Haven't seen one of those in ages. I wonder if the pictures came out alright."

"I'm curious as to what kind of pictures the old man has in here. The poor guy didn't even have any next of kin." Julia frowned. She turned the camera over. Her warped reflection stared back from the lens. "Whatever memories he had in here are gonna end up in the trash. As if he never existed. So damn sad."

"Let's buy it," Rodrigo said placing a hand on her shoulder. "We'll get them developed and go through them all. We'll make an evening of it. I'm sure Mr. Martin wouldn't mind."

Julia didn't know why but she loved the idea. The thought of exploring a stranger's memories had kindled something in her she couldn't explain.

The House of Laments

A longing for a past that wasn't hers and she had private access to it. It would be almost like bringing back someone from the dead.

They asked the woman up front about the camera and she said it must have been an oversight. She charged them ten dollars. Rodrigo paid in cash. Julia didn't even bother exploring the kitchen toward the back of the house. She'd gotten all she needed from this place. As they drove back into town, she clutched the camera to her chest like a little girl with a new book, its secrets awaiting her.

"Let's find a photo lab," she said. As they pulled away from the house, she allowed herself to smile. For the first time in a long time, it was genuine.

⛧

They'd found a place in town that still developed film photography. Rodrigo joked these days it was akin to some archaic proto-science like alchemy. Julia didn't think he was far from the truth.

After they'd dropped off the film roll, they had gotten to unpacking and settling in. Rodrigo assembled a crib in the master bedroom in between website development gigs for his clients back in L.A. Julia set up an office in the corner of the living room and got the cylinders firing on her new romance novel in between the more frequent contractions.

The phone rang two weeks later on a late Tuesday afternoon. The shop had their photos ready. Julia had thrown herself into her new novel and had almost forgotten.

Rodrigo drove to pick up the photos and came back with a bottle of sparkling grape juice.

"I know you can't drink so here's the closest thing," he said pouring them each a glass. He lay the envelope on the coffee table and flashed a smile. They nestled into the couch and pulled a blanket over their laps.

"You ready?" Rodrigo said tipping his glass to hers.

"Yeah," she said. "To Mr. and Mrs. Martin."

She grabbed the envelope and slid out a stack of about two dozen glossy 5x7 prints.

The first print was an overexposed picture of a middle-aged woman, smiling as she clutched her purse in front of the Disneyland Monorail, scores of families jockeying behind her for a seat. She had bushy blonde hair and wore an oversized Minnie Mouse sweater, powder blue jeans, and white tennis shoes.

"She's dressed like my grandma did in the 80s," Rodrigo chuckled.

Julia flipped the picture over. "There's no timestamp."

Pedro Iniguez

"You're thinking digital pictures, babe," he said before sipping from his glass.

She slipped the photo at the back of the stack. The next picture was of a clear, blue lake. In it, a lanky green-eyed man with a warm smile sat on a small boat, his knees jutting out as he waved at the camera with one hand and gripped a fishing pole with his other.

"Cute," Julia said.

Then came pictures of birthdays at the park; candid shots of Phineas and Mabel at home, or toiling on the farm; photos of them, older now, holding each other as they leaned against a station wagon at the Grand Canyon.

"Look at that one," Rodrigo said jabbing his finger on the print. "This must be the place where it happened."

It was a snapshot of Mabel sitting on the bottom step of a steep Mayan pyramid, the jungle canopy shrouding the sun as it fell below the horizon. The trees and fronds seemed to encroach upon Mabel as she sat, her hands clasped on her lap.

"I know this place," Julia said. Her finger traced the crumbling steps of the temple as it tapered into the sky. "This is the Nohoch Mul pyramid."

"Huh?"

"It's in Coba in the Yucatan Peninsula. I've read up on this place. In one of my books, my characters meet on vacation here. Most of the city is still buried underground, lost to time. They've only rediscovered a small portion of it."

"Wild," Rodrigo said, pouring himself another glass. "Wonder what kind of weird things are hidden down there."

Julia pulled out the next picture. It was a snapshot of an elm tree, the stars, like tiny white pinholes, barely visible in the expansive dark blue sky behind it.

"Hm," she said, "looks like Mabel is gone by this point."

Rodrigo pursed his lips and nodded. "Poor woman. Makes you wonder what attacked her."

Julia pulled up another picture; a blurred image of a porch, lit only by the fading light of the sun, which had now mostly sunk behind the plains. It appeared to be the same porch she'd labored to climb at the estate sale.

Another photo: an anonymous rural road at night as it vanished into a horizon where land met stars.

"Weird," Rodrigo said.

The rest were pictures of empty rooms, dark cellars, boarded windows, liminal spaces; even one of an out-of-focus phone booth at night, the distorted light of the flash bouncing off a wet street she thought she recognized from town.

The House of Laments

"This doesn't make sense," Julia said. "These pictures are aimless and dark, washed out, fuzzy."

"Remember," Rodrigo said knocking back the last of his drink, "the man had dementia. It had probably spiraled out of control by this point."

There was a final picture. Like everything before, it was dark, but Julia made it out to be a kitchen. There was an old gas stove with small, soiled rags littering a shadowed section of floor beneath it. And that was it.

She finally came upon the last two pictures they'd taken two weeks prior, clean and clear.

Rodrigo scooched close. "Hey, those came out great!"

"Wait a minute," Julia said pulling back the last picture. Something caught her eye. "What does that look like to you?" She brought her fingernail to the tiny spot where the rags had been strewn below the stove.

Rodrigo took the picture and brought it close to his face, squinting. "That looks like clothing. Children's clothing." He handed the picture back. "But didn't Frank say Mabel couldn't have kids? When do you think this picture was taken?"

"Hard to say," Julia said, her eyes focusing hard on that tiny, occulted spot. It did indeed appear to be clothing. She swore she could make out a small skirt with a dull pink striped pattern. Another article looked like a toddler's collared shirt.

"Why would he have children's clothing?" Rodrigo asked.

"The pictures on the corkboard. What if he wasn't looking for those kids? What if he's the reason they disappeared?"

"You mean those photos on the board were his collection?" Rodrigo shook his head. "No. Can't be. I think we're tired and letting our imaginations create boogeymen that don't exist." He stood and walked to the bedroom. "Come on, let's get some sleep. It's late and we're losing our minds."

"Yeah," Julia said sliding the prints back in the envelope. "Guess you're right."

☆

That night, the terrors found her as she slept. In her dream she was tormented by the wails of children trapped inside a house. Their faces were obscured in a web of shadows behind a window as their tiny fingers clawed against glass. Something loomed over the sky, something great and terrible as it eclipsed the world. Then, she felt cold fingers sliding up her neck.

Julia bolted awake, the nightgown moist and clinging to her body. She placed a hand on her belly and massaged it in a slow, concentric motion.

Pedro Iniguez

Outside, a fresh snowstorm ravaged the house as the branches scraped against the bedroom window.

"Rodrigo?" Julia rocked Rodrigo awake.

"Hm?"

"We need to go back to that house."

"What?"

"I have to make sure. I-I can't shake this feeling that Phineas had something to do with those kids."

"Babe," Rodrigo mumbled. He looked out the window at the violent flurry frosting the window. "It's late. Give it a rest. The old man's dead and this is all in your head."

"I just need to check for those clothes, that's all. I think about Alma, if she were to go missing, I'd want to know. Please?"

Rodrigo regarded her for a moment. "You're serious?"

Julia looked at her belly again and nodded.

Rodrigo frowned, threw on his jacket, and strapped on his boots.

The trek back to the house had been slow as the wind rocked the car. The rural roads had already accumulated three inches of snowfall and the sedan's tires labored to slog through it all.

When they rolled in, they parked directly in front of the house, the car's headlights cutting through the night like a knife. The house had amassed a layer of snow and resembled a phantom rising from the frosted plains.

"Alright," Rodrigo said, reaching into the glove compartment. He retrieved a cheap plastic flashlight, its batteries clacking around inside like loose bones. "Let's go."

He'd left the car's engine running, the headlights guiding their way up the porch. Rodrigo tried the doorknob. When that didn't work, he pressed his shoulder against the frame and pushed. The latch and frame split apart, and the door swung open.

Rodrigo flicked on the flashlight and threw the light around the living room. Motes of dust and snow from outside mingled in the air wherever the cone of light swayed. The house was considerably emptier now, as if ransacked by thieves. All that remained were bundles of old newspapers stacked along the wall.

Julia retrieved the envelope from her coat and brought up the picture. "Let's just get a quick look under the stove and we'll leave."

The kitchen was toward the back of the house. It was cramped, old. Nothing but a pantry, a counter, and dilapidated cabinets. The feint light from the sedan's beams cast their shadows over an antiquated stove, creating a large dark spot in the center of the room.

Julia looked over the image again. The rags were sticking out of the shadows directly beneath the stove, which was slightly elevated off the ground. A cold draft swept in, raising the hairs on the back of her neck.

"Down there," she nodded toward the stove.

Rodrigo sighed as he got on his knees. He aimed the flashlight under the stove.

Julia moaned as she backed against the counter. She dropped the envelope and wrapped her arms around her belly while fluid seeped down her jeans and shoes, pooling on the floor. "It's happening," she groaned.

"Shit," Rodrigo said, jumping upright. He caught her arm and eased her onto the floor. "I won't be able to get us to the hospital in time with that snowstorm. We're gonna have to do this here."

Julia broke into short, labored breaths, the contractions tearing at her insides, the pain sweeping through her whole body like a fire.

"We're gonna do this together, baby."

Rodrigo quickly removed her shoes and pants and squeezed her hand.

The snow began to blow inside the kitchen, flying into her skin like frigid daggers.

She pushed, feeling her muscles expand and contract, her fingers wound tight around Rodrigo's hand.

"I see her head," Rodrigo said. "Keep push-."

Rodrigo squeezed her hand so hard the pain flared like a hot coal in her palm. A pale, naked man had seized Rodrigo by the hair, his teeth plunged into his throat. The pallid man whipped his head to the side and ripped out a chunk of bloody flesh. Rodrigo slumped lifelessly to the floor, his flashlight plunking beside him, its light spinning until it settled on a puddle of blood, now expanding around his body.

"No, God, no!" Julia shrieked, her body still in the throes of giving birth.

The naked man dropped to his knees and lapped from the viscous crimson pool. When he finished, he staggered toward Julia. He bent over her, his pungent breaths shallow and quick as blood seeped down his chin and chest. In the light of the car's beams, she made out the familiar green eyes from the photos, only this man looked withered, his white skin ashy and dry, his ribs jutting from his torso like a malnourished animal.

Phineas' eyes settled on the envelope before his long fingers plucked it off the floor. He sifted through the pictures as his eyes widened and his brows arched, his face painted with the look of pain and familiarity, of things remembered. Thin lips curled to reveal twin spear-like fangs. Then, his mouth twisted into something vaguely resembling a smile.

Julia sobbed as she made her final push. Her daughter slipped onto the floor at her mother's feet, small arms flailing as her wails echoed throughout the empty house.

"Please, don't hurt us," Julia whispered as she tried to sit up.

Phineas stooped, reached out a hand, and slid a long-nailed finger across Julia's neck.

Julia gargled as warm blood spewed from the open wound at her throat and plopped down the sides of her neck. She reached a hand to Alma who was still tethered to her. Phineas followed Julia's gaze and tilted his head. He hunched over the child and severed the umbilical cord with a swipe of his fingernails.

Phineas scooped Alma off the floor and cradled her in the crook of a long, bony arm, their bodies bathed in yellow light.

Hearing the cries of her daughter sent a swell of blood rushing to her head. Julia felt a surge of warm, stinging tears as her heart knocked inside her chest. She wanted to scream and tear out the old man's face. Instead, she felt the rage seep out from her throat until there was only lethargy.

Phineas—the lanky man— crouched low to the floor and scuttled under the oven, baby and pictures in tow, all vanishing into the shadows within.

Julia heard the creak of what may have been the hinges of a cellar door swinging open. Deep within the bowels of the house, the cries of children slithered up the floorboards before they were muffled by the howling wind.

Dark spots filled Julia's eyes as the skin on her body grew cold and numb, as if she were melding into the frigid floor itself. Outside, the car's headlights flickered as the snowstorm continued to rage through the night.

A Pale Stranger

MACKENZIE HURLBERT

Inspired by "Witch Image"

Curled on the shadowed stoop of the grocer's shop, I feign sleep as the constable approaches on horseback. I feel the weight of his gaze wash over me, hear the horse slow its stride. With my face half-hidden behind a ragged scarf, I'm just another bum, forgotten and discarded in the dusty corners of this city. He does not recognize me, but I know him: his name's John Farnsworth. He has a wife and two young daughters. Off horse, he walks with a limp because of a fall he took last spring, and two days ago I treated an abscess on his right shoulder. But that's a different life, a different me. He lets me rest, more likely out of aversion than kindness, and passes on, the clip-clop of hooves fading into the night. Beneath my overcoat, my knife presses like a faithful dog against my hip. My fingers itch to pet it.

When I open my eyes, the square is empty of the day's bustling crowds. The clouds sink low, resting on the tired streets of the city. The gas lamps glow a sickly shade of amber through the haze. The moon above is barely a visible sliver. These are the ideal conditions I've been waiting for. Somewhere overhead, a child coughs. His thick, mucus-filled hacks echo through the night. It continues far longer than normal, his breaths barely interspersed wheezes. My body stiffens. No child should suffer, no matter how poor. I make a mental note to stop by tomorrow. I'll say a concerned neighbor called on their behalf. The child quiets. I wait. I've gotten good at waiting.

The widow appears to me like a specter, the evening fog licking at the hem of her cloak as she glides across the cobblestone street. Tonight, a basket swings from her hand. Her thick tangle of dark hair hangs loose around the pale smudge of her face. As luck would have it, I passed her as she shopped earlier today. Then, she'd worn her locks pinned in a braid coiled around her head like a great serpent and left the alabaster slope of her neck exposed—an unblemished landscape slipping beneath the dark cloth of her dress. She wore no cross around her neck, no locket housing the hair of a lost loved one. Her hands were bare of rings and bracelets. She was so unlike the other ladies in the market who clustered around the jewelers' carts like magpies. No one paid her much mind as she picked her way unaccompanied through the merchants. I stayed a few steps behind, but oh, how my hands ached to settle above the hollows of her collar bone, how I yearned to squeeze, to choke the secrets out of her and feel the fragile muscles tense and strain against the pressure!

As she selected a goose from one of the stalls, I watched and clenched the loose sleeves of my coat in my fists. *You must wait*, I told myself. *The best hunters know when to hold and when to fire.* Now she's only a few footsteps away. The anticipation is almost over, and the handle of my knife warms in my fingers like the palm of a lover. I track her movements with only my eyes, not daring to lift my head off the cold stone of the stoop. She glides through the night as if she belongs here—this pale stranger as shadow-friendly as an owl.

I wasn't always this patient. There was a time when I indulged in nearly two a week, ridding this city of its diseases with the point of my blade. Sometimes I collected the lost souls who sheltered in the shadows of alleys or lingered by the docks—the opium addicts, the gamblers, the thieves. Other times I'd choose girls selling their bodies like ham shanks on the butcher's block. All discardable, all forgettable. Killing them was like feasting on sugar cubes—satisfying and euphoric following the immediate crunch. But afterward, I felt empty, sour-stomached, and desperately hungry for something more . . . substantial. Something more impactful. This city needs a good blood-letting. Something beyond the everyday diseases of whores and scoundrels.

This dark woman, for example, intrigues me. There's the confident angle of her chin, the devious glint in her black gaze, and the way she never smiles, not even for the children who attempt to sell her flowers in the market—a woman that sure and serious is a dangerous creature. I watch her cross the square and disappear around the corner, her steps sound and steady. She wears the night like a second skin, careless of what might lurk in the endless shadows around her. I smile and finger the handle of my knife, picture it piercing the white canvas of her chest and drawing forth droplets as red and juicy as pomegranate seeds. I imagine carving a smile across her pallid cheeks. I count to ten, taking a breath between each beat, then I'm on my feet, a hound after a scent.

Since our paths first crossed, I've seen her make the trek to visit the

A Pale Stranger

grave nightly but for how long she's done it, I do not know. I've staked out the widow's route for weeks now and can easily envision each of her footsteps in my mind. She crosses the square, heads south toward the docks, turns left by the old customs house, and follows Grand Ave. up three blocks until she enters the cemetery. Her secretive strolls in nights past have ended with hushed prayers over a tomb. I could not creep close enough to make out her words but stood entranced by her deep tone, her raised palms, the bob of her head as she emphasized certain syllables with her hair flowing freely around her shoulders—there was something so wrong about it, so disturbingly lewd. No woman of any propriety should walk the streets alone at night, and if this widow was to mourn properly, if she truly had nothing to hide, why would she make these visits under the cover of darkness?

I take deep breaths and force myself to trail her leisurely, my muscles humming with tension. I arrive in time to see the black wisps of her cloak passing through the cemetery gates.

Beyond, the stunted shapes of trees hunch over tombstones crumbled and tormented by the years. She passes under their branches and becomes a shadow within a shadow, a dark wraith-like presence sweeping among stone, root, and grass.

I draw close enough to smell the heavy spiced notes of her perfume as she stops before a large, lidded tomb. Her husband's, I presume, though the stone is devoid of script.

I tuck myself behind a tree and watch as she shifts the basket to the ground and kneels in front of the large slab of dark granite. In nights past, she's bowed her head and prayed, her lips moving in quiet incantations. Tonight, though, is different. She places the items from her basket on the stone: two soot-black candles, a bundle of dried herbs, pale columns of chalk. My breath catches as she tugs the goose from her basket as well. One of her hands smooths the feathers of the bird, its neck stiffly bent over its back like the curve of a shepherd's crook. Her fingers trail over the cold carcass, preening and plucking loose down. Satisfied, she places the bird breast-up on the granite and sketches around it in chalk.

It is too dark to make out what she's drawn, but my God-fearing soul knows, just as I knew when I first saw her that she was my next task. Part of the festering disease within this city that calls for a doctor's touch. A witch. *I've hunted myself a witch.* Who knows what curses she's laid upon the good people of this city. Who knows what kind of evil she's harbored here under my nose. The knife at my side sings to me. My body tingles with the anticipation of darkening the earth at our feet with her blood.

She snaps a match to life and touches the tip to her candles, their soft glow illuminating the tomb, her freshly drawn pentagram, and two adjoining circles of script. Candlelight bathes her face—the black pits of her eyes, the grim line of her mouth—in flickering yellow. I risk one glance toward the street to ensure we're alone.

Beyond the cemetery gates the city is a wall of amber-tinted fog. I doubt the glow from her candles would be visible to a passerby, but even so I'd hate for someone to come spoil my fun. I need to act fast.

My hand reaches to grip my blade but what I see next makes me pause, my palm clammy around the bone handle. She has a knife of her own, retrieved from the folds of her skirts. I watch as she pinches the skin of the goose's stomach and slices an opening. She places her blade to the side, her practiced fingers sink into the cut and stretch it wider, unveiling the dark flesh of the bird's breast. Fluffy bits of down drift to her feet and swirl off into the fog.

Act now, the logical side of me cries. *While her hands are busy and before she completes this depraved ritual.*

But the curious part of me overrules rationality—I'm a man of science, after all and observation is a key part of the scientific method. *I'll just wait a little longer. To see what kind of evil I'm extinguishing. For how am I to cure the spread of the disease without studying it first?*

The witch has ripped the skin to either side of the goose and carefully carves out each breast, placing one on a chalk circle to her right and the other to her left. Next, with precise cuts, she removes the goose's liver. Her eyes glint in the candlelight as she mutters, her voice husky and deep. This close, I can finally make out they're Latin incantations carrying a music of their own. Though I once studied the language in school, my ears only detect a handful of words: *Diabolus. Poena. Vindicta.*

She cradles the liver in the cup of her palms and raises it to her lips, her dark lashes fluttering closed as she bites with tentative care. It's almost ladylike how she tears off a small morsel, chews, and swallows. The bloody meat darkens her lips as she murmurs more words and takes a larger bite, this time pressing her face into the mess in her hands, smearing blood from nose to chin. She whispers a final word and downs the last of the flesh. With one thick gulp, her eyes snap open and the candles flare, casting a sudden surge of heat and light bright enough to make me flinch and jerk behind the tree trunk.

I rub the shock from my eyes and peer back in time to see the goose jolt. The witch rises to her feet and holds her bloody palms to either side. Before her, the carcass twitches once, twice, and lifts into the air, the long strands of its intestines shaking loose and falling in heavy loops to the tomb's lid. The goose's wings stretch out to either side—their soft white feathers angelic in the candles' glow. She stretches her palms out as the goose's long neck uncurls and strains skyward. "Da mihi retributionem,"

A Pale Stranger

she speaks, as if she is addressing me directly, and then it all bursts into flames. The carcass, the chalk outlines, the cuts of meat. The candles glow infernally hot then dim and collapse into puddles of black wax. The witch's head hangs low, as if she too has been extinguished.

I'm beside her in two steps, the knife raised over my head. I can't fight the grin spreading across my face. I crave the soft pop of my knife tip piercing skin. I ready myself to pin her flailing arms, to stifle any scream she might release. But the blade never drops—no, instead I'm frozen there, my arm raised, my right foot mid-step. My pulse thrums yet I'm pinned like a bug in a shadowbox. I strain against whatever forces have their hold on me but it's no use. Not even my smile twitches from the effort.

The witch raises her head, meeting my gaze with a grin of her own. "It took you long enough," she said, sheathing her own knife beneath her skirts. She plucks mine from my hand and tosses it into the bushes. Her teeth are bloody from the liver and my heartbeat flutters as she runs her tongue over them. "I've been waiting a long time to meet you."

She steps closer, stretching one gory palm to cup my cheek. Her touch is slick and warm, like a freshly birthed babe. "You think you're some great protector, don't you? Some Angel of Death. Who are you to deem who's worthy and unworthy of life?"

I strain to answer, to scream, but I stay silent as the tombs around us while I fight to gasp for breath. I manage a thin inhale as tears pool in my eyes. I can't blink them back so they spill over and travel down my cheeks, collecting on the point of my chin. Her power is a cold frost crackling around my joints, seeping into the grooves of my muscles, the darkest pockets of my lungs. I feel as if my entire being is gripped in ice and frozen still, too still to even shiver.

"You killed the wrong girl," the witch says, her smile morphing into something wilder. The bared teeth of a predator. Her hand slips below my cheek and settles on my neck, gripping like a vice. "I'd tell you her name, but I doubt you bothered to ask it."

My mind flashes back to all the girls I killed. The one who wore her hair in two braids like a child. The one with the birthmark right above her navel who'd bit me as I sunk my blade into her. The one with the green ribbon tied around her neck, or the other who wore a locket I didn't dare open, even when she lay still and cooling in the alleyway. There were others—blue eyes, brown eyes, blonde hair, curls black as a crow. I search the witch's face for something familiar and fail.

Her hand drops from my neck and my body falls slack to the ground, knocking the remaining air out of me. Shivering violently, I fight the hollow ache and drag in a ragged breath, my fingers gripping into the earth. I flip onto my back and attempt to scramble away, my feet kicking out against root and toppled headstones. She follows me in slow, steady steps, her thin lips settling into a grim line.

"Get away from me," I cry. My hand lands on a rock, and I throw it at her with all my force. She bats it away easily and barks out a laugh.

"You think you know Death, Angel?" The witch watches me push myself to my feet, her head tilted to the side. "You'll meet him soon enough." With that she tosses her head back and cackles, her laughter ringing out across the cemetery and lingering in the night. I run as fast as my legs will carry me toward the cemetery gates, to the glow of the gas lamps. When I reach the street, I pause and turn back, expecting to see her at my heels. Instead, the graveyard is empty. No candlelight or silhouettes shifting among the shadows. Still, I feel the weight of her gaze and rush forward into the foggy city streets. *The constable. I need to find the constable and report this!*

As if summoned, the clip-clop of hooves on cobblestones sounds distantly in the night. "John!" I scream, running toward the sound. "Constable!"

The galloping grows louder, faster as if he's rushing my way. Relief washes through me like a cool night breeze. "Constable!" I cry again. "John, over here!"

He's no more than a block away now, his horse's pace tapping out the same rhythm as my pulse.

I was in the cemetery paying respects to a former patient of mine, I plan to say. *And I was attacked by a woman performing a satanic ritual.* John might laugh at first, sure, but he'll see the blood on my face and clothes. He'll know I'm not joking.

I hear him slow, and out of the fog he appears, a rider on horseback plodding toward me through the haze.

I run into the street to meet him. "John, my God. You wouldn't believe . . ." My voice falters. John rides a chestnut mare, but this horse is as pale as bone. It trots closer, the beast's long mane of silver flame licking out in all directions. Its eyes, the pure void of a starless night, settle on me as it huffs. The silent rider, a dark hood pulled over his face, circles me. The black cave of his hood pivots to face me with each turn as I swallow back a whimper. His body is swaddled in a great cloak fraying into tendrils of smoke at the edges. In his wake, large flakes of ash drift to the cobblestones like fallen snow.

From the street behind me, the witch cackles again, her laughter ripping through the night and coaxing the shadows out from where they cling to the walls. My nose fills with the spice of her perfume, and I wrench my gaze from the rider to find her watching, silhouetted by the gas lamps' glow.

A Pale Stranger

In one smooth toss, the rider loops a silver thread of smoke around my neck and draws it tight. The pressure of it crushes my throat, and I claw at it uselessly, my nails digging into my own flesh. I can't breathe, I can't scream. I fall to my knees and fight to inhale. My chest burns with the need for air as I pray for death to claim me, to end this suffering. The rider presses his heels into the sides of his steed and takes off at a gallop, dragging me across the city streets and toward a future with no end in sight.

A Sun Within the Fog

COLT SKINNER

Inspired by "Elizabeth"

I watched the fog roll in, standing in front of our tent while wrapped in a thick blanket and wearing three layers of socks. Slowly, the mist surrounded. First it covered the apartment buildings on the other side of the train tracks, turning them into featureless monoliths before swallowing them whole. Then it crawled through the trees and over the fence, caught the glimmer of the waning sun, and ignited the sky in marigold-orange. Finally, it reached our camp and left us blind.

"It's beautiful," said a tired voice beside me. The sound raked a shiver down my spine, and made my stomach roll. It was my daughter, Elizabeth. Her pale face was turned upwards, eyes fixed on the dim glow of the sun, which barely penetrated the gloom.

I smiled, but my lips curled in an off-putting way that was more grimace than anything else. "How are you feeling?" I asked while pulling my blanket tight around my neck.

Elizabeth shrugged. "I feel the same."

The fog carried ice into my lungs as I drew a breath, and bit at my insides.

"Are you cold?"

She shook her head.

"I still have a few of those hand warmers they gave us back at the shelter, if you'd like one."

"I'm okay, Dad, really."

My chest squeezed as I looked at her; petite and delicate, yet her features had become severe since we started living this way, like a flower left out to dry in the late summer heat.

A Sun Within the Fog

Impulsively, I asked, "Are you hungry?", and immediately regretted my question.

Elizabeth turned her attention away from the sun and looked at me. For a moment, one which lasted too long, she was silent and her eyes were serpentine. Then, as a mercy, she grumbled, "I don't need anything right now, but you can eat if you want."

I thought about going into our tent and fetching the bag of potato chips I had stored away there, but I realised how cruel it would be to eat in front of her. "No, I'm okay too."

I walked over to the oak tree which canopied our camp, leaned against the rough bark, and slid down until my butt hit the ground. As my bones fell into rest, I came to realise how sore I was. Everything ached. My joints were stiff, my muscles throbbed, even my skin felt raw. It had been two weeks of sleeping on hard ground with a thin layer of polyester between us and the frost, tucked away from the rest of humanity like a pair of rats. Never resting, never stopping. I'd been plum tired for days. In truth, I barely had any steam left, but I couldn't admit that to anyone; not my daughter, not even to myself.

Elizabeth looked at the dim sun, and we kept a desperate silence between us. The fog grew thicker, until the glowing dot in the sky vanished. I decided I could no longer take the silence between us, so I started to speak. I was awkward, fumbly, and instead of finding words of encouragement, support, or empathy, I stumbled my way into the conversation Elizabeth and I had been avoiding.

"I think we should move on tomorrow."

Her eyes snapped in my direction, and her brow furrowed. "Why?"

I shrugged. "We can't stay here forever."

"Why not?"

"You know why not."

Her lips thinned.

"I'm sorry." I said, shaking my head in annoyance with my own self. "I just think we've been here long enough. It's time to push on and find something better."

She huffed out a laugh filled with disdain, "We don't have anything to *push on* to."

"You think that's my fault?" I barked.

"I didn't say that." Elizabeth sneered.

White-hot fury rose into my cheeks. I slapped the ground beside me, sending a plume of dirt into the air. "I'm doing my best here, kiddo!"

"I AM TOO!"

I put both hands up in apology and steadied myself. "I know, love. I know you are."

Colt Skinner

With a quiver, she said, "I didn't mean too . . ."

Her face softened with a child's worry, which made my guts feel rotten. I stood, with less grace than I would have liked, went over to my daughter, and hugged her. "I know that, lovey."

With both arms wrapped around me, Elizabeth buried her face into my chest and squeezed so tight it hurt. "I miss her so much."

Gently, I kissed the top of her head. "I know."

My arms twitched, then my hands shook, and when my teeth chattered Elizabeth said, "You're shivering," as though I were too stupid to know it for myself.

"I'm okay, just a little cold is all."

She raised an exasperated eyebrow. "You need to *stay* warm. If you get cold, you'll never get warm again. Use those hand warmers for yourself, put them under your arm pits."

"I'm fine." I said, and gave her another crooked smile. "I'll make us a fire for tonight."

"We don't have any wood." she rightly said.

I opened my arms wide and twisted from side to side in an overly dramatic gesture. "Just look around. There's trees and bushes all over the place. I'll cut some wood, and we'll have a fire lickety split."

Elizabeth's lips lifted on the sides, it was subtle, barely there, but it was the first smile I'd seen from her in a long time and it was glorious to me.

"You don't have an axe."

I raised a finger, then raced into the tent. After rummaging through my bag, I pulled out an old hammer with a wood handle, and waved it around as I came back outside. The tool had belonged to my grandfather, and was one of the only personal possessions I had left. It felt sturdy in my hand, and the weight of it grounded me, reminding me I was someone who had once been capable of many things.

"Here!' I said, "I can use this to crack up whatever we need."

Elizabeth nodded. The sight of her head bobbing up and down made the tension in my body relax.

Carefully, I straightened the blanket over my shoulders. "I'll be right back." I made my way into the fog.

While Elizabeth and I were discussing ourselves and the making of a fire, the orange along the horizon changed to fuchsia. Soon, I knew, the sun would be forgotten for the day, and my daughter and I would be left alone in the quiet of the night. I foraged for dry wood by the side of the tracks, careful not to stray too close. Though I had no doubt I would hear a train coming, with the fog surrounding and my mind preoccupied, I didn't want to risk being too near the tracks. Some twigs for kindling and dry leaves for starter was all I could find. There was an empty pizza box by

A Sun Within the Fog

a briar patch, and a plastic bag filled with used tissue paper, but I thought both looked dirty and decided to leave them. With the back of my hammer I removed some of the lower branches from a birch tree, and had an armful by the time I was done, enough to get a fire going and warm the chill in my bones and my blood.

I was about to make my way back to camp when the ground beneath me rumbled. The fog lit up, dim at first, then growing in intensity until it was like an angel ripping out of the heavens. The train blasted its horn. Whoever was on board saw me as a derelict figure by the side of the tracks, an object to be moved out of the way. I waved at the conductor as he rolled by, but his face was sour, and he looked at me like I was lice found in the hair of a dog.

I wondered if Elizabeth could see the behemoth passing by. Curious, I looked back at our camp, hoping I might see her excited face, but the fog was dense, and I couldn't see my child.

A train of passenger cars followed the locomotive. Through the misty windows I saw a man wearing a fedora, a group of teenagers taking up an entire car, and a plethora of folks ignoring the world around them. It was all mundane, until the last car. Towards the back, sitting with her feet stretched over another seat, I saw a woman with chestnut hair and warmly tanned skin. She was reading a paperback novel, and the way her eyes casually focused, both intense and whimsical at the same time, reminded me of my wife.

The branches fell to the ground first, then the twigs and leaves. I followed afterwards.

Gasping for air, clawing at my throat, and pounding against my chest, I couldn't draw breath. Dark encircled and my head wavered. Within this storm I had a vision; my lovely wife, her olive skin smeared with blood, looking at me with those intense eyes of hers, half expecting the horror she had just endured to turn into a joke, and cowering in front of us-our Elizabeth.

When I finally regained my composure the sky was plum in colour. Frantically, I gathered my kindling and ran back to camp, stumbling with almost every step I took. As I approached, the tenor of a man's voice struck me with panic. Who was this person? An intruder? Police?

"Hello?" I called out.

"Hi!" the voice answered, pleasantly.

When I got back to the camp, I saw a young man standing beside our tent. Elizabeth was with him, a gregarious smile plastered on her face.

"Dad!" She said in a chipper tone. "This is Phillip. He's an outreach worker."

Phillip used two fingers to salute me. "Yeah, that's right, from St. Gregory's."

Colt Skinner

I relaxed a little and dropped the makings of our fire onto the ground.

"St. Gregory's," I said, "We were there early this week, got some hand warmers and snacks from you folks."

Phillip reached out and offered his hand, which I shook vigorously.

"Yes," he said, "I think I remember seeing you two there."

"You people do outreach in weather like this?" I asked.

Phillip pulled his hand back, and chuckled. "Not usually, I was already walking around when the fog came in. I do rounds out here two or three times a week."

"By the tracks?" Elizabeth asked.

"Oh sure!" Phillip exclaimed. "There's lot of folks who camp along the tracks. The city's always kicking people out of the parks, and lord help you if you try to sleep any place downtown, but the railway companies won't bother you so long as you don't interfere with the trains. Lots of folks end up around here. Have you met Left-Hand Ed yet?"

Elizabeth and I shook our heads.

Phillip pointed south. "He lives about a mile down, been there for years. He's a good enough sort, talks to JFK, and his dead mother a lot, but he's a kind soul. If you come across him, he'll help you figure out what's what. Which, if you don't mind me saying, you look to be a little bit in need of."

Sheepishly, I scuffed the ground with the toe of my boot. "That obvious?"

Phillip smiled in a warm and bright kind of way. "Well, that tent doesn't look like it's weathered too many storms, and your boots are still in one piece. I'd say you've only been sleeping rough for a couple of weeks at best."

Shame bloomed in my cheeks.

"Not my business to judge or nothin'." Phillip said while raising a hand defensively. "People live the best lives they can, and God throws all sorts of curve balls at 'em. Hell, I've had my share of ups and downs myself. Just saying, if you need help, St. Gregory's has resources, and there's a whole community of folks in similar situations that you can lean on."

"Well, that's good to hear." I said, still kicking at the dirt.

Phillip smiled again. "You trying to start a fire?"

I looked at the pile I had acquired and nodded. "Was hoping to."

"Do you have everything you need?"

"Just about." I answered. "A little lean on wood, but I got some bark here."

"Well, it's your lucky day. I'm handing out fire logs!" Phillip exclaimed. "The ones you buy in a store that are all compacted and glued together. Colin Trepes owns a couple of hardware stores around town, he gave us a skid of them as a donation. They're really good too, last for hours."

A Sun Within the Fog

A ray of hope broke through the fog inside of my head, and with a breath of relief I said, "That's wonderful!"

"I have some in a pile by where the fence opens. I'll grab you one." Phillip nodded.

"I can get it!" Elizabeth exclaimed. "I know where the break in the fence is, that's where *we* came through."

I thought better of letting her go, but she seemed so excited to have purpose, so I nodded in agreement. Her eyes lit up, and she ran off. I watched her run along the tracks and disappear into the fog.

"She's wonderful." Phillip said.

"She is." I replied.

"How is she getting along?" The church-man asked.

I rolled my head. "Better than I thought she would be, but the last two weeks have been really hard."

"Wanna talk about it?" Phillip asked.

I shook my head.

"Well, if you ever want to, we run groups down at the church."

I gave Phillip a smile and nodded.

"Kids are resilient anyways," said the outreach worker. "They go through things that would break adults, but carry on like nothing happened."

"That's probably why there's so many adults in therapy." I replied.

Phillip chuckled; the sound wasn't happy, it was uncomfortable to listen to, as though he liked the thought. "You're probably right about that." He said, then he paused, looked sheepishly in my direction, and then at his feet. "Is she in school?"

I shook my head. "Not at the moment."

"She has to be in school. You know that, right?" The tone of Phillip's voice was suddenly different, no longer friendly and helpful, but condescending and serious.

"I guess so." I answered with a shrug.

"If she's not in school, that's grounds to take her away from you. It's a form of neglect."

I jerked my head in his direction, stunned by the shift in conversation. "What's that now?"

A wickedly cretinous smile came over Phillips face, and he said, "Look man, it's bad enough you're sleeping rough, the state doesn't like that one bit, but if they find out you're keeping her out of school, they'll come after her for sure."

I stood in stunned silence.

"How old is she? Eleven, twelve?"

"Twelve next month." I answered, not thinking before I did.

Colt Skinner

Phillip sucked his teeth and stepped closer to me. "Sheesh, that's young. If she was fourteen or fifteen they might let it slide, but eleven, that's too young to be living this way. They'll take her away from you. I've seen it happen many times."

"Well, we're fixing on moving on anyways, so it shouldn't be an issue."

Phillip shook his head, and once again chuckled in his grating way. "The problem is though, I have to go back and report that I came across you two out here. I have to report any instances of child endangerment directly to the cops."

"Endangerment?"

"That's how the government sees it." He took another step towards me. "Most likely the police will come out tonight to get her, and put her in emergency foster care."

"They can't!" I yelled.

"They have to. It's for her own safety."

"But *you* don't *have* to report that you came across us."

Phillip nodded. "Of course, I do. I could get in *really* big trouble if I didn't. Face jail time even."

"Please!" I begged.

The church-man looked in the direction Elizabeth had run off in, and stared for an uncomfortably long time. "Maybe we could work something out."

Phillip reached into his pocket, pulled out forty dollars, and shoved it into my hands. "Here, take this. Go buy dinner for you and her."

I stared at the money, dumbfounded.

"Just go buy dinner." He repeated, now gritting his teeth.

"Okay?" I said, cautiously. "When Elizabeth comes back, I'll take her."

Phillip shook his head. "No," he said. He pointed in the opposite direction of where Elizabeth had gone. "There's another break in the fence that way. You'll come out in a cul-de-sac of apartment buildings. If you take the first left you come across, walk a few blocks, you'll find this shitty bodega. They have fried bologna sandwiches and waffle fries there, all real cheap. Get dinner, keep the change, take your time . . . and when you come back I'll be gone and there won't be any need for me to call the police on you and your daughter. It's better for both of you that way."

The reality of what Phillip was proposing sunk in. Disgust and betrayal flooded my brain, causing my body to shrivel into itself. I remember a blinding white light, then I pushed the churchman away, grabbed the hammer from my waist band, raised it into the air, and waved it around like a lunatic.

"YOU GET THE FUCK AWAY FROM US!" I shouted. "GET OUT OF HERE RIGHT NOW OR I'LL BASH YOUR FUCKING SKULL IN!"

A Sun Within the Fog

Phillip didn't scare though, he didn't even flinch. Instead, he stepped towards me, grabbed the wrist I held the hammer in, and kneed me square in the balls. A rush of sharp pain spread from my groin, spider webbing through my stomach and making me feel nauseous. I fell to the ground and rocked back and forth while stars rolled through my vision.

A foot came to rest beside my face. I looked and saw Phillip standing over me, holding my grandfather's hammer. During the fray I'd lost my grip on the weapon, and now the churchman had it in his clutches.

"It's a good thing it's so foggy out." Phillip smirked. "Even if another train comes by no one will be able to see us. Left-Hand Ed is the only other person around, and if he hears you or your little bitch of a daughter scream, he'll just think it's a hallucination. When I'm done, I'm gonna strike your tent and bury the two of you, all before the fog lets up. No one's ever gonna know what happened to you."

Gleaming, eyes wild with excitement, Phillip raised the hammer over his head, and then he was gone.

I heard what was happening, but I couldn't see it at first. It sounded like a dog tearing meat from bone and growling possessively. The churchman screamed, then yelped, then whimpered. I heard him claw and gouge with his fingernails, trying to defend himself with what remaining dignity he had left, but when the slurping started he fell silent.

At the periphery of the fog, in the place where the gloom became opaque, I saw Elizabeth. She was hunched over Phillip, suckling violently from his neck, and spasming in ecstasy with each draw she took. I started to reach out towards her, then remembered what her mother had done and drew my hand back.

Another train rolled by, and for a moment I was scared. I worried everyone on board would see us. I thought they would call the police, who would come and take Elizabeth away, making the last two weeks of hiding be all for nothing. But, Phillip was right. The fog was thick and from our camp all I could make out of the train was a cloudy streak of light. No one would see us, no one would ever know what happened here.

When the train finally left, I realised I could no longer hear slurping. I rolled back in the direction of our tent and saw Elizabeth resting on her haunches, blood cascading down her chin, dripping onto her pants and shirt, and pooling at her feet. Her eyes were feral.

A new shiver ran down my spine, not from the cold, but from the fear I held towards my own daughter.

She took a deep breath. Her eyes softened, and calmly, she asked, "Are you okay?"

I nodded. The side of my face smeared in the dirt.

"We'll have to leave for sure now, won't we?"

Colt Skinner

Again, I nodded.

"Can you pack while I finish?"

I placed a hand on my chest and felt the throb of my beating heart. "Of course."

Elizabeth smiled, wide and happy, her crimson mouth covered in pink fleshy shards, and despite the gruesomeness of it all, I saw my daughter once again.

Above us two crows cawed in unison, and took flight into the now black sky. Elizabeth's expression changed. Her face became heavy. In a tone just above a whisper, she said, "I'm sorry."

I stood, wiped the grime from my face, and shook my head. "You don't have anything to be sorry about, he was a bad person."

"Not about him."

My strength wavered as I realised she was speaking about her mother. Tears dripped down my cheeks, and my bottom lip quivered.

"I really didn't mean to hurt her." said my Elizabeth.

"I know baby . . . " I said while taking a step towards her. "I know that, and your mother knew that too. None of this is your fault my love. It's ours."

She closed her eyes, and a dry sob escaped her.

"The night you were attacked," I continued, "it was the worst night of our lives. We heard your window open, and the sound of that terrible *thing* scampering down the side of our house. I knew right away something was wrong. Your mom was about to call the police, but I found pieces of your clothing leading towards the woods, so I pulled her away from the phone and we followed."

"We found you, unconscious, in a heap by the river; pale and bruised, and bloodied at the neck. The thing that took you was already gone, it had everything it wanted, so it left you for dead. We should have taken you to the hospital, but we were so ashamed that we hadn't been able to protect you . . . So, we didn't."

I punched myself in the hip, hard, and took another step towards my child. Elizabeth allowed her face to bask in the newly darkened sky, but kept her eyes closed.

"Your attack seemed surreal, like it couldn't have actually happened. So, when you started to change, we ignored that on purpose. It felt like, if we admitted you were different, then we had to also admit you had been taken from right underneath our noses. That *we* had let this terrible thing happen to you. It would mean we had failed, totally, as parents."

I continued walking, and when I came to her I knelt, and placed a fatherly hand on her shoulder.

"Please, believe me," I told her, "what happened to your mother, it

A Sun Within the Fog

wasn't your fault, it was ours. Our ignorance, our impatience. If we had just listened to you when you told us something was wrong . . . "

Her eyes shot open.

Startled, I recoiled, and made the mistake of removing my hand from the shoulder I had helped create. She looked at me, in a way that penetrated. Her eyes were no longer soft, they were dark, serpentine, and violently feral once again.

On Hollow Pass

MICHAEL BALLETTI

Inspired by "Absolution"

The squeal of braking tires, an awkward pause, and a violent crash didn't surprise Ken, but it jarred him nonetheless. The car had been riding his ass since he left Pop's Bar. When it roared past, Ken knew the guy behind the wheel wasn't from town. The vehicle itself was a major clue (he couldn't remember the last time he saw a Firebird), as were the tinted windows and KISMET emblazoned on a difficult-to-decipher state license plate. But the biggest giveaway was the decision to make a move in the middle of Hollow Pass.

Ken inched forward with high beams blazing and hazard lights clicking. The adrenaline surge he felt moments after hearing the impact was already fading, and it did nothing but intensify his burgeoning headache. This was the last thing he needed. Stopping in the middle of Hollow Pass.

Established in the days of muskets and moonshine to connect the sprawling city of Krawen to its more rural areas—like Birchwood—Hollow Pass was a boon to early traders and settlers. The road cut a path through lush forests and temperate grasslands, creating viable opportunities for the locals, and improving access to markets. But a series of unfortunate mishaps (a polite way to say numerous fatalities) on Hollow Pass led many travelers to deem sections too treacherous. Despite mostly halfhearted alterations and cursory improvements, riders eventually abandoned it for safer, more accessible thoroughfares, resulting in dwindling commerce to Krawen and neighboring towns.

Ken parked his car on an expanse of gravel and dirt that acted ostensibly as a shoulder and walked toward the Firebird, which was smashed accordion-like into a gnarled tree. Armies of densely packed oaks, pines, maples, and shagbark hickories, marred by unforgiving winters and

On Hollow Pass

rain-drenched soil, slanted across both sides of the road, creating an unintentional tree tunnel that looked far from enchanting. Leaves on those knotted and interlacing boughs formed a vast canopy during spring and summer, allowing only glints of sunlight to fleck this ribbon of blacktop. But those warmer months had given way to autumn, and only lonely leaves remained. Moonlight seeped in, casting the road into spidery shades of silver, and high above, barren branches stretched upward, like gaunt fingers grasping for scraps of food.

Ken had made hundreds of nocturnal drives through this area. But now, without the safety of his car to protect him, the angled trees took a more sinister tone, almost as if they were huddling, communicating in furtive whispers, weighing whether to snatch him with their blackened limbs and bury him in their yawning burls. Crickets and night birds were in full throat, most likely intensified by the Firebird's rude intrusion, and Ken imagined the movements of larger creatures scampering and slithering among the overgrown weeds, the dead foliage, the unchecked brambles.

Portions of Hollow Pass were still considered dangerous, even with the demise of horse and carriage, and this was one of them. This narrow scar of road inclined and declined through two miles of twisting, undeveloped woodlands, snaking left and right before leveling off and feeding into tributary outlets. Strange little shacks rested deep in those woods, time-battered and forgotten. Farther down, desolate farmhouses pockmarked segments of Hollow Pass, bleak monuments to a time when everything was used and nothing was wasted. The once rich and fertile soil, long ago reduced to broken dreams and ash, now mimicked graveyard dirt, mute testimony to a failed economic plan. A slice of Americana grown wormy and rancid—a bittersweet reminder of something once revered and now lost.

If not for the Birchwood Preservation Society, Hollow Pass would have been closed to traffic ages ago. But some people have a hard time letting go of the past, even if it's a holdover from a time not worth remembering. For Ken, all that was ancient history. This part of Hollow Pass held more practical value: It was the quickest way for him to get home from Pop's. And perhaps more importantly, it was usually free of cops prowling for speeders and drunks. Hollow Pass was just another backwoods road in the disconnected, depressing town of Birchwood. It fit Ken like a glove.

The stench hit him immediately. It wasn't burned rubber or the chemical smell of deployed air bags, which were present and expected. This was a sour smell, like meat kept too long in the fridge. A dead animal? Maybe, but this seemed different somehow. It was tinged with the unpleasant antiseptic fragrance omnipresent in hospitals and nursing facilities. Its intensity brought Ken to the brink of gagging, forcing him to spit in an attempt to clear his head.

His first impulse was to check on the driver, but it seemed likely the poor slob behind the wheel was in bad shape. And Ken didn't know if he could stomach a bloody spectacle, especially with the booze sloshing through his insides. He looked at the star-strewn sky. There was a time, not too long ago, when Ken would have bolted into that cracked-up car to help the driver, even if the guy was asking for it by speeding around Hollow Pass. But that was before Laura, before . . .

What the hell was that smell?

Ken's mind computed options in the few seconds it took him to examine the scene. With equal parts shame and satisfaction, he thought it best not to get involved. If he called the paramedics, the police would be sure to follow, and he didn't need a cop giving him a breathalyzer test. Those things were so damned erratic. Two drinks and that machine would have his blood alcohol level right up there with what killed John Bonham. The cops might even think *he* caused the accident. And Ken wasn't about to spend time in jail for some dumb ass with a heavy foot.

It wasn't noble, and Ken would wince if he spoke the words aloud, but someone would pass through here sooner or later. Besides, no way anyone was alive. No sense risking himself to save a dead man.

He took one last look at the car. It smoldered like a twisted black claw. That smell. Over and over, his mind repeated:

That smell is making you run.

Ken ignored the voice and started back to his car when something registered in his peripheral vision. At first, he thought it was his imagination or the eerie, pulsing glow of his hazards upon the trees. Ken stood hypnotized amid the haunting effect, lost in the timed bursts of amber light. Click, click. Click, click. Click, click. Then moments dissolved into odd, confusing sounds. Rhythmic rocking. Creaking metal. Shuffling glass. Panic bubbled in Ken's belly like acid, rooting his feet in place, as a nebulous blob spilled out of the Firebird's open driver's side window and thudded onto the damp earth like a birthed calf.

The planet tilted on its axis, and silence fell with the swiftness of a guillotine, obliterating everything but the whooshing of blood roaring through Ken's ears. He took a nervous step backward, animation thankfully returning to his extremities, but never pulled his eyes off the shadowy mass advancing toward him like a thunderhead.

This can't be real, he thought.

Maybe you've finally lost it. Maybe you've finally gone off the deep end.

Ken couldn't believe the thing manifesting out of the ill-defined trees.

On Hollow Pass

It was a woman—tall and lean and wearing a leather trench coat. Her face floated out of the darkness, a porcelain mask bent in annoyance, eyes creased into tiny slits. Shiny jet-black hair poured down her back like a cascade of oil. Hell, she couldn't be more than 20 or 21. Just a kid, probably around the same age as Laura had she . . .

Ken clenched his fists and bit hard on his bottom lip, drawing blood.

Sound returned to the world.

"That's some road you guys got up here," she said, shielding her eyes from his car's dazzling headlights with one long, bony hand. Her voice was light and airy, almost sing-song, but it did not quell Ken's apprehension.

"Yeah," he replied, his fists turning to damp washcloths.

She stopped and grinned. "Listen. Do you know where Woodland Drive is? I was told it was around here somewhere, but . . . "

"Yeah," Ken blurted. His heart was pounding like a jackhammer. It felt like it was going to explode and land right at her feet. And even though he knew it was impossible, knew it couldn't be, Ken felt as if she was watching it pump rapidly in his chest, felt as if she could see through the skin and bone, right to the muscle, gazing with what seemed like a flicker of sexual arousal. For a moment, Ken felt exposed and naked, like she was *reading* his heart. Discovering all his loves, all his fears . . .

All his secrets.

"Great," she replied.

Her voice broke the spell, and Ken regained his bearings. He brought a hand to his chest and rubbed it protectively. She wasn't attractive in the classic sense—much too pale and skinny for Ken's tastes—but she did exude a strange magnetism, an odd quality he couldn't put his finger on.

Why are you thinking about that? You're old enough to be her father.

His eyes shifted over her shoulder toward the mangled Firebird she walked out of apparently unscathed, but her penetrating stare never wavered. An uncomfortable stillness hung in the air, broken only by an intrepid owl's intermittent hooting. Then she smiled, slow and broad, the act cutting two tiny dimples in her heart-shaped face.

"Still got all my fingers and toes," she said, wiggling her fingers in a macabre dance. "Someone must be looking out for me, huh?"

The moon disappeared behind a fast-moving mass of black clouds, and a sudden gust of wind blew through the forest, rustling branches and bending trees left and right before dying away just as abruptly. Ken flashed the woman a dumb smile and realized absently that the smell had faded.

"Could you do me a favor?" she asked.

Michael Balletti

Ken felt the sweat pool under his armpits despite the brisk evening. He lowered the driver's side window and gripped the wheel with both hands.

"Listen," she said. "I really appreciate this." Her words were soft and gentle. "I wouldn't normally ask strangers for rides, but I really need to make this delivery."

"No problem," Ken lied. Delivery? It was 2 a.m. on a Thursday. Ken wasn't the sharpest crayon in the box, but he knew deliveries weren't made in the middle of the night by women like—he didn't even know her name. Great, he thought. He tilted his head toward the open window and gulped the crisp nighttime air.

She was staring out of the passenger side window, a lock of hair curled in her right hand, as Ken's mind raced in a million different directions. How could she have survived that crash? The car was crumpled into a tangled ball of metal. And her face. Not a scratch, a smudge, or a bruise. Nothing! How was that possible? He started to reach for her cheek but caught himself. This is crazy, he thought.

Someone at Pop's must have dropped something in one of my drinks.

He chuckled to himself and looked at the woman.

She continued to stare out the window.

Ken cleared his throat and swallowed hard. "You know, maybe it wouldn't be a bad idea to take you to a hospital, just to let them check you out," he said, hoping his voice didn't sound as shaky to her ears as it did to his own. Something about her gave him the creeps.

Maybe it's because she walked away from a giant metal coffin without a mark!

"No, I'm fine, really."

"That was a pretty bad crash. What about your car? Do you think it's a good idea to leave your . . . "

"Listen," she interrupted. Her voice was a bit harder now. "I really need to make this delivery, so I would be grateful if you could drop me off at . . . " She went inside her leather coat and pulled out a wrinkled piece of paper. "244 Woodland Drive."

Ken's trepidation vanished. Who the fuck was she, he thought, telling him what to do? He had half a mind to stop the car and throw her anorexic ass right out, let her walk out to Woodland. But something stopped him. He couldn't pinpoint it—and his throbbing temples weren't helping him focus—but it felt like he couldn't let her out, even if he wanted to. A strange sense of duty and obligation coursed through him, pushing away the

On Hollow Pass

fogginess encircling his brain. Then as quickly as the sentiment came, it was gone. The haziness returned, but the sudden anger was wiped away, replaced with his usual derisive indifference.

"Well, excuse me, sweetie. I didn't mean to get you all rattled. I was worried about you, that's all," he said, his voice dripping with sarcasm.

"Whatever."

She went into her pocket, pulled out a pack of gum, popped a piece into her mouth, and placed the pack back into her jacket without offering a piece to Ken. Then she shifted closer to the passenger side door. "And my name isn't sweetie," she said. "It's Carolyn."

The name and softness of her voice generated flickering and flashing images, causing Ken to blink repeatedly and bring a rubbing hand to his eyes. The images blew away like tendrils of smoke, but their brief appearance sent shockwaves through his body.

They drove in silence for a few minutes, eventually making their way off Hollow Pass and onto local streets, but Ken's mind was screaming.

Carolyn.

The name hadn't been spoken aloud in years, but it was never far from his lips. My beautiful Carolyn, he thought. Every morning—hungover or not—she would be the first person on his mind. Every morning he would wonder how things could have been different. But he couldn't go back, and even if he could, the two of them would have done the same thing. They both wanted to start a family. And when Carolyn got pregnant, Ken couldn't be happier. A daddy. He was going to be a daddy. And he was determined to be the best daddy ever. Something his father never was.

But complications ensued. The baby was delivered, a little girl, but Carolyn suffered excessive bleeding, something the doctors called postpartum hemorrhage. She died two days after delivery.

The first few weeks were the toughest. Carolyn's brother Dale and his wife Ann were a big help, and Ken appreciated it, even though he never said so. He didn't talk much after Carolyn passed. There wasn't much to say.

But the nights were the worst. Sometimes the baby would wake up Ken with her crying, but most of the time, Ken woke the baby with his sobs. Now he loved his daughter, truly and unconditionally, but he missed Carolyn so much. And no matter how hard he tried, no matter how much he knew it wasn't true, no matter how much he hated himself for thinking it, he couldn't stop seeing his daughter as . . . a replacement.

A few months after Carolyn's death, Ken was alone in the house. It was just Ken. Just Ken and his daughter. His little girl.

It all happened so fast. The baby was crying, and he couldn't get her to stop. He changed her, he fed her, he burped her, but she wouldn't stop.

Finally, he put her in the crib, but the crying got worse. The wailing bounced around the small bedroom, each squeal delivering another blow to Ken's sanity. He wanted her to stop, to stop her crying, because each cry reminded him Carolyn was gone, each cry reminded him how much he was alone, each cry reminded him of everything that was lost.

He just wanted Laura to stop!

So he grabbed the pillow . . .

"Hey, the light isn't going to get any greener."

Ken jumped and looked at the traffic light that gazed at him like an all-knowing green eye. He drove through, made a left on Wainwright Place, and stopped at the intersection. It was deserted, but Ken didn't drive on. Instead, he glared at the woman. Who was she? And why was she doing this to him?

"What the fuck are you delivering at two in the morning?" Ken snarled, his teeth clenched as tightly as his hands on the steering wheel.

"Would it make you feel better if I showed you the package?"

Without waiting for a reply, she went into her jacket pocket and pulled out a thin rectangular box, something that might hold a watch or maybe a pen. It was wrapped in shiny crimson paper and topped neatly with a black bow. She held it delicately in her hands, touching only the corners with the tips of her thumbs and index fingers. Ken leaned in closer.

"What's inside?"

Her face was grim. "That I can't tell you. But it must be delivered. So please, take me to the house."

Ken stared at the woman. The woman with the name of his dead wife. Maybe it was the torrent of emotions surging through him, maybe it was the way the fitful moonlight shined through his car's dim interior, but Ken felt as if the woman's features had changed somehow. Once smooth and spotless, her face now appeared mottled and waxy, resembling a sausage casing stuffed to the verge of exploding. Razor-sharp cheekbones protruded like arrowheads. And in the gloom, her deep-set sapphire eyes shimmered, possessing a quality both wholesome and cunning yet empty as glass marbles.

Ken started to say something but stopped and drove through the intersection. He made a right and rolled down Woodland Drive, a quiet street dotted with shade trees and lined with nondescript ranch-style homes. He came to house 244, the numbers barely visible in the darkness, and parked the car. The porch light was not lit.

Ken turned to the woman. She was staring at the house.

"It doesn't look like they're expecting you," he said.

"They usually aren't," she whispered.

Before Ken could respond, she pivoted and reached for his face. Her sudden touch was cold, but perspiration broke out on Ken's forehead. He felt his eyes grow heavy as she caressed his jawline, manipulated the stubble, and worked toward the chin. A warning bell went off somewhere deep in his mind, but the blackness was taking hold, pulling him down, down, down. Then colors bloomed, blinked like fireflies, and became real.

Somehow, Ken was transported to a sunny park, with Laura swaddled in his arms and Carolyn at his side. *His Carolyn.* She looked so beautiful, so happy, so alive! Her eyes sparkled the way they had on their wedding day. Sounds of children laughing and playing echoed in the distance, and birds chirped in happy high voices.

Without thinking, Ken leaned in and kissed Carolyn softly on the lips. God, it had been so long since he tasted those lips. She smiled, pure and radiant as starshine. The tension in his shoulders evaporated, and the poisoned fist that seized his heart after her passing relented. Ken felt a calmness he only experienced with Carolyn, a sensation that died when she did. She held out her arms for Laura. Ken relinquished their daughter and watched as Carolyn walked farther into the park, Laura nestled safely in her embrace. Cherry blossoms sighed in a warm breeze, almost bidding his wife and daughter a loving goodbye. And even though Ken didn't want them to go, he couldn't suppress a smile, thinking he had finally reached peace with himself.

"Thanks for the ride," the woman said. Her voice was distant, muffled. The park melted away, and Ken was back in his car. His eyes burned, and his shirt and face were soaked with sweat, the sweet fragrance of the cherry blossoms dissipating like dust. The woman's hand fell from his chin, an enigmatic Mona Lisa smile fixed on her face. She opened the door.

"Will I see you again?" he rasped, surprising himself with the question. It felt as if he had gargled with sand. Everything around the woman was blurry and dark.

She turned, her eyes blazing like blue fire, and that light tone in her voice darkened.

"You can count on it," she said and continued toward the house.

Her reply sent shivers down his spine, a mixture of excitement and dread cascading like an icy waterfall. Ken leaned back against the headrest. His head started pounding again.

Am I losing my mind?

A moment passed, maybe more.

Was that business just now with Carolyn and Laura a dream? Has everything since that awful night alone with Laura been one harrowing, mind-numbing dream?

Ken's hands were shaking, and he was nearly overcome with a sudden feeling of exhaustion. Somehow, amid confusing and disorienting thoughts, the region of Ken's brain that controlled action stirred and took command, telling him to concentrate.

Just concentrate. Close your eyes and concentrate, and you'll be back at that park.

Ken obeyed.

One more time. He wanted to look at them one more time.

Ken sat in his car for a minute, an hour; he couldn't judge. Time had lost its hold on him. He centered on his breathing, inhaling and exhaling through his nose, counting every breath.

One more time. One more time.

Inhaling. Exhaling. Inhaling. Exhaling.

Please, God, there has to be a reason for this night! Just one more time!

Ultimately, the darkness behind his eyelids began to churn, twisting around itself until it sparked and flared, erupting into a kaleidoscope of patterns and hues. Those elements coalesced back into that scene at the park, the action picking up where it had left off. Carolyn was still walking away, but it was now twilight, and the shadows were long. Wind hissed through the trees. The sky was a pastel canvas bleeding purple, orange, and blue.

There was a different energy in the air, and Ken felt uneasy, but he called out just the same. Whatever this thing was, it was the only chance to speak to his wife again. Maybe he could explain to Carolyn what happened. Give her his side of things, even though there wasn't anything to say.

It was an accident, Carolyn! I didn't mean for it to happen! And then I didn't know what to do.

I called 911 and told them the baby stopped breathing. I could barely speak! When they came, they knew who I was. They knew about you. I guess they didn't want to believe anything happened, that I could've been responsible. And I just went along. Oh, God . . .

I'm sorry, Carolyn! I'm sorry, Laura!

Please. I need you to believe me. I need you to forgive me! Please!

He just wanted to hear his wife's voice one more time. To touch his daughter's cheek one more time.

But when Carolyn turned, Ken's footing along the rim of sanity—a precarious game he had been playing for so long—finally gave way, and his world plunged into the abyss.

She was still smiling, but it was all wrong. The corners of her mouth were raised too high, as if controlled by a phantom puppeteer, and a frothy, inky foam bubbled down her chin in thick, syrupy globs. The flesh around her eyes was crumpled and bumpy; the wrinkles it caused resembled giant black gashes. Her arms and legs had lengthened into long, spindly stems and lashed out in frantic, spastic gestures. Her eyes were wide but unfocused, like a lunatic ready to strike.

And Laura. Oh, God, Laura . . .

Ken's eyes snapped open, teeming with fear. He was back in his car. His head felt heavy, and monstrous silhouettes blossomed and swirled around him before receding in the brilliant moonlight. A childlike giggle emanated from somewhere near and then fell silent, choked off before Ken could convince himself it wasn't real. He turned toward the house.

The woman was gone.

He scanned up and down the street, but it was empty. Ken rubbed his eyes until he saw stars and shifted the car into drive. As he drove toward his home a mile or so away, he couldn't get Carolyn's ghoulish face out of his head.

And that fetid smell returned, stronger than before. The stench of decomposition. Of decay.

Ken found no respite when he entered his house. Instead, he sat stupefied at the corner of his bed as the sun pierced through the morning haze, the rank aroma intensifying as the hours passed, the vileness mixing and blending with other pungent odors. Spoiled roses. Burnt hair. Rotten eggs. Before long, the foulness oozed from his pores, mixing with the copious amounts of whiskey that usually provided an escape from that horrible night all those years ago.

But there was no escape. Not anymore.

The shameful truth had finally broken through. Worse than that. The self-delusion had allowed it to metastasize in Ken's bones, mushrooming into tumors of grief and self-loathing, spreading and infecting every fiber of his being but only now bubbling to the surface.

His whole body felt like it was on fire.

The solution came to Ken as he wept in the shower, foolishly thinking he could absolve himself with soap and water. The handgun purchased years ago still sat in a dresser drawer. It had been a gift for Carolyn, something to make her feel safe when he wasn't around. But maybe it was always meant for him.

With barrel lodged under his chin and finger poised on the trigger, Ken slid into the corner of his bedroom, a choking miasma of guilt and despair hanging over him. His last thoughts were of his wife and daughter. Wherever he was going, he hoped they wouldn't be there waiting for him.

Ghosted

EVERETT BAUDEAN

Inspired by "Dance Macabre"

Eddie never expected to get rich quick, especially without needing to scheme. His grandmother left him everything even though he hadn't spoken to her since childhood. He had assumed he'd only ever inherit dysfunction—his parents were estranged from his grandmother, and he was now estranged from them. But one surprise call from an attorney, some paperwork, and suddenly he had a mansion and a fortune. Maybe grandma believed that his parents kept him from her? Had they? They hadn't visited since he was six, but as an adult he could have visited. Called. There was nothing stopping him but his own apathy.

He reassured himself that a relationship had been unnecessary since he still ended up with everything. Maybe it had helped that she remembered him as a cheerful six-year-old rather than the overweight, underemployed, and mostly friendless twenty-six-year-old he was now. Life hadn't gone how he had planned because he hadn't bothered to plan. He didn't care that he hadn't finished college. The dead-end jobs he worked were filled with people who had degrees and student debt to match.

Eddie didn't have a love life, either, but didn't consider it his fault. He'd only ever had short-term success with a lot of alcohol involved. He felt he deserved love, but he hadn't met anyone who deserved his. *Women these days are so vapid and shallow,* he'd think. *They never care about nice guys like me. Guys who would actually be faithful and not just out to get laid and move on. They'd rather whore themselves out on TikTok or Instagram for quantity over quality attention. That's all anyone wants now: the instant, constant gratification of new clicks and new dicks.*

Now he might be able to play that game. With wealth and property, he would be more desirable in the turgid flow of *thots*. The house was a stately, early 19th Century Victorian, and while it had never been fully renovated,

Ghosted

it was well built and it didn't look like it was going to fall down any time soon. Eddie inherited more than enough money to fix and maintain it, but didn't intend to do more than the bare minimum. If he played his cards right and didn't get greedy, he wouldn't have to work. Part time at worst. Plenty of time to devote to his true passions: online gaming, endless Reddit scrolling, and porn.

Though Eddie mostly kept to himself, on his few ventures into town for microwaveable 'groceries' he couldn't help but learn about the history of the house. When people heard that he was the new owner, they were always curious to ask him about the supposed haunting. Eddie didn't care for small talk with strangers, but he had a genuine interest in this piece of lore. He had always been curious about the paranormal and macabre, but never experienced it himself. The grocery store manager was older and looked like he'd lived in town his whole life, so he decided to ask him what the story was.

The manager seemed excited to tell it, though it looked like it was the thousandth time repeating the tale. "Supposedly the guy who built the house had a daughter that vanished just before her wedding. It was supposed to be a very big to-do, so it was a huge scandal that the family never recovered from. Your relatives ended up buying the house after that for a steal. The ghost story goes that she was murdered by her fiancé's jealous rival, but the skeptical story is that she eloped with the guy."

"Yeah, sounds like something a woman would do," Eddie said, chuckling. The manager politely returned a chuckle at this 'joke,' but it didn't sound genuine.

"Who knows," the manager continued. "But they say her ghost wanders around in her wedding dress, trying to find her way to the altar."

"Well, if I see her, I'll ask her for the truth and let you know." Eddie said, knowing he wouldn't follow through even if he did see a ghost.

Eddie returned to his dated and dusty home and upstairs to his arbitrarily-chosen bedroom. He didn't have to worry much about keeping the spacious house clean because he barely moved from his computer desk. His room could be a wreck, because if he ever had company, he could pretend one of the other bedrooms was where he slept. While he'd quit his job to 'work on the house,' that only meant that he'd started to preface his online political rants with 'as a homeowner.'

He tried putting more of an effort into dating apps, but putting variations on 'has money and a cool house' in his profile wasn't working. He needed to look like he had more to offer, but he didn't have looks, hobbies, or even an impressive reason behind his wealth. While he didn't want to swipe on sluts who were after his money, he also didn't feel like any of these girls *deserved* any more from him. If he had to be as fake as they were, why not skip the bullshit and look at porn instead? The pornstars and cam girls were more honest about what they were doing, even when they were pretending to be someone's stepsister inexplicably stuck in a dryer.

Something else was bothering him, though. Despite the size and solitude, the house didn't feel private. He had a newfound self-consciousness about jerking off. Maybe feeling more adult didn't mesh with constant masturbation. Perhaps the ghost story was getting to him. Or maybe he'd been spending too much time on incel pages which were inexplicably getting more and more puritanical. He wasn't sure. He only knew that he'd tapered off in his habits, and it was another one of those nights where he couldn't quite muster the enthusiasm to rub one out.

He zipped up and made his way down the stairs to heat up some pizza rolls. A full moon was rising outside the window atop the stairs, shining brightly enough that he didn't need to turn on any lights. The house was so quiet that the humming of the microwave was the only perceptible sound. What kind of haunted house didn't have constant unexplained noises? He fixated on the countdown until the silence was broken by the piercing *ding!* He removed his plate and headed back upstairs. He wasn't surprised to burn his tongue as he took a premature bite at the base of the staircase, but he was surprised by the ethereal figure of a young woman, silhouetted in the stark moonbeam at the top. He dropped his plate on the step, the sound of his gasp drowned out by the shattering porcelain.

The phantom gazed forlornly at him, or rather *through* him, as if he was as transparent as she. Eddie stuttered and mumbled, struggling to speak, eventually coughing out a weak "h-hello?" There was a sudden change in the expression on the apparition's face, as if her cheeks blushed, becoming slightly less translucent. She put her hands to her mouth and silently passed through the door and into the hallway.

"Wait!" Eddie finally let out, not fully believing what he'd seen. He hurried to the top of the stairs faster than he'd ever moved before, entering the hallway completely out of breath. The hallway was darker without the direct moonlight, and he couldn't see anyone. With an exhilarating mixture of fear and excitement, he opened the doors to each bedroom, but found all of them dark and lifeless.

In the last bedroom he thought he felt some kind of presence but couldn't parse sensation from imagination. He could barely see, but remembered this room looking like it hadn't been used for decades. An antique four-poster bed, complete with gauzy bed curtains, dominated the space. In the dim light, he thought he saw a flutter of her ghostly dress, but it was only the bed curtains moving slightly as he disturbed the still air. He turned on the light, but it felt incompatible with searching for a ghost, and

Ghosted

none of the ubiquitous dust showed evidence of movement through this room for quite some time.

He turned the light off and opened the drapes of the large bay window on the far wall, but there was still less moonlight than on the stairs where he'd seen her. He spent a few more minutes looking around the room in the dark but felt more and more foolish. Maybe he hadn't seen anything after all, and the isolation was taking its toll. He returned to the hall and sat for a while on an old upholstered bench, looking at the moonlit doorway that the ghost had passed through. He lingered there, trying to remember the details. Aside from the initial shock, she had seemed sad rather than frightening. As strange as it felt to admit, he had actually found her beautiful.

He wasn't sure how long he waited there, but it was long enough that the moonlight had slowly retreated. He rose and sighed, taking one more look into the abandoned guestroom. There, in the sliver of light through the open curtain, he convinced himself that he caught a glimpse of her face, the sadness replaced with a cautious smile.

Eddie saw no more apparitions that night, but the experience had stirred something within him. He spent the following nights stalking through the house, searching for signs of this moonlit maiden. Strangely, he felt that she was somehow avoiding him, like she was shy and hadn't expected to be seen.

He researched paranormal investigation techniques and tried all of them with no success, becoming disheartened as none of it proved more useful than a Ouija board. He felt more alone every night until, on the night of the new moon, he found himself sitting in total darkness and isolation. Having no leads than this growing feeling of absence, he decided that the moonlight must be the key. He spent the next week researching lunar cycles and charts, learning where and when the moon would rise, and making a detailed map of which rooms would get the best moonlight. With this knowledge, he resolved to wait wherever the light would be strongest. He would always be in the right place at the right time.

At the next full moon, he tried to suppress any appearance of excitement and expectation. He positioned himself in the large bay window of the dusty bedroom where he'd last seen her, occupying one end of a bench that spanned the entire niche. He had thoroughly cleaned the window to best let the light in and sat facing the spot where he was certain it would be brightest. He waited, his impatience threatening to turn to disappointment and shame for believing any of this was real.

Everett Baudean

As the moon surmounted the treetops and shone through the window, he saw her. She appeared gradually, barely perceptible at first, nothing more than a vague outline of a face refracted on the glass. Her image intensified with the moonlight until he could make out her cautious expression. He did not wish to startle her, but wanted to let her know that her presence was felt, and eventually mustered the courage to speak.

"Hello," he said, unsure of what to expect. The spirit looked frightened, as if she had a lump in her immaterial throat.

"H-h . . . " she struggled, slowly whispering a full "Hello" like an echo without a source. She paused, as if doubting she could be heard. "You . . . can see me?" she asked.

"Yes," he replied, "and hear you." Not knowing what else to say, awkwardly added: "Thank you for coming."

"No one has ever heard me. I think people have seen me, but they always . . . look away. Like they would prefer I did not exist. This is the first time . . . since . . . " she trailed off.

"I understand that feeling," Eddie said, reassuringly. He was surprised at the silence from a spirit that had gone unheard for nearly 200 years. "What's your name?"

"Abigail."

"I'm Eddie. Um, Edgar I mean. Eddie is short for Edgar . . . " He was unsure what formality was proper.

"Pleased to meet you." Her voice grew more confident and her image more substantial as the moon rose further, and she appeared to relax slightly.

Eddie was at a loss for how to continue this conversation. He wasn't great at talking to living women, and here was one dying to meet him. Talking to a spirit in the first place was unbelievable, but to communicate so normally was unimaginable. He managed a smile. He had so many questions but felt it could be unwise to push past pleasantries.

"I'm very pleased to meet you," Eddie said in return. "You're the first visitor I've had here, but even so, I know you'll always be the most interesting."

Abigail's demure smile grew larger as she averted her eyes and brought her hand to her mouth, seeming to blush as the pale light shimmering through her cheeks brightened. When she recovered from the effect of this long-awaited attention, she looked at him again and spoke. "You must be special to see and hear me. Not like other men at all. I am so glad to have made your acquaintance. Some things are worth waiting for."

Eddie's heart fluttered. No one had ever said anything like this to him before. He felt hot blood rush into to his cheeks and looked away, unsure what to make of this strangely coquettish interaction with a ghost. He looked at her again, paying close attention as her form grew more distinct, and more appealing, in the intensifying light. She truly was beautiful, with soft but defined features looking at him as if he were the only man in the world.

It was strange to behold her, so clear yet still immaterial. She wore an elaborate dress trimmed in lace, with a piece of sheer fabric stretching from her bust to a collar with an ornate broach. The effect was entrancing. The sheer fabric would have been translucent when she was alive, showing enough to entice while staying in the bounds of her reserved society. Now that it was sheer *and* ethereal, covering breasts that were translucent themselves, it made every glance feel voyeuristic. Eddie caught himself wondering if the layers of transparency would make it possible to see what she looked like naked, then began to panic as he felt himself becoming erect.

He straightened up and tried to resume polite conversation, hoping to deflect any awkwardness from his staring by complimenting her dress. This elicited more charming expressions, and he thought he caught her looking him over as well, so he stayed the course. He beat around the bush about the story he'd heard but avoided the topic of her death, even though that's what he was most curious about. He learned that her father had made his fortune in textiles after the turn of the 19th century, and had begun to build the house around 1820, when she was a little girl. Eddie wished he'd paid more attention in history class, and if his teachers had looked like Abigail, he might have.

She asked about him in return, and politely listened and smiled as he tried to explain the modern world, though she clearly understood little. She didn't ask much, and her apparent lack of curiosity about 200 years of progress surprised Eddie. He could only assume this was due to social conventions of her time which were completely alien to him.

The conversation faded along with Abigail's form, and the sorrow that he saw in their first encounter was now in both her face and her voice. "The moonlight is waning. I will not be able to stay with you much longer."

"I would very much like to see you again, Abigail. Will I be able to?" he asked hopefully. "Please?" he added, trying not to betray his desperation.

"I can return with the full moon. If you wait for me in the moonlight, I will find you." Her voice trailed off as her form became nearly imperceptible.

"I will wait," he said quickly. "I'll be where the moon is brightest!" Abigail vanished, managing another final smile, this time more hopeful than the last.

Eddie sat frozen as disbelief swelled within him. He returned to his room, head spinning and heart racing. Lying down in his bed and feeling so much less alone, he fixated on the image of Abigail. This beautiful girl thought *he* was special. Was he? Yes, he must be. He was the first to see and hear her in two centuries. A euphoric shiver ran down his spine as he recalled every detail of her face, her body, her voice, and for the first time in a while, it felt incredible to masturbate. He didn't know if her presence was still in the house and if she could see him, but that thought only excited him more.

Eddie struggled to wait for the next full moon. He read about contemporary issues during Abigail's life to help him converse with her. He bought new clothes for the first time in as long as he could remember, though wondered if this effort was necessary as she had no other options in men. When the full moon came he could barely contain himself, but he still had to try and maintain his composure. It wouldn't do to spook a spook by being overeager. He didn't know if she had a perception of time in between her manifestations. A month later could be her tomorrow.

Eddie found the best window for the coming moonlight and again waited, his heart in his throat and sweating despite how cold the house was at night. His fears were unfounded, and she again took shape as the moon crested the tree line. They both smiled with relief. She still looked beautiful, though wearing the same dress. He was glad for it despite his wasted money and effort on new clothes. He'd fantasized about seeing her so much that a change in appearance would have been disappointing.

Eddie was prepared with several topics of conversation that would be right for a girl from the 1820s. He filled their limited time as fully as he could, and she became gradually less reserved.

"Abigail, can I call you Abby? You can call me Eddie, we don't have to be so formal, now that we're friends." He hoped to make the right moves toward more personal conversation.

"Yes, you may. Thank you, Eddie!"

As she opened up more, it was Eddie's turn to politely pretend to understand what she was talking about, despite his advance research. She spoke of people she'd known in life and long-dead gossip. As the conversation turned more personal, according to plan, he noticed that she placed her delicately-gloved hand on the seat next to her. This seemed like an invitation. Her hand was well within his casual reach, and their time was growing short. He decided to follow his heart and go for it, pushing further into the intimacy of their private conversation.

"Abby, I'm so happy to have met you. I think you are a wonderful person." He placed his hand where hers lay projected by the lunar light. He felt a chill as his flesh entered the space where her hand would be, but he enjoyed the sensation. It was clumsy to position his hand as if he were holding hers, but she did not recoil from it.

"Eddie, I wish I could stay with you. You make me feel like I'm no longer trapped in this place, but that I want to be here."

"I want nothing more than to see you again. I just want to be with you in the moonlight," Eddie told her as she started to fade. "To be with you all night."

"I will see you again," she said, her voice growing quiet as the light faded. "Wait for me!"

His hand warmed as her image flickered from view, and he rued that warmth. Abigail said she was trapped in the house, and that stuck with him uncomfortably. He resolved that the next time they met he would no longer avoid the difficult questions. Maybe he could help her. Was meant for it. She needed him and had no one else.

Another month until another full moon. Eddie didn't worry about whether she would appear, but how it would go when she did. He'd thought of little else than Abigail. It was bizarre to develop feelings for a girl long dead, but he had watched enough Tim Burton movies to cope. When the time came, the moon would most clearly shine through the window above the bed in that room where he first felt her presence. He waited, making little effort to contain his anticipation.

When she appeared, seated next to him on the edge of the bed, the smile she arrived with quickly faded to concern when she saw his face.

"Eddie, are you well? You seem upset. I'm sorry I could not come sooner."

"No, I'm sorry. You haven't done anything wrong. It's just that we've been getting to know each other and, well, I have concerns for *you*." He gesticulated emptily, unsure how to proceed but worried he was wasting their precious time. "One of the last things you said was that you're trapped in this house, and I want to know if I can help you. I care about you, Abby."

Abigail looked surprised, but her expression gradually shifted to cautious gratitude. "Perhaps. My life was . . . it was incomplete. That is what binds me here."

"You have unfinished business," he said, answering, not questioning.

"Yes."

"Abby, what can I do to help you?"

Everett Baudean

"It . . . It is sad to discuss."

Eddie reached his hands to hers and felt the chill he'd longed for. "Please, you have to tell me."

She gestured to her dress "This was to be my wedding dress. I was engaged and in love." She waved her hand in a slow arc. "This room was being renovated for us to live in after the wedding. One of the men doing the plastering, I came to know him during the work. He . . . " she trailed off, pain growing in her voice.

"It's okay," Eddie said. "Take your time." He was growing impatient but knew he couldn't force it.

"He said only he truly loved me, that my fiancé was only interested in my father's money, and that though he was poor, we could run away together and be happy."

"What did you do?"

"I told him no. I had made a promise to my fiancé, and I could not break it. He returned here the night before the wedding, saying he needed to retrieve something. I was home alone, trying on my wedding dress to make final alterations. He again implored me to run off with him, that it would kill him to see me married to another, that he could not bear to see me in the dress." The pace of her story quickened as she relived the trauma. "I told him I could never, that I did not love him, and that he must leave and never return. He flew into a rage and he . . . he killed me." She hid her hands in her face and sobbed. There were no tears and no breath, but sobs nonetheless.

Eddie tried to put a hand on her shoulder, but could only hold it where the edge of her body appeared to be, feeling for the familiar chill. Eventually, he managed to speak. "I'm sorry, Abby."

"I never wed. Trapped here, I heard people say that I had eloped, and saw my reputation sullied." Her tone went from anguished to grave. "I died so close to happiness. I never got to know the touch of a man but was accused of throwing my life away for it." She paused uneasily. "I'm sorry, that was inappropriate to say. What must you think of me?"

"Abby, I think you're the most beautiful and pure girl I have ever met, and what happened to you was a tragedy. How can I help you?"

"It isn't possible."

"Nothing is impossible."

She hesitated. "I must marry. But how could anyone marry me? I am dead!" she wailed and began to sob again.

Eddie was at a loss, but an idea began to take form. He could be the hero and finally get the recognition that living girls never afforded him.

"Abigail," he said, standing from the bed. "I will marry you."

"B-but how?" she stammered.

Ghosted

"I know I haven't been good at explaining how the world works these days, but you can get anything on the internet. I'm sure a wedding ceremony is easy."

"You . . . you would love me?"

"Yes," he said, firmly. "I love you."

Abby smiled with a joy he hadn't seen in her before.

"Wait here. We should still have time. The moon has only just come up."

He dashed down the hall and across the landing into his bedroom. He grabbed his laptop and quickly searched YouTube for wedding ceremony videos. It wasn't long before he found a short, generic one that looked like it was meant for couples to practice a rehearsal. He wasn't sure what he was doing or if this would help, but he didn't have much time to think about it. It wouldn't be a legally binding marriage, but if there was a chance it would work he would try it. As macabre as the idea was, he would *technically* have a hot tradwife that he could brag about online. Much better than a pillow waifu.

He rushed back to the room where she awaited him, put the laptop on the bed, and asked her to stand facing him. She wouldn't have time to marvel at the technology, and he hoped she could follow along with the cues as he hit play on the video. He smiled, holding his hands where hers would be. She was brighter and more visible than ever before, as if the fulfillment made her glow independent of the moonlight.

The virtual officiant went through the motions, and they repeated standard vows in a nameless ceremony, all the way through "until death do us part," not thinking of whether that made sense in the context. They both exchanged "I do," and the recording pronounced them man and wife. Eddie leaned in for their first kiss and felt her chill on his lips, like the first taste of a flavorless ice cream.

"Oh, Eddie, thank you so much."

"Anything for love." They stood for a few more moments, Eddie unsure of what to do next. "So, is that it? Is your soul at peace now?" he asked, suddenly afraid it meant losing her and having nothing to show for it.

"No," she said, looking down at her feet. "My body must be," she said hesitantly, "laid . . . to rest."

Eddie's heart sank, and the chill he felt down his spine was not the pleasant feeling he'd come to crave. "What do you mean?"

She pointed at the far wall, the long thin finger of her gloved hand now seeming ghastly. "I am in there. My body. He plastered me in, and I was never found. You must lay me to rest."

Eddie gulped, unsure of what to do.

"Please!" she said desperately. "This is the last part. I have waited so long. We have come this far. I need to be released."

Everett Baudean

"Okay," Eddie said, words failing him. He went downstairs then down to the basement, where he found an old square hammer among some long-forgotten tools. He returned to the bedroom and raised the hammer. It was heavy in his hand, but his heart was much heavier. "Here?" he pointed at a section of wall.

"Yes, please," she said. "Please. Remember, I love you."

Eddie struck the wall. He broke the plaster and the backing boards in a line between studs, then worked down the edge of the stud until the plaster started to come away. He dropped the hammer and squeezed his fingers into the gap he'd created. Looking away from the wall, he wrenched the section of plaster and thin wood away. It came off in a great sheet and crashed to the ground, kicking up a cloud of choking dust.

Eddie slowly opened his eyes after the dust settled and he could breathe again. There, in the newly torn alcove, was the withered, mummified body of a young girl. Her skin was brown and drawn, causing her teeth to jut out like a piranha, and the few strands that remained of her black hair were mingled with the cobwebs. He recognized the tattered, yellowed dress, the sheer fabric long since rotted away. The neckline had collapsed down to her waist, bearing shriveled masses unrecognizable as breasts.

Eddie gagged and turned from the body to the spirit with a horrified look.

"I'm sorry," she said. "Both are the real me. You're the only one who has ever seen . . . "

"What do . . . Do I have to bury you? Call the police?"

"No, that won't be necessary, please just lay my body on the bed."

Eddie crept to her corpse, averting his eyes from the gaze of her hollowed sockets, and gingerly put his arms around her, pulling her from the wall. She hardly weighed anything, and he was afraid that she'd crumble to pieces and join the dust. He carried her to the bed and carefully laid her in the center. The moonlight was at its most intense now, and he saw every dreadful detail, crack, and missing piece of her.

He turned his attention back to the Abigail he knew, trying to forget what he'd seen, and struggling to recapture the feelings of love from moments before. For the first time, her fixation on him made him feel haunted.

"Be at rest," he said, not knowing what else to do.

"There is one last thing," she said with hungering urgency. "My husband, my love, our marriage must be consummated."

"What?! You can't be serious! I can't . . . not with . . . "

Abigail's specter brightened intensely as her expression darkened. Her voice boomed: "YOU MUST! NOW IS MY TIME OF NEED AND YOU

Ghosted

PROMISED! YOU SAID YOU CARED ABOUT ME! LOVED ME!" Her voice crescendoed into the shriek of a banshee. "YOU MADE A VOW! TO HAVE *AND* TO HOLD!" Eddie felt a tremendous pressure surround him, as if the air was closing in and crushing him. "I HAVE GIVEN MYSELF TO YOU AND YOU TO ME! COME AND GIVE ME WHAT YOU OWE!" she continued, grabbing his hand, and this time he felt her pull, as if the bonds of matrimony formed unseen chains.

He climbed on to the bed, powerless to resist, and found himself looking down at the desiccated remains of his new, old bride. The moon felt like a spotlight catching a crime in progress. Abigail's spirit form laid down, superimposed on her physical body, so that Eddie could see both simultaneously: the woman he'd desired and the horrible reality in which he was now trapped.

"There, you can see that I am beautiful. You can see the one you love," she said, softening her voice. "I love you. I'm sorry I shouted. Please, give me release. I need you. You are the only one. Kiss me again."

Eddie leaned down, trying to focus on the face he once found so beautiful, but the vile visage of her corporeal form lurked below and could not be ignored. Compelled by an otherworldly force, he closed his eyes and tried to kiss her ghostly lips again, but his mouth felt only brittle teeth. He shuddered as he felt them shift from their sockets and fall, but he was unable to withdraw. Tears soaked his cheeks and dripped on to hers where the moisture was instantly devoured.

"Now, make love to me! Bring this to completion!"

He was unable to move, held there by what felt like a cold spike impaling him to the bed. He unbuckled his pants mechanically as he'd done so many times when thinking about her. When he was finally fully revealed, she lifted her ghostly hands to his arms and grabbed him. His blood ran cold yet still surged into his loins and formed an icy erection like rigor mortis. He did not have to remove her dress. The fabric crumbled at the touch of his rigid appendage.

Abigail threw her head back in ecstasy. He assumed he was penetrating her, but all he felt was a dry crumpling and the occasional scratching of her bones on his. After too many crunching thrusts through her frigid spirit and into her desiccated husk, she let out an orgasmic wail as he felt her entire pelvis collapse into shards of bone beneath him. With her release, he felt he was freed as well. He scrambled off the bed, falling into a twisted heap of numb limbs and half-removed clothes. He dragged himself across the floor at a crawl, pants trailing around his ankles. He escaped to the bathroom, and gripping the toilet like a life raft, vomited and cried profusely.

After he was dry of all tears and bile, he peered cautiously out of the

Everett Baudean

bathroom and back toward the bed, but couldn't see or hear anything from the floor. The room had grown quiet and dark. He struggled to stand, and pulled his pants back up so that he could walk. He approached the bed slowly, where a final fading shaft of moonlight illuminated the wretched scene. There, where their bodies and spirits had briefly conjoined, was only an outline of ash, as if some tinder had been burned to kindle a fire that would never be.

Commendation of the Dying

LAUREN BOLGER

Inspired by "Deus in Absentia"

Someone shoved Aidan Scott's skull so hard against a brick wall, he saw stars. Traveling a darkened backstreet close to home, he'd mistaken his assailant for an opium dealer, and approached him.

A simple mistake made in a shadowy alley. And now, a hand as solid as the hull of a ship held him there for as long as its owner pleased. The gloved fingers tightened around his throat, throttling his breathing. His heart beat harder, a rabbit in a trap, as he kicked at the assailant with his long legs again and again, missing each time.

As the veins in Aidan's neck rioted, throbbing hard against the unrelenting pressure, as he wondered if he'd ever take another breath, he swore he heard a choir singing. Voices lilted, joining, dancing higher and higher into the night sky.

As though in revolt of his current circumstance, some corner of his mind drifted, wanting to find them. That part of him climbed higher, until he recognized the voices were coming from below. From the basement entryway not ten yards to his left. *I must join them. I must descend,* he said inside his own mind, his mouth lifting, delirious, into a numb smile. A familiar feeling stirred deep in his gut, like a percussion born long before any mortal life. Every organ in his body began to fashion a rhythm.

"Wrong place, wrong time," the attacker informed him, jolting him from his reverie.

His body was his again. All sweating face, loss of breath; his adrenaline racing, climbing, claiming him. "Release me," he tried to say, but nothing resembling words came out. He tried once more, to no avail.

His skull swam dizzy, a bell rung too hard from the impact. A bright white bled into his world from the corners, inward, and his energy, his cares, any sign of wakefulness began to fade. As easy as falling asleep.

Lauren Bolger

Sleep did not come easily to Aidan. A virtual recluse, he only ventured out to obtain drugs that would aid him. When he was alone, his head ached, his heart swelled, and his veins surged with a literal pounding, like drums. The earth seemed to shake underneath him, like he was detecting, or even conducting a shared rhythm. He felt his body, his being, bending the tempo of the earth. From there, his body grew hot. Some kind of infernal longing overtook him. Something he'd never been able to appease.

When he described his malady to doctors, they looked at him as though they found him insane. The last one had asked if he had any immediate family, had insinuated paying his elderly aunt a visit, the only one left alive besides him.

The physicians in this town were close with the sanitarium operators, and he could no longer risk sharing these details, lest he be locked up for the rest of his life. So he took to buying drugs on the street to quell his suffering, if only temporarily.

The man dropped him roughly onto the stone path, his knees, bashed to hell, pain jolting up his legs, battering him delirious. He gasped, drinking the cold night air. Aidan pressed his hands to his throat, and recoiled instantly. His neck was tender, bruised.

A stocky shadow loomed over him, still. The sharp sting of moonshine overcame him. His heart galloped harder. "What do you want?" His voice was taken, and it hurt to speak. Only a whisper was left. He lifted himself tenderly to his hands and knees, reached one hand weakly towards the man, in surrender, in pleading, frankly in whatever would make this stop.

When no answer came, amidst the panic, he tried to remember a prayer, any prayer, from his time spent in church as a boy. "Though I walk through the valley of the shadow of death, I will fear no evil: for thou art with me—" he started, but something bit him, deep between his ribs. Pain branded his guts, seizing his middle. He slumped over, curled his fingers protectively over the hilt and handle of a dagger.

His breath was gone again. He managed shallow, sharp groans as the man made quick work of emptying his coat and pants pockets. He heard the quiet rub of paper as the man relieved him of all his bank notes. As the stranger's footfall faded, all he could do was hold as still as physically possible, take and expel the night air with great labor, and try to remain alive.

"—thy rod and thy staff, they comfort me," he continued the prayer in his mind, though the words didn't ring true. Not even remotely. He waited for someone to find him, hoping to God they wouldn't make him move.

A fool's prayer.

Though he lay down the street from the church, only three doors over, it felt as far away as the other side of the Earth.

Commendation of the Dying

Aidan Scott awoke in his own bed, to find the pain in his side had doubled, perhaps tripled. Or maybe reached some kind of ceiling. Sharp shooting agony grabbed his middle like a giant fist. He leaned to the side and after gathering all the spit left inside him, vomited.

A glass of water waited for him at his bedside. A glass of water, a bell, and a note.

A note he was afraid to read. That paper was a faded yellow, from the physician's pad.

"I'm so very sorry, Aidan. I've sent for the priest. I will return shortly, as I had to attend to a birth."

This means I am dying, he recognized. *I'm dying.* His life had been for nothing. He hadn't a memory to hold on to. A person to send for.

He'd always imagined he'd die in a king sized four-poster bed, in a room so large it dwarfed the furniture. But he also dreamed of sleeping peacefully in one, if only for one night. Consecrating a marriage there, producing an heir.

Too late for all that, now.

The sky showed gray and unremarkable between the heavy sapphire curtains. *Why be there at all*, he wondered at the sky, *if you will not hold any color.* Wincing, he smiled sadly at how perfectly that described his life. He swished his mouth with water and swallowed it. With great time and care, he arranged the pillows so he could sit more upright. Every movement hurt.

Aidan feared death like any other, but he'd also given enough thought concerning his deathbed to have pictured it many times over, due to the malady that plagued him, only increasing with each year that passed. That infernal racket within his skull, claiming his body.

At least I will not have to struggle at night any longer, he tried to tell himself, but a desperate longing to extend his life, to have time to find another solution gripped his throat like a vice, and tears came.

He allowed them to stroke warm rivers down his cheeks. Felt them cool, then dry, stiff against his chin, and thought about the voices he'd heard in the alley.

What had he told himself after? "I must descend."

At those words, that same warmth spread within his chest, and he found himself smiling again. He bit his bottom lip. The pain was there, still, but it felt like something he could control. Something he could roll up. Could hold in one place. Invite other feelings to lay alongside it.

He felt alive. Happy.

"My, my. You're really going through it, aren't you?" A deep, honeyed voice came so suddenly, he shouted out, banging his elbow against the headboard.

His eyes slipped to the source of the sound. The easy chair across the room, to the side of the picture window.

The priest, he told himself. *It's the priest*. At first, he felt relieved, but dread filled him quickly. His last rites. This was why he was visiting.

The heavy black vestments, shiny, like silk, with sleeves adorned in gold told him otherwise. Not the priest. Or, not Father Paul, at least. Whoever this was, why were they dressed this way? As though this were some holy occasion.

The room was dim, and he squinted, trying to see better. To make sense of this presence in his bedroom. The man's face seemed painted in white, with the eyes blackened out by shoe polish. Like some ghoulish jester. Aidan squinted to inspect further, but the figure's left eye gleamed a bright white, blocking out his vision.

"Aidan?" The person moved to stand, holding his hand out. "Don't get up." His accent was Italian. His voice, deep and . . . soothing, somehow. Smooth.

Too practiced, Aidan thought, wary. "Why are you here? What . . . who . . . are you?" He started to turn, to sit up in bed, but groaned, leaning back against the pillows.

"Please, don't get up. You've been through enough." The man sat back down, his hands settling regally on the armrests, like a subject on a throne.

The man hadn't answered his question. "Did my physician send you?" Aidan asked. "Where is Father Paul?"

He chuckled slowly, resting a curled index finger against his lip, clearly enjoying the error. "Oh, dear. I am *not* a priest."

"You find something funny about that?"

The man tipped his head, raising his eyebrows. "You're looking good." He held his hands out, as though presenting Aidan's condition to himself. "Considering." He quirked an eyebrow. "You're *very* tall."

"You're aware I am bleeding to death, then?" Aidan's reply was curt. "I assumed that was why you were here." *Cut to the chase*, he thought angrily. Commenting on the physical appearance of the dying. This isn't a reunion at a god-damned pub.

"Oh, it is why I'm here, yes. I was nearby during your . . . accident." He hiked his robes. Crossing his legs, he steepled his fingers. "When I am so blessed to come across someone like you, Death does me a little favor."

"Someone like me?" Was that in a good, or a bad sense? Was this man aware he was trying to purchase drugs illegally? Was that the answer?

Commendation of the Dying

"Yes. We'll get to that."

And wait, what had he said? Death does him a favor? What did that mean? "What did you say about death?" That eye was shining at him again. Aidan's heart slipped to his stomach.

"Unfortunately, this is the hard part. I mean that in the only sense you'd understand it. Death is allowing me to come here and talk with you. He's given me a chance to make my case."

"Make your case? For what?" *Jesus Christ.*

"Do me a favor now. Indulge me. Let me talk with you a bit. Let the conversation progress naturally and you will discover what this is about."

It may have been the head trauma, or the delirium of his body coaxing him into death, but the question poured out of him. "Are you trying to get me to come with you to Hell?"

"Now tell me. How could you possibly have guessed that, darling?"

"Don't call me that."

"Well what shall I call you, then?"

A costumed stranger with an eye shining like a star, who talked about Death like an old friend. All this, while Aidan lay dying. Not good. Maybe he could make him leave. Hadn't he learned something in Sunday school about giving permission?

"You don't need to call me anything," Aidan said. "We're just talking. And soon? You won't have what you're looking for. And when you realize that, you'll be on your way."

"I haven't much rope with you, do I?"

"I'd venture to say none. No rope, whatever." Aidan swallowed. "Can I ask you something? Are you the Devil?"

"The Devil?" he chuckled, low, shaking his head. "Gods, no. Though I suppose you could say I'm in his sympathies." His lip lifted ever so slightly. A curtsy his mouth made against his teeth. Shy, but salacious. An invitation.

Warmth coursed through him; desire, like brushfire in his guts, barreling down his length, taking everything to the tops of his knees. "What have you done to me?"

"I'm sorry." He hid his teeth again, pressing his lips shut. "I don't do this with living humans often. This one-on-one . . . ritual, I'll call it."

Fear gripped Aidan, tightening his skin. *Get him to answer you. Get just one blasted answer.* "If I were to tell you to be gone, would you have to leave?"

"I'll elect not to respond to that. All I can do now is implore you to hear me out. I must follow rules in these matters. I cannot tell you what comes after this life, but I can tell you *some* things. Most importantly, I can advise you that you have choices."

"Choices?"

"You haven't done anything, Mr. Scott. You haven't lived. You've spoken to your God, just yesterday, in your hour of need. And where was this God, then?"

"He probably didn't answer because I don't go to church."

"Hm. You see your God as an absent grandfather who shuns you for not visiting? You still wish to close the door on an unfulfilled life, and then transcend to the heaven your church promises? Maybe your soul will melt. Will meld with all the others, like liquids in a barrel. Your individuality, your will, everything will be gone."

Aidan shook his head, trying to clear it. Why was this making sense? Were his instincts betraying him? Who could he trust if not himself? "Why would you care about what happens to me?"

"Oh, don't say that, darl—" He shook his head again. "It pains me that you think I don't care about you. Why else would I be here?" He bit the corner of his lip.

Aidan's desire called him again, twisting his lungs, making his breath even shorter. "I'm very aware that you still haven't told me why you're here." Sweat prickled at the back of his neck. "I haven't forgotten. I know you're tricking me. I know it. I am not stupid."

"I'm here in celebration of you." He opened his hands, gestured at his ceremonial robes, and in one fluid motion, held his hands out towards Aidan. "There is so much to discover, Aidan."

"Are you taking me on a vacation? To celebrate my Death Day?" He spit, bitterly. "To call this a celebration is macabre, at best."

The man ignored him. "There's so much you've never experienced. Remember where you were last night?"

"Remember? I will never forget. It's what will be my demise."

"And that's just it. Remember how you felt last night when you heard the singing? Pure happiness. You felt called to the sound. Even in the face of mortal danger, that was what you focused on. You've only just begun to live. It isn't fair, is it?"

How could the man possibly know that? Aidan closed his eyes. Instead of darkness, all the veins in his eyelids lit up fire-red, like swirling with dye. Dye made by his body. His *own blood* saying hello.

Was this death's doing? This pleasurable delirium? Was he just one trembling step closer to the end?

He pressed his fingers, hard, against his brows, trying to return to himself. The man was awaiting an answer. "Of course it's not fair," Aidan said. "It's not fair at all. But that's hardly a concession."

"You all right?" The voice was a heady whisper. Soft and deep; genuine concern. Tenderness. Like a post-coital lover offering a refreshment.

Commendation of the Dying

"No. I'm dying, remember?" Aidan said tersely. He'd thought this was all wrong, but what if it was the only good thing to ever happen to him?

"Aidan." The voice was grave, now. No hint of playfulness.

"Mm," he replied.

"We haven't long. I must cut to the chase, now. I know you. I *see* you."

Nobody had ever told him that before. His blood surged. The warmth in his chest bloomed anew. "Do you mean it?" He was still puzzled, though. Hesitant. "Wait. What do you mean 'see me'?"

"I know your secrets. You hear something nobody else can."

Aidan bristled. "I don't know what you're talking about."

The man shook his head. "You mean you won't *admit* you know what I'm talking about. Your skull, your veins, your heart, they talk to you, no? Do you know what that is?"

Aidan's heart stuttered, then throbbed. The earth-shaking, mountain-splitting sound he knew so well was threatening to insinuate itself again. He rubbed his face. "Some previously unidentified medical ailment, I'm sure."

"I ask you again. Do you know what that is?"

He let out a sigh. Covered his face with his blanket. "I assume you are about to tell me."

"Your blood. It is singing to you."

He scoffed. "Singing. That's ridiculous. Singing!" Again, how did he know these things? Yes, the sound plagued him. Every time silence settled upon a room. He didn't know if he'd trust this man's story, but if he sent the man away, he'd die not knowing.

Maybe he was dreaming.

"You aren't dreaming, Aidan." The voice from outside his makeshift tent, said. "You are chosen."

"Chosen? By who?"

"Who even knows. Someone all-knowing, or someone who slipped when carving the contours of that clay snake coiled inside your skull. The point is, you have a gift."

"Funny, I always thought of it as a curse. It's deafening. It robs me of sleep."

"Maybe we can call it a cursed gift." He chuckled, quietly.

"Can you tell me what it is I'm hearing, then?"

"It is the skin stretched taut over the drums of chaos. Beaten by the fists of the wicked and the suffering. The random battering of the universe, begging to be gifted with rhythm."

"What does that even mean."

"My crew and I. Hellions, all of us. We embody chaos but we write its name with sound, in the air. With our instruments, our voices."

A short sigh escaped Aidan's lips. "That was you? Last night?"

The man nodded. He stood, then walked towards Aidan. "Ignore the call of the gods, my dear, for they are absent. We need a percussionist. Join us."

The warmth encased Aidan again. He didn't understand any of this. But he'd never felt this way before. He didn't want to die, but he felt embraced. Loved, somehow, and so suddenly and fiercely.

Everything in Aidan surged. Energy. A waterfall of liquid fire in a loop, feeding itself.

"Show me how," he said.

Hallowed Ground

DAVID D. WEST

Inspired by "Death Knell"

My mothers burst into my room as the church bells began to chime. I was still awake, even at this late hour. I rocked back and forth on my cot, knees pulled tightly to my chest, as my mothers crossed the room and sat beside me. A lone candle flickered in a sconce, sending shadows dancing across the stone walls.

"Did you not get any rest, my dear?" Mother Zeena asked. She wrapped an icy hand around my arm. "We have a long night ahead of us."

I shook my head.

Mother Blanche was less compassionate. Her perpetual scowl deepened at seeing my state. "Come," she said, grabbing my other arm and pulling me to my feet. Mother Zeena watched from the cot as Mother Blanche sat me in a chair. "The bell now strikes midnight, and you are of age at last."

Mother Zeena leaned back on the cot. Her dark clothes made her body disappear in the shadows and I could only see her pale face staring at us. Mother Blanche ran her fingers through my hair, doing her best to comb it. I winced as she tore through knots, tears welling in my eyes.

"We must look our best," Mother Blanche said. "Zeena, don't let sloth overtake you in this final hour. Stand up and help get the girl ready. Eighteen years we've been preparing for this night, and you're lounging there without a care in the world."

I could see Mother Zeena roll her eyes. She stood from the cot and crossed the room. Her frigid hands grabbed me by the cheeks, and she lowered her lips to my forehead. "Are you nervous, dear?"

I nodded, then yelped as Mother Blanche's fingers tore through another rat's nest in my hair.

David D. West

Mother Zeena smiled before turning around. She spoke as she dug through my top drawer, objects clattering around. "Forgive your mother." Her voice was delicate. The more passive of the two women, I'd always clung to Mother Zeena. "It took her decades to conceive. When you came screaming into this world, I knew you were the one we'd been waiting for all of our lives. We couldn't be happier with the girl you've become, but tonight it's time for you to become a woman." Mother Zeena turned and held a few makeup brushes in her hand. She set to applying various powders and pigments to my face.

I'd dabbled with makeup a few times, but Mother Blanche had always rebuked me, dragging me to a washing basin and scrubbing my face until my skin turned red. "Now's not the time for that," she'd always say. "When the time comes, your mother and I will doll you up. We know what he likes."

Mother Blanche's gravelly voice made me jump. "Where is the dress, Zeena?"

Mother pointed over her shoulder, at the door leading out of my room. Mother Blanche disappeared through it, and I felt some of the tension drain from the room. Mother Zeena leaned back from my face, studying her work. The smile that stretched across her face told me she'd done an exemplary job. She stepped aside and I saw myself in the mirror. Shadows from the candle flickered across my face.

I looked like a ghost. My face was whiter than my bedsheets, though two rosy patches stood out on my cheeks. Contour had been added to highlight my feminine features. I looked nothing like myself. A stranger stared back at me from the dirty glass and I felt my skin start to itch at her gaze.

My eyes darted to Mother Zeena. "What's it like?"

She ran her fingers through my hair. They glided through it easily, as all the knots had been worked out by Mother Blanche's calloused fingers. She wrapped her hand around the base of my skull and her tender touch gave me the smallest amount of courage.

"It hurts a little at first," she said. "Then after that, you'll be in heaven."

Ever since I could remember, my mothers told me I was destined for greatness. My first memory was of them describing some grand ritual I would someday be a part of, an act that would cement my role not just as a woman, but as the bringer of glory to this world. Trepidation and exhilaration were constant since my first bleed as I inched ever closer to that day. Now that it had finally arrived, I couldn't settle on any one emotion. My heart was aflutter with conflicting sentiments, each clawing their way to the forefront and demanding to be heard.

But one of those emotions stood above all the rest.

"Do I have to do this?" I asked. I felt drops of snot running from my nostrils as emotion started to overcome me. I sniffed, trying not to cry, lest I ruin the portrait painted on my face.

"Of course you do, dear," Mother Zeena said. Her voice was comforting, though I yearned for different words to come out of her mouth. "Your mother and I have prepared for this night for your whole life. I don't think we have enough life in our old bones to start over from scratch. I understand the reservations you have, as any young woman might on the night she fulfills her destiny. But if you just make it through tonight, all will be well in the world."

Her words did little to ease my anxiety. Before I could protest further, the door flew open and banged against the stone wall. The sound echoed in my small room. Mother Blanche came forward carrying a white dress. She tossed it onto my bed and grabbed Mother Zeena by the hand.

"Change," she demanded. I wished Mother Zeena had been in charge of this whole ordeal, but as the one who birthed me, I figured it was only natural that Mother Blanche took on this role. "When you are finished, you are to leave through the front doors of the church. The path weaves through the woods. As long as you follow the sigils, you will find us."

My mothers exited my room hand in hand, leaving me alone.

I stepped into darkness, letting the church door slam shut behind me. A cool breeze caressed my cheek, lifting my veil and exposing my chin to the elements. I had never set foot outside of the church before. I was born within its walls and knew I was destined to remain there until this day. I had glanced through the windows, of course, but the view from every window was the same.

The church sat in the middle of a thousand-acre forest. No matter where I looked, all I could see were paper-white birch trees rising from the soil like a million fingers, clawing their way to the heavens.

I breathed deeply, taking in the woody aroma of the world I had been sheltered from for eighteen years. Leaves crinkled in the breeze and branches clashed against each other. The moon sat high in the sky, full as if she were pregnant with her own young, shining just enough light to reveal the sigils on the tree.

His cross was carved into it. The same cross that branded every single room of the church. A long vertical line with a shorter crossbar through it. The crossbar sat on the lower half of the line, as if it were an arrow pointed to the ground. I could see the inverted cross carved into the bark of other trees. A path forward. The one my mothers had described all my life.

David D. West

The path to salvation.

I started walking. Leaves gathered at the hem of my dress as it swept across the earth, leaving a mark on the dusty forest floor. My hand reached out and caressed the stiff trunks, fingers feeling the swirls and burls defacing the bark. Sharp stones stabbed into the soles of my bare feet through the decaying leaves. Everything in the church had been so stony and cold that I always thought the outside world would be softer in comparison. Other than the leaves crumbling under my feet, everything in the forest was as rigid as the church itself.

Following the crosses through the woods would lead to my mothers, who would be busy preparing the arena for the ceremony. They only had a ten-minute head start on me, so I knew the path had to be safe, but the dark and isolation forced my mind to wander. I clasped my hands beneath my chin, certain I would come across a wolf or some other beastie around every corner. I would meet my demise on this path tonight and my mothers would be left unfulfilled, their only daughter robbed from them by the terror that lurks in the woods. At least then I would be free from the horrors that were to come. The church was safe, the church was my home, but for some reason we were needed out here, away from everything I knew.

As if to accentuate my fears, a sharp yipping sound tore through the silence in the forest. I cried out, frightened, then clasped my hands to my mouth. Bushes rustled in the darkness as a chase took place. The yipping was replaced by snarling, and finally a screaming as the predator found its prey and tore its throat out. That beast would surely smell my fear and turn its attention to me, another easy target in the woods. I started running. Twigs snapped under my foot, a deafening sound in the otherwise silent forest. The path was dark but the inverted crosses on the trees shone with all the glory of the moon above us. Something bounded along behind me, feet stamping against the hard earth as it pursued. I didn't dare look over my shoulder. One glance at the fangs, at the savage look in its eye, would spell my demise. I would trip over a wayward branch and it would be upon me, and the darkness of the forest would wash over me. God, I wished my mothers were here, I wished they hadn't left me to this task alone, I wished this fate had been anybody else's, I wished I could be safe in my room in the church's basement, I wished–

Trees shrank away around me. A small clearing lay ahead, lit by torches. I could see two shapes. My mothers, surely. Safety lay ahead. I threw myself forward, body crashing into the soft grass that lined the meadow. My mothers looked down at me, each wearing a matching quizzical look. My chest heaved, desperate to replenish the oxygen I'd expelled running through the woods.

Hallowed Ground

"My dear, what has you so worked up?" Mother Zeena crossed the clearing, her dark robes swaying in the breeze, and kneeled beside me.

I looked over my shoulder. Two small orbs shone in the darkness, reflecting the flickering light from the torches. Mother Zeena made the symbol of the cross, fingers tracing first from navel to forehead, then from shoulder to shoulder. Mother Blanche stepped forward and raised her hands above her head. An intimidating gesture, something to ward off the evil behind the ring of light.

"Be gone!" she shouted. Her gruff voice matched the growl from the beast that watched us. "She belongs to some other beast. If you have your fill of her, what will be left?"

The orbs disappeared. The beast retreated into the darkness.

Mother Zeena lifted me to my feet, brushing dried leaves from my dress and smoothing the wrinkles. "I told you we should have escorted her," she said.

"And who has done this before?" Mother Blanche snapped back. "Who knows the customs, the rituals, better than me? You dare jeopardize our mission?"

No response from Mother Zeena, but her eyes dropped to the ground.

"Here," Mother Blanche said, handing me a small sack. She produced her own, as did Mother Zeena. "We don't have much time. Already the moon starts to fall from the sky towards the horizon. As I do."

Mother Blanche dipped into her bag and pulled out a handful of white powder. Salt. Mother Zeena and I followed suit. We walked in a circle, letting the salt fall from our hands to outline the arena. The crystals shone in the torchlight. When the circle was finished, we each took a spot equidistant from each other. Mother Zeena nodded, then we moved in tandem, crossing the circle, then back again, all the while letting the salt fall from our hands. Our sacks emptied and the final sigil was complete. A salt circle ran the length of the clearing, and a star had been fashioned inside of it. Another of our master's marks.

"And now," Mother Blanche said. Her voice wavered as she spoke, matching my own racing heartbeat. They'd described the ritual to me hundreds of times throughout my life, but to see it playing out was something else entirely. "To the bells." She reached out and pointed. Sure enough, three bells had been fastened to trees that surrounded the clearing. They sat outside the salt circle but were close enough that the ring could still draw power from their knell.

We took our places, me in the middle.

"Zeena, you start."

At Mother Blanche's request, Mother Zeena pulled her black veil over her face and started humming. It was a low, solemn sound. One that made my bones ache. Mother Blanche joined in. The humming rose in pitch. Mother Zeena started speaking, a language I'd never heard before. The tones were low and guttural, as if she were speaking from the back of her throat. Mother Blanche hummed the whole while.

The first bell chimed. Mother Blanche pulled the cord and the sound reverberated around the arena. Mother Zeena sounded her own bell. I rang mine, and the triple knells joined together and became an uproar. I winced at the deafening sound. Yet it was still not enough to drown out Mother Zeena's chanting, Mother Blanche's accompanying hum.

The bells chimed again, one after the other.

And again.

And again.

Six times each our three bells chimed. As the clapper on my bell rang out for the final time, my mothers' chanting and humming stopped at once. The knell echoed around the forest. I felt the vibrations running up my arm.

And then the earth began to shake. Branches swayed overhead at the quaking and a fresh covering of leaves fell. The pentagram began to glow, the white crystals becoming a deep crimson color. The ground fell away within it, leaving only the salt behind. I heard fire crackling within the pit.

A hand reached up, then another, and set themselves outside of the glowing pentagram.

A monster pulled itself from the earth. My heart stopped in my chest when I saw it. My first thought was this had been the beast that chased me through the forest minutes ago. Why didn't it take me then, when the darkness surrounded us and the true terror that would surely befall me?

The beast snorted. It looked like the crudely drawn sketches Mother Blanche had shown me through the years. Despite the cloven hooves that sank into the ground, the creature resembled a man. I had never seen a man before, apart from the photographs Mother Zeena kept stashed away underneath her mattress in the church's atrium. This creature was better endowed than any of those photos; the pale pink protuberance dangling between its legs was as thick as my wrist and almost as long as the cross that adorned the wall in my bedroom. Even though it looked male, a pair of supple breasts grew from its chest.

Above the neck was anything but human. A black goat head sat on the creature's shoulders, wiry hair falling in curls around its neck. Two horns grew from its head, twisting and rising skyward. Its rectangular pupils studied me with a cold, uncaring gaze that chilled my blood and froze me in place. I wanted to turn and run, not stop until I reached the church, until I locked myself in my bedroom and never came out, but my feet wouldn't move. One of the creature's ears twitched, an involuntary gesture, I'm sure,

Hallowed Ground

but unsettling nonetheless. It only served the contradiction that was this creature; part man, part woman, part goat.

"My Lord!" Mother Blanche cried. She abandoned her post at her bell and stepped forward. Mother Zeena followed suit. They flanked the creature, mouths agape in reverence behind their black veils. "For eighteen years we've raised your child. Prepared her. And now, we return her to you."

My mothers bowed their heads.

It stepped forward, closing the distance between us. I could smell its rancid breath and my stomach curled.

"Mother Zeena," I whispered.

"Shh." She kept her head bowed, indifferent to my change of heart.

And it was a change of heart. All my life I'd prepared for this, and now that it was time to complete my destiny, I couldn't do it. I ripped my veil from my face and tossed it to the ground.

But maybe I didn't have a choice.

Two hands, softer than anything I'd ever felt, reached out and grabbed my cheeks. Its touch was warm. Welcoming. Heat spread through my chest, then worked its way elsewhere in my body. It tilted my face up until I stared it in the eyes. The beast bleated, a soft sound, and a faint mist flowed out of its mouth with its breath. I inhaled it deep into my lungs, an involuntary action, and felt a new change come over me. My skin buzzed as if my whole body were vibrating. The edges of my vision grew blurry until all I could focus on was the creature in front of me, my Lord, as I fell under his spell.

It lowered its head. Its fur brushed against my face as our lips met. The rancid breath breathed new life into me. Its tongue, thick and long, probed my mouth, exploring every part of me. Its hands left my cheeks and wrapped around my waist, pulling me closer to it. Our breasts pressed together through my dress as our kiss continued. A yearning awakened inside of me.

I could do this after all. How could I resist my destiny? How could I resist my Lord, now that his power was flowing through my veins, drawing me ever closer to him?

I pulled back from its embrace. Mother Zeena crossed over to me and helped with my dress. She pulled it over my head. The cold air raised goosebumps over my naked body. It had been years since I'd been completely nude in front of my mothers, but this occasion didn't bring the usual shame. Instead, pride welled up in my chest. They were getting to witness history, the fruits of their labor over the last two centuries. I was going to make them proud. I was going to be a mother, just like them.

The grass was soft beneath my back, tickling my skin. The beast knelt between my legs, already erect in anticipation of claiming its bride. I grabbed it, ready to guide it home.

Mother Blanche cried out. "Wait!"

The beast lifted its head, breaking our concentration on each other.

"I've toiled for you my whole life," Mother Blanche said. Her black veil hung in front of her face, but I could see the desperation that bled from her every pore. "Take me instead of this girl. She has no idea how to mother your young."

Her fingers ran down her dress until they found the hem. She lifted it up and tossed it aside. Her naked body shone in the moonlight, orange light from the torches flickering across her wrinkled and sagging skin.

The beast throbbed in my hands. It started crawling, eyes set on a new prize now. Anger burned through my chest. I'd spent my whole life preparing for this moment, groomed by my mothers, and now one of them was trying to take it away from me. I rolled to my stomach to get a better view of Mother Blanche, hate furrowing my eyebrows. Her hand tore the veil from her face and her eyes shone with yearning. The beast approached her and wrapped its arms around her, feeling of her skin, of that gentle palace between her legs.

I opened my mouth to protest, to scream, when Mother Zeena interfered.

Without a word, she grabbed Mother Blanche by the shoulders and pulled her away from the beast. A line of spittle connected their mouths, glinting in the torchlight. It severed, sending moist drops to saturate the salt circle. Mother Blanche stumbled backwards, losing her balance. Before she had a chance to react, Mother Zeena grabbed her head and slammed it into one of the bells. Her head made a solid thunk as it connected with the metal and resounding chiming echoed around the words. The beast sat and watched the events unfold. The goat's eyes were emotionless, but I thought I saw a small smile stretch across its lips.

Mother Zeena pulled back and slammed Mother Blanche's face into the bell again. A final knell went out as blood splattered from Mother Blanche's fractured skull. A thin spray swept across the beast and it shivered underneath it. Mother Zeena dropped her dead lover's body to the ground and regarded the beast.

"That girl there is yours. We've raised her from scratch. Preparing her for you. No harlot shall come between you."

It swiveled, turning its attention back to me. Mother Blanche's blood covered its chest, and its cock was slick with it. I rolled to my back and it settled itself between my knees again. The act itself was quick; with one quick thrust, I felt the beast stab into me. Pain flared inside of me and I felt something tearing. The filling sensation was quickly replaced by a vacated yearning as the beast pulled out, its member slick with both my blood and my mother's.

Rearing its head up to stare at the moon, the beast bleated, satisfied with its work. It fell backwards into the salt circle, disappearing back beneath the earth. Soil rose from the abyss to close the gap between our worlds.

I lay on my back, regarding the moon and the stars above me. My hands rested on my navel, pain and pleasure both rippling through my body. His spell wore thin and I felt a cold chill running the length of my body. Mother Zeena knelt beside me and placed a cool hand on my sweaty forehead, brushing away loose strands of hair. I could see a faint smile behind her black veil.

"We need to get you back to the church, dear," she whispered. There was an excitement in her voice that I hadn't heard in a long time.

I turned my head to the side and saw Mother Blanche's body lying in the clearing. The salt turned red where the blood flowed from her shattered skull. Her eyes remained open and they stared right at me.

As I felt the transformation happening in my body, as some unknown entity started claiming my own life force as its own, I truly wished I could have switched places with my slain mother.

Mother Zeena pulled me to my feet, grabbed a torch from one of the sconces, and led me away from the clearing.

Any thoughts of beasts or terrors in the forest were long gone. I had looked the beast in the eyes, taken his seed deep within me. I had his protection now. Nothing in the forest could hurt me.

We turned a corner and found a wolf standing in the path. Blood crusted its muzzle, surely from whatever kill I'd heard it make on my journey to the clearing. At the sight of Mother Zeena and I, the wolf lowered its head and uttered a thin growl of submission. It stepped aside and let us pass without issue.

In the church, I started down the stairs towards my bedroom before Mother Zeena's hand on my shoulder stopped me.

"The atrium, dear," she said.

She led me to Mother Blanche's room, which was in better condition than my quarters had ever seen. Her large bed was fitted with velvety sheets which kissed and welcomed my skin as I slid into it. Mother Zeena hovered over me, tucking the blankets underneath my body. Something she'd always done, ever since I was a child.

Tearing the veil from her face, Mother Zeena planted a kiss on my forehead. "You did well tonight, daughter."

"I'm sorry," I whispered. Tears finally fell, now that I'd had a little time to process everything that happened in the clearing. "For Mother Blanche. I mean–"

"Hush," she said, stopping my mouth with a quick kiss. "Your mother let her lust take control. All these years we've been preparing, she'd prattle nonstop about the beast. It was never about you, or what would come of your coupling. Her thoughts were hers and hers alone. When she saw our Lord, she let her own fancies get the best of her. I simply did what had to be done."

Something swirled in my stomach, a seed coming to fruition. My eyes grew wide and my hands went to my navel. The skin moved underneath my touch, a slight distension.

Mother Zeena laughed at my confusion. "This won't be a normal birth," she said. "It'll happen much quicker. I'd wager it won't be a week before you're a mother."

Euphoria and misery rushed through my body in tandem at those words, and the growing mass in my stomach celebrated with a fresh flurry of kicks.

"The world will soon be yours, little one." Mother Zeena kissed my stomach through the blankets before exiting the room. My son squirmed in delight at my mother's touch.

Mother Zeena left the room, leaving me alone with a stack of books that belonged to Mother Blanche.

I read what I could, with what little moonlight shone through the windows. I read the diaries Mother Blanche had kept since I was a little girl. I read every entry, the last one scribbled in a frantic hand earlier this morning. Beside the diaries sat a stack of mythology books, containing various diagrams, spells, incantations, and various languages I couldn't decipher.

But paired together with Mother Blanche's diaries, they painted a clear picture.

I wept in horror when I realized what was growing in my stomach and what would befall the world. Through the door I heard a gentle tittering as Mother Zeena stood guard. She wouldn't allow me to leave this room until I gave birth, just as she never allowed me to leave the church until it was time to take the demon seed.

As I lay in bed, only two days past my insemination, stomach prematurely ballooning with the world's demise, my thoughts kept flashing back to Mother Blanche, lying in the clearing with a broken skull while the knell echoed all around us, as if her soul was putting up a final fight. If only I could be in her place. I would hear those chimes again, once my son is born and free to conquer the world, as all the bells in the world would chime to signal the end of everything.

Even now I can feel him inside of me, twisting and writhing, waiting for the day he bursts forth from my wretched womb and wreaks havoc on the world.

Hello Darkness

BRIAN J. SMITH

Inspired by "Spillways"

Hello. It's me. *Your old pal. The Darkness.*
I like to pop in occasionally and remind you I exist. You can take all the new or old age anti-depressants you want but they have no effect on me. They all taste the same . . . like Skittles.

I'm the one who reminds you of your bad days, the things your parents or siblings did to you when you were vulnerable and clueless. I keep you awake at night, pulling skeletons from your closet to show you everything you've tried to quell. Alcohol and drugs will not hinder my presence nor will it silence me.

I'm not your brother, your mother, or your guardian angel. The only person I care about is Me; *Numero Uno*.

Well, you could say I'm like a guardian angel of sort. I'm more like a shadow living inside of your actual shadow. I'm nothing more than a puppeteer of an emotion you never knew you needed or only existed in other faraway places.

I'll remind you of all of your breakups from the first to your last, the affects they have on you, and how happy *they* are without *you*. I'll remind you of your failures but never your accomplishments and twist the knife when you're already wounded and *bleeding*. I'm the voice that sits on your shoulder and tells you to have one more drink, snort one more line, fill your veins with that insatiable shot, say what you don't want to because you know the consequences of it; kick the dog but don't kill it, seize your phone and slam it on the floor, grab a chair and–

Well, I think you know. You think its anger driving you to do those things because you allow people to get under your skin. Nope, not at all.

It's always been me. The Darkness inside of You and there's nothing you can do that'll send me away.

Brian J. Smith

I am Forever, my friend.

Forever.

I will remain here when You die and another sad soul takes your place, and so on.

I don't know You but I know you've lost someone recently. A beautiful and loving spouse with whom you've loved for years because of the happiness you'd given to each other.

And the way they went. I wouldn't wish that on my mortal enemy.

You were on your way to The Langston Pumpkin Show, walking across the street like the other happy couples that'd trotted past you that day. Your Better Half stopped in the middle of the crosswalk and told you they forgot their cell phone back home and looked so ashamed because they wanted to take plenty of pictures. It wasn't until they'd patted their pockets when the bright yellow school bus broke through the ROAD CLOSED barrier and crushed them like roadkill.

Their spine crack like a dry twig; their eyes had that bug-eyed look. Their limbs twitched as if struck by an electrical charge and their intestines burst from their stomach, spreading below soft flesh now mashed into the pavement.

You go through the motions of crying, grieving, and loss of appetite. That is where I come in. I've been away for too long and my appointment with you is long overdue.

The first day you woke without your Better Half, you wake up alone. Well not alone but with me festering in your mind.

You accentuate their absence by reaching over and palming at the pillow on the opposite end of the bed, filling yourself with an emptiness you've never felt before. You sigh, roll onto your back, bury your face in your hands and moan.

You wipe the tears from your eyes with the back of your hands, toss the blankets aside, and make the long walk across the hall toward the bathroom. Once you've done your business, you collect yourself, parade downstairs, and mosey into the kitchen. The brown countertop is cluttered with half-eaten casseroles in someone else's casserole dishes from days ago.

You did not bother to clean because that was their job. You've been eating off of them from time to time, a little here and a little there but it doesn't stay down. You think you'll feel better once you eat but then I send it right back out of you.

If I don't eat, you don't either. You don't take a piss unless I know about it.

You saunter over to the countertop, withdraw a knife from the wooden block sitting next to the blender and feast your eyes on a half-eaten tiramisu. You cut a generous piece and shove it inside your gullet. You

𝕳𝖊𝖑𝖑𝖔 𝕯𝖆𝖗𝖐𝖓𝖊𝖘𝖘

ignore the nest of flies hovering and buzzing over the other casseroles, tainting the green bean and tuna noodle ones you've failed to stomach.

I let you have this one because I know you'll feed me soon enough. You close your eyes, savoring every bite of spongy caffeinated cake and hold the knife loosely inside of your hand. You hope you won't regurgitate this because you've done enough of that to last a lifetime because Your Better Half would never want you to prolong the misery of their absence.

Pardon me while I don't shed a tear for your poor damaged soul. People like you are a dime a dozen. They keep internal and psychological things like me alive, allow me to fester inside of your brain, and fill you with images you'd never believe, feeding my insatiable appetite.

You turn back to the tiramisu and cut another piece. Instead, you jam the tip of the knife into the back of your left hand and hear the sweet sound of torn flesh.

You jerk back and drop the knife into the casserole dish. You raise your hand toward your face and glance at the pinprick below your left thumb.

An overwhelming sense of joy and cleanliness washes over you from all sides. Although it is supposed to hurt, you do not feel any pain because you have been through worse. Your brow furrows with confusion as you lick your finger and swipe it across the back of your hand.

Oh yeah. That's what Daddy likes.

You lick the blood and sigh, letting the rich coppery odor ride on your tongue and fill your mouth. You reach across the casserole dish, wrap your right hand around the handle of the knife, hold it above the tiramisu, and jam the tip back into your hand again and again. A wide pleasing grin spreads across your face as tiny droplets of blood trickle onto the stale dry dessert and dowses its soft brown surface to a rich peppermint color.

There you go.

Feed me oh please feed me. Bleed for me and feed me. I haven't eaten in years and I'm just so fucking hungry.

Now, eat the tiramisu.

There you go. Eat every blood-drenched piece and savor every bite.

You're so good at this.

You finish the tiramisu but I force it back out of you.

You hurry back upstairs, run into the bathroom, and hurl until it hurts. You wipe the saliva off your mouth, gurgle some water, and spit it in the sink. You notice you've lost a lot of weight, in fact you've lost so much you despise your reflection in the mirror.

You strip off your bedclothes and masturbate twice because it feels so good to get out all of the tension that's been festering inside of you. You think that'll get rid of me? There's only one way for you to purge me, but I'm not gonna tell.

Brian J. Smith

You dry off, dress in a nice tee-shirt and jeans, and go back downstairs in hopes of starting the day anew. You cannot brush off the thought you'd eaten a blood-drenched tiramisu in a matter of minutes and never once stopped.

"Not today, Satan." You said. "Not today."

Satan? Really? That big red bastard wishes he were me.

You enter the kitchen, throw all of the old casseroles away, clean the house from one side to the other, brew a fresh pot of coffee, fire up the Boob Tube (a television for all of you who don't know), and walk into the living room.

You think cleaning the house and getting dressed was going to bury me? You think you're gonna get rid of me that easy, huh? You don't know who you're fucking with.

You don't have a casket big enough to hold me, motherfucker.

A sudden realization strikes you like a brick to the face, stopping you in the middle of the living room. Did you know it takes you seven steps to go from the kitchen doorway to the couch? Retrace your steps not once but twice and again and again to see if I'm right.

What's half of seven?

Those are some beautiful toes, you've got there. When was the last time you trimmed those toenails, huh?

There is another alternative to taking care of those, isn't there? The only way to take care of me is for you to take care of you and you need to take care of those toenails, am I right?

Stop counting your toes and do something about those nails. It's what Your Better Half would want you to do. They'd want you to take care of yourself, wouldn't they?

You walk back into the kitchen, approach the countertop, and slide the big wooden drawer beneath the microwave open. It's America's Junk Drawer; everyone has one but this one has what you need for this little dilemma. There's a ton of shit lying inside that drawer, isn't there?

You search it every which way you can until you find the metallic pair of slip-joint pliers and snatch them in your right hand. You close the drawer, even though you don't have to because there are other things you can play with; a proverbial toolkit for the everyday at-home handyman.

You sit on the edge of the right cushion of your overstuffed blue couch, perch your right foot onto the edge of the coffee table, and take a giant swig from your steaming hot mug sitting on the opposite end. The blue veins streaking through your feet are accentuated by the golden sunlight pouring through the living room drapes. They look so beautiful it's going to be an insult what you're about to do.

You clamp the pliers onto your big toe and squeeze the handle until those tiny teeth give a loud splintery crack. Your skin bristles and your heart leaps with a mixture of pleasure and adrenaline. A jagged crack splits the nail in half, spreading a river of sharp pain down your foot to the center of your heel.

You give a maniacal snicker, grip the toenail as tight as you can, and tug the pliers back. With the soft sound of torn flesh, it slides free from your toe. A current of cool air wafts across the house and teases the pocket of wet flesh once hidden behind your toenail.

You let out a lungful of air you didn't know you were holding and slide the pliers onto the next toenail. You lock the pliers onto it without waiting for the same guttural crack and tear it free, releasing more hot pain. You remove the next one and the next one and the one after it, flooding your entire foot with anguish.

Your lips trembling, you fall back onto the couch as waves of pleasure ripple through your entire body. Your crotch twitches with excitement, your right leg curls inward and draws itself toward your stomach. The pain is unbearable but at the same time it is so reassuring.

Oh, that's what I like. Pain is pleasure. Your pain feeds me and as long as you continue this little soiree of ours, we can stay friends.

You scratch my back and I'll scratch yours.

That's what friends are for, right?

Your toes are bleeding, aren't they? Wow, that's a lot of blood. They're not gushing but there's enough there to let you know you did some damage.

You feel a whole sense of ecstasy from that little operation, don't you? You enjoyed it, huh? This is gonna be easier than stealing candy from a corpse.

This is only the beginning.

You take a sip from your coffee mug, gather your bloody toenails into a pile, and sweep them into a nearby trashcan. Your stomach utters a low guttural growl, but you ignore and keep drinking your coffee because it is the only thing I've allowed you to drink all week.

Besides, I wouldn't want you to fall asleep on me.

Outside of your house, a car rolls down the street and backfires. You jerk for only a second, but the sound is deafening. Birds burst from the evergreen bushes lining the concrete sidewalk and give a loud squawk.

How can the world be so damn loud?

You slide your hand down your ears and glance over your shoulder. Something glints out of the corner of your right eye; a pair of scissors with black plastic handles.

They look sharp, don't they? Their sharpness tugs at your curiosity like a child begging for sweets before dinner. You down your coffee in one swig, lean forward, and pluck the pair of scissors from the cup.

Brian J. Smith

I was going to have you pull your teeth out with the pliers but who am I to argue.

You pull your left earlobe away from your face and slide the scissors onto it. You draw a large breath and brace yourself for what's to come.

You squeeze the handles and hear the hiss of tearing flesh. Pain slices across your jawbone and squeezes lucid tears from your eyes. You drop the severed lobe into your coffee cup and move on to the right one.

You don't hesitate when you cut this one off. The *shunk* sound explodes in your ear canal as the scissors sounds like a broken record; one you cannot stop listening play. Another wave of pleasure ripples throughout you, traces the contour of your spine with its icy finger, and curls your toes.

A coppery odor stings your nostrils and tingles the back of your mouth. Something wet trickles down your cheeks. You breathe a sigh of relief and drop the scissors ignoring them as they slide onto the floor by your feet.

You run into the guest bathroom and stare at yourself in the mirror. A river of blood courses down your neck and greets you with a pleasing grin of stained teeth. You snatch a rag off the wooden shelf above the toilet, douse it in cold water, and press it against your earlobes to try and slow the bleeding.

You wait for the bleeding to stop enough to fit each tattered ear with a thick strip of gauze and medical tape. Your makeshift earlobes look better than the ones you had before. The sounds barking from the television are muffled and distant.

Your stomach grumbles again but you know you can't leave. You cannot eat because I won't allow you. Oh no, I need you in a malnourished state for when the police find you, and they will find you.

You know what would hit the spot? A big juicy BLT.

You return to the kitchen to refill your coffee cup and search the cupboards, ignoring the array of casserole dishes. You scan the fridge for what seems like hours before you find the plastic container sitting on the second shelf. I like where you're going with this; I really do.

You turn the stove on, place a cast-iron skillet onto the stovetop, and drop five pieces of bacon into the skillet. You may want to turn the heat down or you're gonna burn the fucking house down and then we're both screwed. I have to admit though, it does smell good.

You fry the bacon and kill the burner. *Don't you dare eat one bite of that bacon.* You place the bacon onto a paper towel and peer at the river of grease popping and crackling inside the skillet.

Tip it over and pour the grease on your arm. Oh yeah. You feel it?

You feel the burn, huh? It feels so refreshing, doesn't it. It fills you with a sense of . . . relief.

Searing pain streaks across your arm and spreads blistering patches

Hello Darkness

across your skin. You drop the skillet into the sink, waves of ecstasy coursing through your veins and draw a cloud of bacon grease and burnt flesh deep into your lungs.

You leave the bacon on the countertop, refill your coffee cup, and plop down on the couch. You rest your left arm upon your lap, peer down the length of your legs, and feel a slight throbbing in your toes. The sunlight seeps through the drapes and glints off of your plump red nubs.

You see your reflection in the television and greet it with a toothy grin.

Keep bleeding and you'll never hear from me again. Of course, darkness never leaves the body after you've done all of the bleeding, but I think you knew that. You and I are joined at the hip; we have a deep connection nothing can sever.

And those teeth? Oh, how they look so beautiful. So yellow and bright.

You grab the pliers off the table, flexing them back and forth. The metallic jaws fill you with an interstellar ecstasy.

Those teeth are looking pretty bad, aren't they?

You open the left side of your mouth, and clamp onto a back tooth, squeezing will all your might as you yank the pliers out. A loud crunch that resembles broken glass follows and you hold the jagged tooth in the light.

The familiar coppery taste slides across your tongue. A laugh escapes your bleeding mouth as you place the tooth onto the coffee table. You move onto the next one. And the one after that. And the one after that.

The pain makes your mouth numb, sending a caustic bile tingling down your throat. It fills you with an overwhelming sense of satisfaction. Your skin bristles again; your crotch twitches once more.

You place the pliers onto the coffee table and turn to the television. This time, you greet it with a gummy grin. You stare at the row of teeth lining the coffee table and admire your handiwork.

Warmth radiates across your face. It feels good, huh? It feels good to open yourself up and enjoy all of the finer things in life, including pain.

Money cannot give you all of this, can it? It can buy all sorts of things, but it doesn't do what I do.

A rerun of an old eighties program flashes across the flat screen. Something glints in the corner of your eye and draws your attention from it. The slip-joint pliers sit on the coffee table, their jaws glinting in a thin film of sweet, red blood.

Your tongue slides out and pushes past your lips. The pair of scissors still lies on the opposite end of the coffee table, their metallic blades also coated with a bloody film. What could you possibly do with those you have not done already?

You have done magical things to yourself so far. Why stop now?

Brian J. Smith

Pain is addictive, isn't it? Remember, pain is also pleasure. Everyone needs pleasure once in a while.

You should do something about them, shouldn't you?

We'll have so much other possibilities in mind. So many things to explore. Each limb and hair on your body opens a fresh paradise.

You hold the pliers in your left hand and gather the scissors in your right. You give an innocent chuckle and–

What are you doing?

Not that.

Put those down right now! I'm ordering you to put it down right now!

You're just teasing me, aren't you? You wouldn't cut off your own tongue. I mean, we've been the best of friends, haven't we?

I've never done you wrong at all. I'm just a tour guide taking you through a museum of maniacal madness and filling you with the knowledge of pain you did not know was possible. I'm innocent in all of this!

I was trying to be a good friend.

Why would you ever want to end what we—

Wrapped

ROBERT BAGNALL

Inspired by "Darkness at the Heart of my Love"

Jesus Christ, *Joseph, Mary, and all the angels . . .*
There was no other words for it, for what was spread out on the sidewalk.

You asked what the strangest case was we ever wrapped up. It had to be that one.

I was a beat cop then, the first to the scene. Nobody wanted to go near it. Taping it off was easy; the gawpers hung back on instinct, all except the office drone who called it in. He remained like a dumb dog by its dead owner, his girlfriend cradled close, head buried in his chest, eyes averted. Innocents, they'd been on their way to a date night movie. It happened right in front of them, something they'd never be able to unsee.

The lashing rain carried the blood and brains away in rivulets over the curb and into a storm drain. "Somebody get a sheet or something," I shouted at the chalk-faced onlookers at the building's front door, neither in nor out. I could have sung a verse of the *Star-Spangled Banner* before anybody forgot their fright and moved.

Madeline Pincoe, the mother, was upstairs. I didn't believe she was forty; I'd have put her at least half that again. She had a haughty look, which could have translated to high-cheek-boned beauty but, grey-haired and sallow-skinned, came over as haggard and haunted. She'd collapsed against the kitchen doorframe of their seventh-floor apartment, sightless eyes wide open, jaw sagging, utter disbelief etched across her face. She looked like her world had unraveled in the blink of an eye. Which for her, I guess, it had.

We only learnt their story through the half dozen shorthand notebooks Mrs Pincoe left, almost a thousand pages of spidery writing all told. If she hadn't bequeathed us those, I have no idea how we'd have pieced together their shared history. There was precious little else to go on. A home-working freelance bookkeeper, standoffish with colleagues and clients, her rent was always paid, checkbook balanced, and she never received a red bill. Neighbors described her as polite but diffident, an introvert. Nobody had seen the daughter for years. There were memories of a father; some wrongly assumed he had taken custody of the child. The only curious detail was the bales of raw cotton she carried up, like she had some industrial process going on, and the over-stuffed rubbish sacks she transported back down daily, three at a time, to the dumpsters.

Some, of course, say Mrs. Pincoe's narrative was a total fiction, a diversion, that the truth is something far stranger, something not yet even guessed at. And, whilst I do not subscribe to that view, there is, of course, no way for me to disprove it.

Kelley Pincoe was born at three in the morning one crisp October, some fifteen years earlier. She weighed just over seven pounds, typical for a newborn. Madeline Pincoe spent ten hours in labor, average for a first child. It was an unexceptional birth, in so far as the miracle of birth is ever unexceptional.

At first, the labor pain was a continuation of the discomfort of pregnancy, dialed up. She waddled back and forth in the delivery room, sat on the edge of the bed, stretched with her hands against the wall. Anything to find the Shangri-la of a comfortable position.

Then the contractions kicked in, firstly like menstrual cramps, but worse. John's massaging ministrations helped, but only so much. Before long, all the muscles in her lower back gripped, twisting harder and harder, like a cloth being wrung out. Which was exactly how Madeline felt, but whenever she was measured, the noises the midwives and obstetrician made suggested she had further to go. Her vision tunneled. She called for her husband to rub her back and then, cursing, sent him away. Nothing helped.

Only when they applied the epidural, did the pain subside. It was like she'd been standing staring at a wall; only by moving back do you see the building. Now Madeline could see the size of what she was fighting. It was big, but no longer overwhelming.

And then, this whole having-a-baby thing, backed up and blocked solid for what felt like a lifetime, was happening double quick, new life was slithering out of her all raw and bloody. The feeling of being forced apart from inside vanished, and an aching hollowness followed.

𝔚𝔯𝔞𝔭𝔭𝔢𝔡

She'd run a half-marathon once, ended wheezing, sweat running down her, limbs burning. That had nothing on this. But the feeling of elation was similar.

John said something and his tone, rather than his words, alerted her. Scared, she felt like she was falling, the room suddenly out of focus. Something was wrong with the baby. It was whisked to the other wide of the room, to a trolley of instruments and monitors. Things were done, out of sight. The midwife and elderly obstetrician conferred in low voices and then—*slap*—the baby screamed and, mysteriously, this was a good thing.

Madeline screamed. As the doctor smacked her newborn's rump, she had felt a sharp pain. The midwife glared at her as if she had committed a social faux pas, somehow betrayed womankind, but the doctor grinned from over his half-moon specs. And then the baby was on her, skin to skin, its crying ceased, and it started to feed.

"It's a girl," John said.

"Kelley." Had it been a boy it would have been Maurice, after her father.

"Welcome to the world, Kelley Pincoe."

Madeline was only dimly aware of the medical staff exiting as she watched Kelley explore with tiny fingers. There were other babies to slap in other rooms.

"I really felt it when he hit her," Madeline whispered.

"I know."

"No. I *really* felt it."

John smiled benignly. Madeline didn't want to get cross at him now, but he didn't get it. The epidural had softened the pain, made it fuzzy and faraway. But the slap to get Kelley breathing, that cut through the fog. Madeline knew the bond between mother and child was special, but never that they would be so incomprehensibly connected.

She was wheeled to a recovery room. With John watching the infant, Madeline drifted off to sleep, gratified by the esoteric knowledge of the sisterhood so unexpectedly shared with her. Only when the nurse came the next day for Kelley's heel-prick test, and Madeline felt it as clearly as if somebody had jabbed a scalpel into her own foot, did she wonder whether all was as it should be. Surely, this mental connection would have been cited in one of the childcare guides she'd crammed. It would have come up in her Lamaze class.

Wouldn't it?

John stayed until teething. Up to then, it had been Madeline's eccentricity, even a useful barometer when forcing a tiny limb into a tiny Babygro, when trying to guess what was wrong. But teething was something else. It was constant. Continual. Madeline was in eternal discomfort. And when discomfort ratcheted into disabling pain was exactly when Kelley needed her most.

"Why don't you fucking go to her for a change?"

Madeline knew exactly how it looked to John, baby Kelley crying whilst she clutched her own jaw and moaned, face down in the pillow. *Psychotic.* That was the word John used. Was she a bad mother? How had this happened?

She went to the dentist whilst John cuddled and bounced Kelley, distracting her by letting her chew on his fingers. In the dentist's chair, Madeline grimaced. Five miles apart, the psychic bond remained. The dentist shrugged: the x-rays showed nothing. He prescribed her OxyContin.

They had discussed having a second child, but they weren't even sleeping facing each other anymore. Soon, they weren't even sleeping at the same address.

The OxyContin had a strange effect on Madeline, reminiscent of the epidural during labor. Except now it wasn't the pain that felt dislocated but every sensation and emotion. She could function, keep books for her clients, but her face kept an impassive concerned frown. She wasn't washing as often as she used to. Make-up went unreplaced when it ran out. It took a moment for her to construct a response to anything half-challenging, her previous spirit and wit now hopelessly extinct. Friendships drifted.

Only one aspect of life remained in high-definition technicolor. Whenever Kelley trapped a finger or bumped her head or her bath was too hot, it shot through Madeline like lightning through an August night's sky. And every time it happened, she held Kelley tight and vowed she would never let it make her hate her baby.

One day when Kelley was two, Madeline took her to the park. Early autumn leaves fell but the sun was still warm. She liked to chase the ducks. Glassy-eyed, Madeline watched her, drawing a mental line which, when crossed, would be the moment she would lever herself from the bench, run, and gather her daughter before she could reach the edge of the lake.

But the lake wasn't the problem.

Tottering after a mallard, Kelley collapsed, tears erupting on impact. Madeline felt a blowtorch pass across her knees. She doubled over, let out a howl from the pit of her stomach, face contorted like Munch's *Scream*. Opening her eyes, through tears she saw Kelley wailing too, an undirected bawl at the sky.

Wrapped

Madeline hobbled to Kelley, winced at the sight of her daughter's two bloody scraped knees embedded with grit, flinched at the thought of the iodine to come. Her own knees were, of course, unharmed. She tore a handkerchief in half, bound the wounds and held Kelley tight and rocked her until the storm passed. As she did, a plan formed, a plan that struck her as wrong, but in her mental fug, as also both coldly logical and oddly alluring. And, excepting suicide or infanticide, as the only way forward.

When she first wrapped Kelley in layers of loose raw cotton, secured with surgical tape, the child thought it a game. She grinned and burbled, sang *mommy look, look mommy*, bounced around her room. Madeline laughed and wondered who Kelley reminded her of. The Michelin Man? Pillsbury Doughboy? A mummy, the ancient Egyptian embalmed kind?

The mood had changed when they returned from the park. Kelley, restricted by the wadding, waddled uncertainly from pushchair to play equipment. She fell, but onto padded knees and thick gloved hands. Madeline felt nothing. Other parents looked askance, assuming something medical they shouldn't ask after. But other kids, lacking social filters, were crueler, pointing at the wrappings around Kelley's head, laughing and name-calling.

Madeline extracted Kelley from the pushchair too roughly, taking out her anger on her two-year old, who was too much of a marshmallow ball to notice.

"Mommy?" Confused, Kelley looked to her mother to explain.

"I'm never gonna let you get hurt." She hugged her tight.

The novelty, the sense of it being a game, was truly over by the following day. Madeline refused to take Kelley outside. Kelley threw a tantrum, banging fists against the floor. Mrs. Schweppenstette downstairs would be complaining again. Madeline could feel the tattoo of pain Kelley was beating out on herself in her own hands. In her mind, she calculated the number of mattresses required to cover the floor. *The lower walls, too,* she told herself.

As Kelley sat, red-eyed, snotty nosed, emotionally exhausted, Madeline calmly, mechanically worked out practicalities. She could home school Kelley. Not yet at kindergarten, it should be easier to fall out of a system you weren't already in, right? Kelley was almost out of nappies. Should she buy a chemical toilet? She couldn't get a plumber in. Her grandparents had had ponies. She'd mucked them out. She soured at the prospect. Perhaps better to keep Kelley in nappies, even, ultimately, those adult sizes for incontinent geriatrics. But she'd need to keep Kelley wrapped in cotton. She was going to need lots of raw cotton.

Her bookkeeping background enabled her to play the role of buyer with credibility. She negotiated an FOB price of less than fifty dollars a ton but even the smallest order necessitated hiring storage. And waiting for a boat from Turkey and for the consignment to make its way through customs. She jotted numbers down. Yes, she could make it work. She would have to bulk buy retail at fifty times the price for a few months, but that would give her time to locate a convenient lock-up.

Friends could be told John had taken Kelley. That would be plausible. As for neighbors, this wasn't a 1950s sitcom, nobody knocked on doors for cups of sugar. Did they ever? And Kelley would be getting her room done over. Didn't every kid want their room remade every so often? They could make a game of it . . .

And so became life in the Pincoe apartment year after plodding year. Madeline not daring to open the door until Kelley's screaming abated in case the neighbors heard. Madeline feeding Kelley with a plastic spoon because when she had dared give the child proper cutlery and the use of her own hands, she had tried to stab Madeline, then succeeded in stabbing herself. Madeline's arm, although unmarked, lit up like a firework and she had slapped Kelley and felt that fizz on her own cheek as well. And, in any case, Kelley's hands were now wrapped in cotton because, out of frustration and anger she'd forever smash them into the single gap in the padded walls which allowed the door to open.

But what Madeline was most proud of was that she changed Kelley's cotton wool wrappings every day, and the bedding on the floor each week. She no longer saw it as strange or weird or iniquitous. It had helped Madeline shake loose of the meds, so it couldn't be all bad, yes? It had become normalized. It was what they did.

Even when she drilled the rings into the walls to keep Kelley loosely chained, but away from that doorframe, she still couldn't see anything wrong with what she was doing.

As to what exactly happened that day, we can only speculate. Tales of abductees' escapes often hinge on a moment of trivial inconsequentiality. A phone call upsets the routine, and a door is accidentally left unsecured. Or a minor repair necessitates the power being turned off; an escape route presents itself, and the prisoner takes their chance.

Whatever the exact sequence of events beforehand, it culminated in Kelley Pincoe not just jumping, but *projecting herself* from the apartment's seventh-floor window. She cleared the stoop to land head-first, face-down on the sidewalk. I sensed her aim was quite deliberate. She had concertinaed on impact, her broken back drawn up and legs pulled in, like

Wrapped

an escapologist about to amaze. Which, I guess, is exactly what had happened. Her long black hair was spread out in front of her, and in it were caught the remains of her head, black blood, orange skull, grey brain, the colors all wrong under the sodium streetlamps.

The raw cotton wrappings, which was all she wore, had soaked in the rain. What had been a thick, wooly layer had become lank, transparent strands that slid off or stuck to her pale, thin body which had not seen the sun for fifteen years or more. It was obvious I didn't need to call a doctor, at least for nothing more urgent than to officially pronounce her dead.

And the mother? I know what you're thinking. In her rage at a lifetime's mistreatment, the daughter grabbed something blunt and heavy and brought it down on her helpless tormentor's skull until it cracked like a watermelon. You're thinking I spared you the grisly details of Madeline Pincoe's head bashed in, even though I painted you a picture of Kelley Pincoe, naked except for a swaddle of raw cotton.

Not so. Mrs Pincoe slumped, rag-dolled against the architrave, much in death as in life. She'd upset a jar of pasta on the way down, covering the floor with broken glass and macaroni, but she herself appeared quite uninjured, externally at least.

As the first officer on the scene, the one who kicked down the apartment door, I was also the first to see the single windowless room Kelley Pincoe had called home for a decade and a half. All I remember is the stomach-dropping sense of something being terribly wrong. That, and the nose-tickling, faintly perfumed, smell of cotton dust mixed with piss.

When volunteers were called to read through the Madeline Pincoe notebooks, I raised my hand. For me, it offered closure. I can't speak for the other two. I suspect ghoulish voyeurism. So there we were, the three of us huddled around a small table, reading—or, rather, not reading because every two minutes somebody would interrupt with *JesusChristyouain'tgonnabelievethis*—when the lieutenant called me outside.

He asked me to describe the scene, exactly, in detail. A curious request, given it was all in the report. When I'd finished, he stared into the middle distance, like he hadn't been listening.

"Sir?"

"Strangest thing. Just had the autopsy results on the mother. No drugs, otherwise healthy, no reason for her to die except . . . " He shook his head with disbelief.

"Sir?"

"Her skull was untouched, but within it, her brain showed blunt trauma, like she'd been in a head-on automobile accident. Or suffered a sustained and brutal beating."

"Or fallen seven floors headfirst onto concrete," I added. Exactly like her daughter.

He nodded and went, muttering, "You can't wrap a kid in cotton wool . . . not for life . . . you can't . . . " and, after a whispered *Hail Mary*, I returned to reading the journal of the woman who had tried just that.

Her True Calling

DORIS V. SUTHERLAND

Inspired by "Call Me Little Sunshine"

The girl's name may have been Elizabeth, it may have been Faith, it may even have been Mary. She may as well have been nameless. She lived in a nameless house in a small civil parish in the middle of a nameless stretch of the English countryside.

The land may have once had a name, but it was a name that people today feared to speak. The area had been one of the last in the country to accept the New Faith. It had clung to the old ways: to ancient creeds condemned by the newcomers as demon-works. Julius Caesar had witnessed those age-old rites firsthand but was thrown into a fit of convulsive shudders when he tried to describe them. The man who had written freely of the Gauls burning sacrificial captives in towering men of wickerwork found himself in fetters when he tried to write of the-land-without-a-name.

The area in which the girl lived had seen many visitors over the ages. Matthew Hopkins had gone there to hang witches, but fled in a fear that consumed his dreams for every following night. Aleister Crowley had made his pilgrimage there and left a pitiful gibberer. Harry Price had investigated a reported haunting in the house where the girl now lived, only to spend his train ride home uttering and re-uttering a certain Bible verse concerning the Prince of the Powers of the Air.

It was nighttime, and the girl sat in a room lit only by the laptop screen before her. She watched as a priest in flowing robes, Father Something-or-Other, strode to the pulpit of a majestic church. He opened his mouth and warned of dark powers and principalities. The girl's body trembled with a lifetime's worth of rage as she listened.

The priest spoke of mortal sins. He said that the mortal sin of pride could cause demonic possession. He claimed to have seen the mortal sin of pornography lead to a terrible fate. He described demonic possession being brought about by the mortal sins of fornication, of witchcraft, of reading forbidden books. From his high pulpit, he related incidents in which he met with violated women and told them that their ordeals had filled them with demons and that they should pray to the Holy Father. These were the words that he inflicted upon the world. His voice was level and dry when he spoke his obscenities. His congregation listened, without objection, to the foul speech of Father Something-or-Other.

 The girl growled under her breath: "Father Motherfucker."

Come the red-skied morning the girl strode on her way to work. Along the streets, she was surrounded by the acolytes of Father Motherfucker. It had not always been this way, but once the changes began, she had seen them happen piece by piece: one person would watch the priest's videos, and recommend them to a neighbour, and the contagion would spread. The people of the civil parish began adopting Father Motherfucker's mannerisms, his tone of voice, his speech patterns, his rhetorical style, his turns of phrase, his uncompromising condemnation.

 The girl walked past a man who bent to speak to her.

 "Little heathen," he said, the transatlantic twang in his voice a result of mimicking Father Motherfucker's accent. The girl knew this man: he was sure of his own salvation, having avoided all of the temptations and sinning and swearing that he believed would beckon demons to his door.

 She hastened her pace to escape the man's sight. A woman turned the corner: she wore glasses in the Father Motherfucker fashion, her hair close-cropped and pink-hued to evoke Father Motherfucker's bald pate.

 "Little harlot," she said. The girl knew her, as well. The woman was satisfied of her safety, having celebrated All Hallow's Eve in the most pious fashion: by dressing her children in the garb of sainted martyrs, filling their minds with sanctified nightmares of arrow wounds and flayed skin.

 The girl turned up for her job at the convenient little shop. One by one, the scions of the Father filed in to buy their wines and wares.

 "Can I have a bag with that, you little blasphemer?"

 "Any chance I can have 50p off, you little pagan?"

 She replied to each epithet with a smile and a polite nod, a response that she had practiced and perfected years beforehand, back when they called her by a different name. When they knew her as Little Sunshine and nobody knew of Father Motherfucker.

Her True Calling

At the end of the day, the girl went out back where her manager was waiting. This stern-faced and pious individual was hard to recognise as the woman who had first given her the job. When the girl had started work, her boss had been full of life and laughter, ribbing the regulars and putting up staffroom posters showing members of the royal family with unflattering captions daubed below. But things changed once she became a daughter of the Father.

"Sit down, you little heretic," said the manager with a sad smile.

The girl obliged, a premonition of unemployment washing over her.

"Now," continued the manager, "I really do appreciate the long hours you've put in here since you joined us. I'd be committing the sin of deceit were I to say anything else. But the fact remains that over the past year or so your presence has become unsatisfactory."

The girl felt a creeping sensation across her face as her skin turned green. "Did I get here late?"

"Oh, your transgression was nothing so tangible, I fear." The manager stood and wandered around the staffroom until she settled behind a stack of crates that—whether by accident or design—formed a shape of roughly the same size as an average church pulpit. "It's not so much what you've done as what others are saying about you. This wasn't a problem at first, because you were Little Sunshine. The customers loved having you serve them! Now, though, you're something else. You're . . . "

"The little demoniac," mumbled the girl.

"Yes, well, that's one of the names I've heard used. There have been reports that our regular customers can't even load their purchases into the refrigerator without uttering a Hail Mary over every free-range egg. I'm afraid that's simply not good for business, and it's hard to justify keeping you around when we've been getting so many fresh applicants. I mean, look at this CV."

The manager held a sheet of A4 paper. The girl squinted to read it. Beneath his name, the new applicant had listed his education history, work experience and favourite video sermons by Father Motherfucker.

"I understand," said the girl. Without another word, she collected her coat and left the shop for the last time.

⛧

In her home, the girl curled around her laptop. She decided to play a video to take her mind off things. When the algorithm directed her towards a sermon by Father Motherfucker, she felt tempted to look elsewhere, but she was unable to do anything other than watch the video and allow a seething rage to fill her.

The topic of the sermon was fiction. The Father warned his flock away from stories that dealt with wizards and goblins. He assured the faithful that such novels were written by true sorcerers—by witches and warlocks who studied the blackest of arts. He revealed that the spells in these stories were not children's fancy, but true spells; that the names granted to the characters were not whimsical wordplay, but the names of true demons: princes and marquises of Hell. Even to touch such a book, said Father Motherfucker, was to open a doorway to the demonic realm. Only a qualified exorcist such as himself could be entrusted with carrying the books to their purifying bonfires.

Had she not been so consumed with anger, the girl would have laughed at this statement. She had read books of black magic, and she had also read children's stories of goblins and pointy-hatted magicians. The two had precious little in common.

The sermon moved from the topic of novels to that of games. Father Motherfucker warned that role-playing could become an addiction, and like any addiction, could push open a portal allowing the influence of the demonic. The trouble with such games, he argued, was that they encouraged disassociation from reality: players would enter fantasylands of dragons and sword-wielding barbarians, cutting themselves off from the real world of demonic possession and prayers to saints and the protective influence of St. Christopher medals.

Again, the girl felt an urge for a sardonic laugh. The urge went unfulfilled.

Finally, the sermon addressed the topic of films. Father Motherfucker declared that the filmmaking industry was a hotbed of Satanism; that studios and directors hired dark magicians to place curses upon master copies, to insert demons into digital video files. Why, even going to a movie theatre was a grave risk. There were demons between the frames, and with 24 frames a second, that allowed space for at least 23 demons a second. Instead, viewers should stay at home and watch the videos of Father Motherfucker, which contained a subliminal Lord's Prayer delivered on a stuck-record loop across a frequency discernable only to the higher part of the human soul. The video ended with a notice that Father Motherfucker's new book, *The Truth Behind the Influence of Demons*, was available in hardcover for $79.95, hurry now while stocks last.

The girl had heard enough. She slammed her laptop shut, stamped over to the nearest wall, and punched it. Her knuckles left a small smear of blood. She gazed around the room, searching for an item of furniture to pick up and hurl as far as possible. She threw pillows, but this made her

Her True Calling

feel childish, so she graduated to chairs and stools and the scratching-post reserved for the cat that she hoped to someday adopt. She hefted the table and shoved it onto its side, sending crockery and glassware to the floor. She screamed and yelled until the inarticulate cries left her throat sore, at which point she drank four pints of water. Refreshed, she dug her fingers below the sofa and heaved until it was turned upside-down, scattering cushions and magazines.

There were moments when she began to calm, but her anger would soon return. As much as she wanted to laugh at the absurdity of Father Motherfucker's declarations, the laughter always died when she considered how many people saw him as infallible, untouchable; as a man who only the self-evidently broken and irredeemable could doubt for a second. How many people were there among his faithful? How many had come to accept his claims that violated women were infected with demons? How many failed even to doubt his ludicrous assertions that role-playing summoned demons, that Hollywood actors in costumes were inflicting dark magic on audiences?

This last thought had entered her head for only a split-second when the girl froze. She stared, but her focus was not on the disarray in her home. Images were running through her mind—pictures and ideas and plans for action.

If Father Motherfucker and his flock were so afraid of role-playing and play-acting, she realised, then she had a role to play for them. She smiled at the thought.

The sound of her laughter, unheard since the days when she was Little Sunshine, echoed through that nameless civil parish.

☆

Drama had always been one of the girl's strongest subjects. While still in primary school she relished the role of Lady Macbeth, washing her hands on stage, her face contorted by every conceivable anguish, a performance so impassioned and persuasive that the entire audience hallucinated blood on her palms. The faculty members who witnessed the spectacle ran to their offices and typed out letters of deepest concern to the girl's parents. The staff printed out and proceeded to eat these letters in despair, so vivid were the play-images in their memories.

She was forbidden from ever taking the role of Lady Macbeth again. She responded with another performance in which she played *Macbeth*'s witches—all three at once—and used as many of the arcane ingredients as a child with unfettered internet access could manage. From here she progressed to the part of Lavinia in *Titus Andronicus*, scrawling a tongueless-handless indictment that prompted intervention from social services. Her next performance was in Dryden's seldom-revived *Amboyna*, where she simulated a seventeenth-century torture method by pumping a lifelike dummy with water, swelling it into an obscene parody of the human form.

She had been delving into pre-Christian pageants of a Dionysiac bent when the school finally put its foot down.

"We recognise your talent and your passion," said a teacher wearing a plaster mask of insincere avuncularity. "Perhaps you would like to perform Marlowe's *Faustus*?"

A traditional story, a story with a message, a story of which even Father Motherfucker might have approved. The girl had agreed with this choice and every teacher sighed in the most profound relief.

What none present knew was that *The Tragical History of the Life and Death of Doctor Faustus* had been performed before in that little civil parish—long, long ago where a theatre stood on the flatland that now housed the local inn. The actors who had starred in that bygone century were far from God-fearing: their revision of Marlowe's script contained forbidden utterances and rites in the honour of dark beings, and those that watched could have sworn that Mephistopheles himself trod the boards. After that, the faithful trembled at the sight of that shunned theatre: once Mephisto had been called, he was hard to send away.

The little girl's school was not so far from the spot of that old theatre. She had donned the costume of Faustus, she had summoned Mephistopheles, and she had executed the Pageant of the Seven Deadly Sins. This had been her final year at primary school, and when she walked out the door for the last time, the entire faculty took part in a solemn mass.

※

All of these memories were running through her mind as she headed to the quiet inn on the grounds of the old theatre. She asked for a room to spend the night. The landlord glared at her from behind his Father Motherfucker square-rimmed glasses and called her a little degenerate, but he accepted her money and handed her the key. When she got into her sparse room she began unpacking her rucksack, taking out her camera, mounting it on a tripod and connecting it to her laptop. She commenced the livestream and went to the middle of the floor.

Then she began performing.

She re-enacted Lucifer's fall in *Paradise Lost*. She recreated the pranks

Her True Calling

of Loki that had shaken Asgard. She paid tribute to Set by dismembering a bleeding effigy of Osiris. She performed an elaborate mime in which she drew the sigils of all seventy-two Goetic demons, her movements burning livid lines into thin air.

All the while, she was aided by unseen beings. A chorus of infernal voices sang in harmony with her every movement. Impish grips manipulated her camera and added to the lighting effects under orders from a gaffer of Gehenna. A make-up department reached down from beyond all things material, painting her face and styling her hair with elements that had no place on the terrestrial periodic table.

The room had a mirror. The girl caught a glimpse of her new look in the glass, and she liked what she saw. This emotion provided the finishing touch to her portrayal of Lucifer in his capacity as Prince of Lust.

She cycled through the other six sins, making a sunshine-smiled princess out of each unholy prince.

As Beelzebub, girlboss of gluttony, she consumed a dish that had been prepared only once before: on the table of England's maddest king, a man who went on to devour every text and fragment that documented his existence.

As Sathanas, the most wrathful of WAGs, she screamed an irate oath in the direction of Father Motherfucker, one loud enough to give him a reflux-awakening in his bed an Atlantic Ocean away.

As Belphegor, that envious virago, she simmered with resentment as she visualised the royalties that Father Motherfucker received from each $79.95 book of lies. This made her segue into a mammary-laden Mammon, and her heart was filled with avaricious thoughts of her latest performance receiving clicks by the ten-thousand with an accompanying stream of advertising revenue.

Finally, as the slothful slut Abadon, she allowed herself ample rest while her familiars did the remainder of the work. Wi-Fi devils and pucks-of-the-code wove the algorithms to ensure that the video was spread far and wide.

The world over, screens that showed Father Motherfucker delivering his sermons on cleanliness and fidelity were corrupted and disrupted. Those watching could no longer see the holy Father, with his bald scalp and square spectacles. They saw the girl. Even if they didn't know her name, they knew full well what lay within her.

Some screamed, and continued screaming until they had forgotten their birth-tongues and could speak only languages inherited from ancestral memory. Some stared until their vision was expanded, allowing them to see for the first time the sundry trans-dimensional species that had been following their every move since conception. Some threw their devices to the ground and broke the screens underfoot, only to realise that the girl's performance would haunt their waking hours like a permanent night-terror.

And every word of the holy Father was erased from their memories, replaced with the girl's silent blasphemies.

※

Father Motherfucker got out of bed, stretched, and yawned. He had a memory of a strange event in the night, of a voice yelling from nowhere and bile filling his throat, but he dismissed it as a nightmare—and nightmares were hardly bad for his business. He chuckled at the thought of his flock-members coming to him with their own bad dreams, and how he had always set their minds at ease with a few chosen words of Latin. He gave a deeper chuckle when he remembered that his latest book was going to be out today, his publisher having guaranteed him the largest portion of its hefty cover price.

He sat at his computer. His smile of confidence faded when he saw the screen. Pontifications had been replaced with notifications. Alerts across social media showed that his empire of dogma was crumbling.

He watched video after video, eyes staring behind his square glasses, mouth agape. His faithful had become faithless, and he knew that no words in Latin would bring them back.

Across each video, in every tab and window, was the face of one girl.

He spoke. A quaver distorted his voice almost to an inarticulate moan, but he was able to utter a single question: "Just who are you?"

Smiling back, Little Sunshine gave a truthful answer.

Peering Through the Blazing Gates

DAVID COSTA

Inspired by "The Depth of Satan's Eyes"

Cries of horror echoed throughout the ruins of the Cathedral of Our Lady of Grief like ghostly wails pervading a crypt. Haunting screams bellowed from every direction, a chorus singing an anthem of torment. The agonizing voices were accompanied by the Cathedral's own instruments: the subtle scratching of disintegrating mortar falling down the walls; the violent crashes of collapsing columns. Together, they created an eerie symphony that brought chills to their unfortunate listeners.

Afraid of an aftershock, Sister Annette clutched her bible and mumbled a prayer as she ran down the stony stairwell. A whirlwind of emotions was tearing her apart. Fear for her own life pulled her in the opposite direction, the respect she had for Pastor Lewis almost forced her to stop and cry, but, in the end, her devotion to His Holiness overwhelmed all else, urging her forward. The pope might still live and, if Sister Annette was unscathed, it was all part of God's plan. She was meant to find him and help him out of the falling cathedral. She was meant to save the Church.

Guided by faith, trusting the Lord, Sister Annette delved into the catacombs. Numerous cracks split the ground, and tombs lay completely broken, the corpses of the ancient priests spilling out as if they too had been trying to escape the crumbling cathedral. Sister Annette signed the cross as she passed them, heading towards the Hall of Reliquaries. No matter how violent an earthquake was, God would never allow that many relics to be destroyed. It was the safest place to be in a time of crisis.

Dust showered down on Sister Annette as the ground trembled once more. Instinctively, she pushed herself against the smooth stone walls, praying with fervor. The cries that came from above were so low they might be her imagination.

As soon as Annette could safely walk again, she strode into the circular hall. Several shrines lined the walls, displaying statues of angels, skeletons of saints, and holy relics. The low domed ceiling was painted with ancient frescos depicting God triumphing over Satan, locking him in a cage; a motif also present in the designs of the marble floor.

The Hall of Reliquaries was a breath-taking place, but what truly shook Annette was that the pope was nowhere to be seen. She had believed the holiest of men would seek shelter in the holiest of places, but it appeared she was wrong. *Was I wrong about leaving the rest of the congregation to search for the pope?*

"Why couldn't I save him?" Images of Pastor Lewis crushed by a falling pillar flooded her mind. "Will I find His Holiness like that as well?"

Sister Annette stared at her bible, seeking answers. "Have I failed Your trial, oh merciful God?"

The light in the hall grew dimmer, the air colder, as she mentioned the Lord.

Annette lowered her bible and noticed something strange. The marble floor, the dark circular cage that restrained an image of Satan, was cracked. A faint red glow emanated from it.

She fell to her knees, placed the bible on the floor, and pulled the broken slab. It was heavy, but it budged slowly revealing a glowing ruby and–

A sudden crash made her scream.

Startled, Annette noticed a stone had fallen from the ceiling, smashing her bible. A couple of inches, and it would've been her head.

Puffing, Sister Annette pushed the broken slab away. Her jaw dropped as she saw the macabre statuette that lay beneath. Winged like an angel, with a horned goat's head and blazing rubies for eyes, the demonic figure sent shivers down her spine.

Drawn to the precious gems, Sister Annette focused on the creature's eyes. The damp catacomb's air grew hot. Flames began to dance within the rubies. A terrible dread shook her innards.

There was an immense cruelty pouring out of those entrancing eyes. Something so vile it fixated her gaze on the rubies. She recognized those convulsing flames. They matched the descriptions in the bible. Sister Annette knew she peered into the blazing gates of Hell.

Peering Through the Blazing Gates

Annette's room grew colder as she locked the vile statuette in a box and hid it under her bed. Feeling unclean after touching the demonic figurine, Sister Annette recited the Lord's Prayer. When she finished, she looked at the crucifix on the wall, wanting to feel Jesus' cleansing gaze.

She would hand that unholy idol to Bishop Reynolds as soon as possible. Until then it was her sacred duty to keep its dark influence from spreading to the rest of the Church. Just thinking about the statuette made her skin crawl.

Sister Annette left her simple room and headed towards the monastery's cloister where funeral arrangements were being prepared. Luckily, His Holiness the Pope survived the earthquake that devastated the Cathedral of Our Lady of Grief, but he was among the lucky few. Just like Pastor Lewis, many people, including churchgoers, died a horrible death last night.

Echoing steps joined hers as she strode along the ivory archway. Brothers and Sisters exited the dormitory, joining her in her march, some in mournful silence, others murmuring prayers. Annette kept to herself, eyes on the floor, her mind on the object she hid under her bed.

"Annette?" A man spoke quietly beside her. That soft voice belonged to the recently-ordained Father Morris.

"Oh, good morning," she said. "How are you doing, Father?"

Sighing, he raked his short dark hair with his fingers. "It was a terrible night for all of us. In moments like these I fear it is harder for those who remain than for those who were carried to Heaven." Father Morris' lips twisted in a sad smile that failed to break the harmony of his handsome face. "They are in a better place. And all we can do is mourn."

"It makes me wonder, Father. Why did I survive and someone like Bishop Johnson didn't?"

Morris' firm hand fell on her shoulder. "You don't need to call me Father, Annette. I'm still the same person who skipped school to go to the movies with you." His joyful laughter echoed throughout the archway. "And as to your question: God works in mysterious ways."

"He does, doesn't He?" *If He didn't, why did I find that horrible artifact?*

"Morris." Annette stopped walking. "Can I talk to you in private?"

"Now?"

"Yes." She pulled him by the cassock's sleeve, heading towards the empty refectory.

The ivory archway led to a hall with angels and cherubs rising from the painted walls, their gilded wings contrasting with the tones of white and blue that dominated the room. The hall was spacious, with wooden benches and long tables adorned with silver candleholders that were as old as the monastery itself.

When she came to a stop, Father Morris frowned. "What's the matter Annette?"

She stared at him for a moment, then shook her head. "How much do you know about the Cathedral of Our Lady of Grief?"

"As much as any other priest, I suppose. Why?"

"Because . . . " Sister Annette sighed. There was a fine line between evading the truth and lying and, friend or not, she didn't want to lie to a priest. "Do you know if there was anything secret about the Cathedral?"

"Secret?! Annette, what are you talking about?"

Hands shaking, Annette suppressed her nerves and spoke. "When I was looking for His Holiness in the catacombs, I found something. I don't think anyone was supposed to find it. A secret compartment that was revealed when the stone floor cracked open. Do you know anything about it?"

"Can't say I do . . . " Father Morris scratched his shaved chin. "Why would there be a hidden compartment in the catacombs?"

"That's what I want to find out." *That, and why it contained a satanic idol.*

"We could talk to Bishop Reynolds about it. Perhaps you made a great discovery."

Sister Annette grabbed Morris' arm. "I don't want to talk to anyone else about it. Talk to whoever you want, but please, keep my name out of the conversation."

Father Morris' frown was worth a dozen questions.

"Please," Annette insisted. "Trust me on this. That compartment reeked of trouble."

The priest nodded. "I'll see how much I can find without raising suspicions."

A bright red light emanated from under Annette's bed, its unholy touch tainting the nun's entire bedroom. Sister Annette made the sign of the cross as her mouth went dry and, for an instant, it seemed the light wavered.

The light shouldn't be visible, not with the box closed. Sister Annette was curious, but also afraid. In the end, curiosity won out and she removed the box from under her bed. Two scarlet beams pierced the box's solid wood. To Sister Annette it defied all logic, but logic didn't need to be present when Satan's hand was at work.

Annette's fingers seemed to burn as she touched the lock, yet she

Peering Through the Blazing Gates

ignored that disturbing feeling and opened it anyway. The figurine's defiling gaze set upon her, its rubies glowing like hellfire. The flickering flames within the gems entranced her, each flicker making her heart clench with fear.

Then she heard screams. Awful screams like those that echoed when the cathedral fell. Screams full of terror, full of pain. But there was something eerie about them. Loud as they were, they belonged to a single person. Someone she knew.

As the eternal flames danced, she saw Pastor Lewis' plump body sizzling. Women in provocative clothes approached him. Two of them massaged his ample belly while a third stroked his hair. The rest started undressing in a sensual manner, taking off their tops. Their tight miniskirts. Their G-strings. Their flesh.

The macabre orgy started and Pastor Lewis howled in pain. Sister Annette shut the box. But that hellish vision didn't fade. Nor did the soul-crushing screams.

⛤

The mild rain falling over the cemetery hid the tears shed by the congregation. Hundreds of members of the clergy came to pay their final tribute to the victims of the earthquake, leaving bouquets by the coffins and candles by the crypts. They also left donations for the restoration of the Cathedral of Our Lady of Grief, an initiative started by His Holiness the Pope, to show that even in the darkest times hope shone like a beacon.

If there was a beacon in this dark afternoon, it was Bishop Reynolds. Tall and skinny, the man resembled a lighthouse, the gold embroidered miter on his head reflecting the weak sunlight.

"Pastor Lewis was a true man of God," the bishop said from his portable podium, "an example for all of us. He died a martyr, trying to protect an innocent woman from a falling pillar, doing more good in his final moments than many do in an entire lifetime. Let us pray for his soul."

Sister Annette's voice joined the buzzing murmur of hundreds of prayers. It was a solemn moment, devoted to a great man, but in her mind all she saw was the depravity revealed by the satanic figurine.

She thought it odd that if those ruby eyes showed what happened in Hell, why were those horrifying women sharing their bodies with him? It was a macabre punishment she didn't understand.

When the eulogies ended and the coffins were buried, Sister Annette threaded through the crowd toward the bishop.

"Your Excellency," she said with a bow of her head. "Your inspiring words were a gift in this troubling time."

"Thank you, Sister Annette." Though he didn't smile, an air of satisfaction surrounded him.

"There's something I must talk to you about in private, if possible."

"I'm afraid privacy is something we cannot have in the near future. The congregation looks to me for guidance, and I must always be available." Bishop Reynolds opened his arms wide. "We are among God's people. It is safe. Whatever you need to say can be said in front of them."

Annette gulped. She surely wasn't going to mention the statuette in public. "I've always admired Pastor Lewis," she said instead.

"May his soul rest in peace."

Annette's mouth went dry. She knew for a fact his soul would never get the privilege. "Was he as perfect as he seemed? I've heard . . . rumors . . . about his lust."

The bishop's face contorted with anger. His eyes burned as the rubies on the statuette but when he spoke, his voice was ice cold.

"Whatever indiscretions Pastor Lewis committed do not tarnish his name. Only God Himself can judge the actions of His flock." He dropped his voice to a whisper. "Remember that pride is a sin and all I hear is a *nun* judging a dead *priest*. After the ceremony, pray ten Lord's Prayers and ten Hail Marys as penance for your sin."

⛧

Sister Annette prayed fervently on her knees to the crucifix hanging on the wall. She did her penance, and she felt a fool. The statuette was a vile creation that had to be shut away from the world, and she fell for its tricks. Satan could not be trusted. He was the Deceiver, the one who would do anything to undermine the Church. *It showed me a lie and nothing else!*

But then again, Sister Annette thought, eyes on the floor, *Bishop Reynolds confirmed that Pastor Lewis broke his vow of celibacy in such a debaucherous way.*

"Is he really down there?" She knew the answer but was too afraid to acknowledge it. "Is he burning for all eternity?"

Annette was startled by a soft knock on the door.

"Come in," she said between puffs as she got up.

Father Morris entered her room, his countenance strangely somber. He closed the door quietly behind him, as if his visit were in secret.

"Hello Annette."

"Morris. Did something happen?"

Peering Through the Blazing Gates

"Not exactly," he said. He walked toward her bed, getting dangerously close to the statuette. He sat on the edge and shook his head. "I spoke to Bishop Reynolds about your discovery."

"Did you–"

"No, no. Don't worry, your secret is safe with me."

"What did he say?"

"He refused the idea of a hidden compartment, but I got the feeling he wasn't telling me something. So, I dug a little deeper. According to Bishop Andrews there were some hidden compartments in the Cathedral. Father Ambrose said that the Hall of Reliquaries was kept in the catacombs for a reason; his best guess was some of the relics had been stolen from other cathedrals during the Middle Ages, so I see a pattern here."

"The compartment," Annette said, feeling an unnatural warmth emanating from under the bed. "I found it in the Hall of Reliquaries."

"Curious." Father Morris looked her straight in the eye. "Tell me one thing, Annette, did you find anything in that compartment?"

"No," the lie escaped from a strangled throat. "It was empty."

"Good. Because I called in a favor and managed to speak to one of the Bookkeepers of the Vatican Library."

"You did?"

"Yes," he said with a delightful smile. But the smile faded as he continued. "According to her, some cathedrals were built on top of unholy artifacts to keep their dark influence away from the world. The Cathedral of Our Lady of Grief was one of them."

"You mean that . . . "

Father Morris nodded. "It makes complete sense. The relics in the Hall of Reliquaries were meant to protect us, to suppress the evil that lay within the compartment. And now that evil is loose."

Annette tossed and turned throughout the night, unable to fall asleep since Morris told her about his discoveries. She knew the Vatican Bookkeeper was right because she felt the devious influence of the satanic statuette. There was only one thing to do. *I must give it to Bishop Reynolds right away.*

She reached for the box, took hold of it and–

A deep, red light radiated from the lacquered wood. Annette looked away, but the glow grew stronger, illuminating the room. Images of crackling flames danced on the walls. Bishop Reynolds stood surrounded by an all-consuming inferno.

"No!" Annette screamed. "Enough with your lies!"

But the image remained unwavering, the bishop's pontifical vestments growing more detailed as he started walking. Unlike Pastor Lewis, the flames dodged him, revealing his surroundings. Bishop Reynolds seemed unsurprised when he saw Father Williams relentlessly beating a man with a baseball bat. Untouched by the flames, the bulky priest grew angrier each time the pitiful man promised to pay his debt. *Everyone knows Father Williams has a bad temper, but would he really do this?*

Before Annette could get her answer, Bishop Reynolds moved on, and the flames illuminated Sister Velma. The large nun was sitting by a window, gorging on roasted beef and lobster, her eyes occasionally drifting to the African children she'd been sent to feed. Annette gaped in disbelief, and she was stunned as the fires of Hell revealed many other members of her congregation.

Why don't the flames consume them? And why am I seeing them? They are all alive, they can't be in Hell. At least, not yet.

Altar cloths appeared in Bishop Reynolds' hands. He strode to Pastor Lewis, who continued to burn with the lecherous women, and placed one over the writhing pile of bodies, covering the priest's sins. Bishop Reynolds covered Father Williams and his violence but grunts and screams still came from under the cloth. He did the same with Sister Velma, yet even concealed, her gluttony and selfishness were revoltingly apparent.

Bishop Reynolds advanced through the flames, hiding the sins of the congregation. They were horrifying. Rapes. Violent deaths. Acts that would result in imprisonment, or worse, had Bishop Reynolds not veiled them from the world.

"This cannot be true," she said as tears fell down her face. "He would never—"

But he already did. He told her that much.

Sister Annette took a deep breath as she stood in front of the studded door to the bishop's office. She stared at the box in her hands. The demonic figurine had to be turned over to the religious authorities, but those same authorities were as corrupt as the minions of Hell.

The problem was she only knew they were corrupt thanks to the idol. *Could it be trusted? Were those satanic visions real?* There was only one way to find out. Sister Annette knocked on the door.

"Come in," Bishop Reynolds said.

She entered and to her surprise the bishop was not alone in the

Peering Through the Blazing Gates

elaborate room. Sitting in front of a grand painting of Jesus ascending to Heaven, on ornate chairs with red cushions set in front of a rich blackwood desk, were Father Williams and Bishop Johnson. The first was a bull of a man, with his muscles threatening to tear his cassock open, while the second was a feeble old fellow with a compassionate and patient look.

Bishop Reynolds motioned towards an empty seat. "Please Sister Annette, join us." The other two men smiled welcoming grins and nodded. "What brings you here?"

The chair looked more comfortable than the ones in the dormitories but Annette wasn't here to relax. She stood straight, staring him in the eye. "A grave matter. One that requires a certain amount of privacy."

"Again with this, child?" Bishop Reynolds shook his head. "You can speak freely in front of these men."

"What's in the box?" Father Williams asked, leaning towards her.

Sister Annette ignored the question. "Your Excellency, I need you to confirm if these rumors are true."

Bishop Johnson interrupted, coughing into his hand. "This is not the place for rumors, Sister."

"No. No." Bishop Reynolds' voice was calm, but his face remained stern. "Let her speak."

Sister Annette met his gaze. "Is it true that Sister Velma feasts while children starve at her doorstep?"

Bishop Reynolds' eyes widened with shock, but he regained his composure. The other two members of the Church did not.

"That's outrageous!" Father Williams spouted.

"Is it true that you, Father Williams, beat a man to death?"

"He was—"

Bishop Reynolds placed a hand on Father Williams' shoulder and silenced him.

"Those are serious accusations," Bishop Reynolds said, rising from behind his desk. "Especially coming from a nun." He circled around the desk, drawing closer to her. "Last we spoke I noticed that you were harboring pride in your heart, and now I see that the penance I ordered was not enough to expunge it."

"I didn't accuse anyone," Annette said. "I just need to know the truth!"

"The truth," Bishop Reynolds spat, inching his face closer to hers, "is that none of this concerns a woman of your station."

It's all true! Father Williams committed murder, and Bishop Reynolds covered it up.

Sister Annette held them with her gaze and retreated to the door. "What you did is a much greater sin than mine." She pointed an accusing finger at them. "I'll report this to His Holiness. I swear to God!"

"You will do no such thing!" Bishop Reynolds slammed his fist on the desk.

Father Williams glared at her. "What's in the fucking box?"

"Enough proof to take you all down."

Sister Annette jammed her clothes into her small suitcase. She placed the lacquered box on top. She fetched her favorite rosary, spared a last glance at her room, and abandoned the dormitory.

The monastery was quiet and still under the morning sun's glow, and the few people she encountered greeted her with oblivious smiles. *Good*, Annette thought, hastening her pace. *No one knows what I did.*

She knew Bishop Reynolds was going to punish her for confronting him, for accusing him of something vile. The fact that she was right didn't matter, which caused her blood to boil. She didn't care if Bishop Reynolds forced her to clean the privies for the rest of her life. She didn't even care if he banished her from the monastery. Sister Annette wanted what was best for the Church. That was why she had to go against the people she once idolized. Why she had to see the pope.

Before she left the monastery, Sister Annette passed by the chapel. Paintings hung in its grand halls depicting Jesus' life, leading to His crucifixion. The sight of the golden altar at the end made her heart tighten. To save the Church, she had to denounce some of its members.

It was a trying task, and Annette needed spiritual cleansing if she was to meet His Holiness the Pope.

Her steps echoed as she marched towards the confessional. It was archaic, with incredibly detailed spiraling columns that were so detailed they no longer appeared as wood. Annette entered and knelt, her heart pounding with anxiety.

"Forgive me, Father, for I have sinned. It's been four days since my last confession. These are my sins: I have hidden a great secret from my congregation. I have lied, to priests and bishops. I have accused members of the Church, including a bishop, of horrible sins, with nothing to back those accusations. Worse, I accused them based on satanic visions provided by an unholy idol."

There was a long silence and it seemed to gain form in freezing hands

𝔓eering 𝔗hrough the 𝔅lazing 𝔊ates

closing around Annette's throat. The suffocating feeling intensified when the priest finally spoke. "Those are very serious sins, and I must admit that I need to do some research before I can determine the appropriate penance."

"Morris?"

"Please Sister Annette, in the confessional I insist that you call me Father."

"Morris, you don't understand!" Annette pushed her face against the latticed opening. "Pastor Lewis indulged in orgies, Sister Velma is a glutton, Father Williams killed a man, and Bishop Reynolds covered it all up. They're all corrupt! I'm going straight to the pope!"

"Annette please think this through," he tried to sound calm, but there was agitation in his voice. "You are going against the Church based on information you claim came from the Devil. Can't you see how this looks?"

"I'm sure they are corrupt, Morris! I saw Pastor Lewis burning in Hell with his harlots, and when I spoke to Bishop Reynolds about it, he knew! He knew and he tried to hide it!"

"Annette, I'm asking you to be calm and–"

"My confession is over, *Father*." Annette strode towards the chapel door. She couldn't stand another person turning a blind eye towards the sins of the Church. They might want her to do the same, but she had her integrity. She had her pride.

Sister Annette felt her eyelids grow heavy as her head rested against the window at the back of the bus. A curtain of night enveloped the bus and not even the moonlight could pierce through the dense forest that lined the road. Besides a few huddled bodies, she was alone in the bus. Annette yawned unabashedly. This whole ordeal had been exhausting and she finally had a moment of peace.

Her tired body relaxed against the cushion and she closed her eyes.

A red glow shown through her eyelids.

Her eyes shot open, and she saw the rubies' glare piercing the suitcase.

"Impossible," she muttered, but the glow grew fiercer, and flames appeared on the surrounding seats. They burned brightly, fueled by sin and torment.

Annette stared at the other passengers, at the driver, but they were all unaware of the blazing inferno that consumed the bus. She clutched her rosary and prayed like she never prayed before. She felt panic when the earthquake hit the Cathedral of Our Lady of Grief, but this was different. The earthquake was an act of God. The statuette's visions however . . .

"Please, God." Annette's lips quivered. "Please aid Your faithful servant. Please! Help me God!"

And then she saw a man with a golden crown of three levels of gems and a magnificent cross atop his balding head, wearing a gold embroidered vestment that seemed heavy enough to bend his spine, and holding a staff topped by a crucifix. His Holiness the Pope walked through the corridor between the seats. As he advanced towards her, the flames parted. His humble smile creased his old face and Annette wept.

"Thank you, God," she murmured, drying her tears.

His Holiness stretched a hand towards her, the flames vanished without a hiss, and an oversized check appeared out of thin air. A stunning amount of money was written on it and toward the rebuilding of the Cathedral of Our Lady of Grief. The pope's smile turned into a sinister grin as he plucked the check from the air. When he disappeared, the flames of Hell returned.

The bus reached the airport and all the passengers shuffled out, except for Annette. The vision of the pope stealing enough money to save millions from the cruel grip of poverty haunted her. *If the leader of the Church is corrupt, then is all the Church corrupt?*

No, it couldn't be. God wouldn't allow that, and Sister Annette was the proof there were still righteous people among the sinful.

"Hey, lady!" The bus driver shouted from the front. "Last station, you gotta go."

She left her seat on gelatin legs as she crossed the once ablazed corridor, the suitcase with the statuette weighed as much as a mountain. When her feet touched the road she suddenly felt doubt creep into her mind. She wasn't afraid she was doing the wrong thing, but uncertain of her next move, of who she could trust. The pope was now out of the question, yet somehow the Vatican still seemed the answer. Surely some of the archbishops could be of help.

A strong hand closed around her shoulder.

"Sister Annette." The strict voice belonged to Bishop Reynolds. The massive hand to Father Williams.

"I'm sorry, Annette," Father Morris said as the enormous priest dragged her to a nearby van. "You must understand that I had to tell them!"

Annette went to protest but Father Williams' other hand brutishly covered her mouth.

Bishop Reynolds opened the van's door and she was pushed inside.

Peering Through the Blazing Gates

Her skull struck the top of the van and she landed with a thud. White specks danced in her vision. Her ears rang.

"A shame that it has come to this, Sister." Bishop Reynolds took a seat. The van started moving. Annette weakly screamed for help.

"The windows are soundproof, not that it matters." The bulky priest cracked his knuckles. "But I would prefer if you were quiet."

"Check her suitcase," ordered Bishop Reynolds.

Father Williams removed its contents one by one. When the lacquered box appeared, Bishop Reynolds grunted in surprise.

The muscular priest slowly opened the box. The satanic statuette's hellfire eyes glared at everyone, and the two priests made the sign of the cross.

"I feared as much," Bishop Reynolds muttered. "Sister Annette, for conspiring with Satan against God, you are hereby excommunicated from the Holy Church." He turned to Father Williams, his face somber. "She is an enemy of Christ. You know what to do."

Father Williams fell on her like a vicious animal, raining blow after blow. Annette tried to resist, but it was impossible. The man was immense, and his rage unending.

She pleaded for mercy, begged God for help, but a devastating fist was her only answer.

Blood flooded her mouth, and through her bleary eyes, a light shone. Its touch was warm, familiar, and the radiance so bright she might be staring directly at God. The grand presence comforted Annette for she knew Heaven awaited her.

The light shifted as something hit the statuette. From its ruby eyes the blazing fires of Hell spilled, engulfing the van. The dancing flames revealed Satan, looming behind the priests, eagerly watching the life being squeezed out of Annette.

The Goat Priest

MATTHEW M. BARTLETT

Inspired by "He Is"

Where the heck was Henry?
    He said he was going to check the mail. How long ago was that? It seemed like he should have been back before now. But time seemed to move at varying speeds these days, irrespective of the circumstances, and more so the older she got. Annie draped her needlepoint over the arm of the chair, and after a few tries, straining with her arms and rocking her body, she lurched to her feet. Through the rain-smeared picture window she saw Henry standing next to the mailbox, a blue and red plaid blur, facing the road. The damn fool was getting soaked. What was he . . .
    . . . and then she saw the catalogs and flyers scattered around him on the driveway. And that his hands were up, covering his face.
    Oh lord.
    Annie plodded down the porch steps, the sounds of Henry's sobbing carrying up the driveway, striking fear into her heart, quickening her step. She hadn't seen him cry in over thirty years, back when the shop had laid him off. That had been a helpless weeping, and she had been surprised by the revelation of his hidden weakness. The spell hadn't lasted long, thank the Lord, and he'd found new work in a matter of weeks. During those weeks he'd gone back to being his stoic and resolute self, and she was relieved to see him once again as strong, to reinterpret the transgression as a brief, shameful lapse that could happen to any man.
    But even then, he hadn't *sobbed*. She'd never in all of their fifty-nine years together heard him do so until now. The helpless hitching and croaking stirred in her an atavistic revulsion. Further, it hinted at larger troubles than whatever it was that had caused him to react that way. She worried often that dementia would strike him. With both of them in their eighties, she had to count on him more than ever to be in control. The

The Goat Priest

steady hand at the helm. He was in charge of their money, of their medications—their future. Jesus would see to their salvation in the afterlife, but surely He was far too busy to prevent their ending up in some horrible cesspool of a nursing home, with godless, unhygienic attendants, left to rot.

"Henry!" she called. "Henry, what's the matter?"

He turned just as she reached him. He looked stricken, his face red, wrenched into a grimace that looked nearly like a savage grin. In his large hand he held a tri-folded letter, held it delicately, as though it might shatter if his grip was too tight.

"Our angel is redeemed," he said, his voice gruff, as though he were fighting to keep it from trembling. "His light has shined upon her."

He lurched forward and embraced her so hard she feared her arms might break. She opened her mouth to ask what on earth he was talking about, *who* he was talking about . . . and then it hit her, and she embraced him back, squeezing handfuls of his flannel shirt in her hands, arthritis be darned.

Maxine.

Their only child, their daughter.

They had cast her away when she was sixteen. She was no longer the sweet, docile, loving little girl they once cherished, the little girl who loved church, excelled in her catechism classes, who couldn't sleep the night before her confirmation. Annie didn't know what more they could have done. They filled her life with the Lord. They forbade her the sinful indulgences with which other parents spoiled their charges and forbade her from communing with children they knew to be bad influences. Strict, but loving, they cocooned her in their omnipresence. They wielded the switch and the rod only when she backtalked, denied her supper only when she fussed or fidgeted. Most importantly, they brought her up to be upstanding and ladylike, not spoiled.

Her wildness, her delinquency, had seemed to bloom overnight. It was too much for them to bear, especially when the neighbors saw her in her cut-off jeans and her torn shirt, saw her with this and that disreputable boy, heard her coarse talk and her cursing and her casual blasphemies. Such shame they felt when their fellow parishioners looked at them with prideful pity, noting Maxine's conspicuous absence in the church pew.

And of course she had caused one final scene, out on the front lawn, cursing and spitting and screaming so loud the neighbors watched through their windows and some even came out to look on from their porches. She hated them, she said. They'd never see or hear from her again, she screamed. She hoped they were happy, she shouted. Her boy of the week, a greasy, unwashed fellow in a half-tee shirt, made obscene gestures and told her to get in the god blanked effing car. And with a screech of tires and a string of departing curses, she was gone.

It had taken years to dismiss any hope she might see the error of her ways, might awaken to the sure damnation that awaited her eternal soul, her *tainted* soul—that she might find Jesus and He might guide her home.

And now?

"She's getting married," Henry said. He was back in his chair, back in control, his eyes dry (but red), a grin on his face, the letter still in his hand. "This man, Simon, he met her at her work, took her to his church—he brought her back to the light."

"And now back to us?" she said.

"Back in our lives. They don't live far away, pet. Less than a half a day's drive!"

Annie clasped her hands at her breast—she dared hope she might actually live to have grandchildren to dote upon, family holidays in which to luxuriate, saying Grace together, kneeling as a family in prayer, the years apart erased. And now Annie felt her own eyes welling up, her own voice hitching. "I thought we'd lost her forever."

"So did I, pet. May the Lord forgive us our faithlessness."

From his framed picture upon the wall, Jesus, all beatific blue eyes, swept-back hair, and dainty hands pressed together, gazed upon them, bestowing his grace. Annie would swear she could feel his love entering through her pores, strengthening her heart, swelling her very soul to bursting.

"Get your best clothing together for the dry cleaner, my dear," Henry said, clapping his hands together and holding them palm to palm in unconscious imitation of the Savior. "We have a wedding to attend."

A week later, seven days of blissful anticipation and meaningful gazes passed between the newly hopeful pair, their silver Chevrolet Tahoe pulled out of the driveway, Henry Gossineau at the wheel, left arm cocked out the window, Annie in the passenger seat, looking worriedly from side to side for oncoming traffic, of which there was none. *We Support Law Enforcement*, their bumper proudly stated. *It's a CHILD not a CHOICE*, it asserted. *Are you following Jesus this close?* it ungrammatically queried. The SUV rumbled down the quiet street, then swung slightly leftward before turning right, hailed by a chorus of surprised car horns, onto the long road that led to the interstate.

And so, for the first time in many years, the Gossineau house stood

The Goat Priest

empty. The tattered, faded American flag sagged limply atop its pole. The untrimmed hedges hunkered. Dried leaves lay in unkempt piles. Inside, Jesus continued to stare blankly yet handsomely from the wall, bestowing his grace upon unwashed teacups, shelves of Hummels, China plates propped up behind the glass walls of their cabinet, carpeting and couches and a sprung recliner. The wall-mounted television stared back, silent for the first afternoon in ages, bereft of its preachers and politicians and offended commentators. A copy of Country Living magazine lay open to an ad for 9/11 commemorative plates. Annie's needlepoint—a rippling American flag—lay over the arm of the chair. The ticking clock seemed to boost its volume to fill the space. From time to time, the refrigerator raised its voice to compete, then fell back into cold silence.

The front door opened slowly, with a creak, admitting a widening wedge of afternoon light, fragrant autumn air, and not a few dried, curled-up leaves, which skittered down the hall and came to rest along the baseboard. In his haste to reunite with his once-estranged daughter, his mind buzzing, assembling the words he'd say to her, imagining what she might look like after these many years, Henry Gossineau hadn't closed the door all the way.

"Here, Henry, turn here!"

"There's no *turn* here!"

Having gotten off the wrong exit, which had deposited them unceremoniously onto a car-jammed interstate heading in the wrong direction, the couple's nerves were frayed, their patience with one another eroded, the unthinkable thought of arriving late or, worse, missing the ceremony altogether putting them both into a near-panic. But they were near. They were just going to make it.

"HEEEERE," shrieked Annie, clawing with her left hand at Henry's outstretched arm and gesticulating wildly at trees and houses with the other. The car jolted leftward as he removed his hand from the wheel to slap away her hand.

"What the hell is wrong with . . . oh."

He returned his hand to the wheel and jerked the car rightward, sending it careening onto a broad street—not coincidentally called Broad Street—lined with tall trees whose leaves and branches gathered at the tops of the bare trunks as though frightened of the ground below. The houses, white and brick, mostly Colonial or Victorian, sat tastefully back from the street, immaculately maintained, with rolling lawns of deep green and lush, flower-choked landscaping. Marble birdbaths. Leafy trellises. Fences of gleaming black iron, or low stone walls. *Rich people*, thought Henry. *Oh, to be rich. One day, one day.* The street ended at a cul-de-sac at whose outer curve stood a tall church that at first both Henry and Annie Gossineau thought was the scorched remains of a burned building.

But it wasn't, of course. It was an edifice of uneven grey stone stained dark in places from recent rainfall, and had the look of a kind of abbreviated castle, narrow and tall, complete with a front-facing tower, arrow slits, and battlements. Behind the tower stretched a high-vaulted, gable-roofed section, also of stone, but with conspicuously updated windows and framing. The church looked old and a little out of place. Neither Henry nor Annie observed the absence of a cross; neither noticed that the stained glass of the windows was black and red only; they did not catch the lack of a marquee, or even of a sign proclaiming the church's name. Annie noticed a large and bowlegged goat meandering by the tree line. It turned and regarded her balefully, then squatted and released a thin stream of black diarrhea into the leaves, maintaining eye contact the whole time. Annie looked away quickly, embarrassed.

Henry parked the car crookedly, to Annie's verbal consternation. Ignoring the scolding and refusing to right the vehicle, he clambered out, and just as he did, the sun broke free from a morass of retreating black clouds. It shone strongly on the dew-garlanded grass, the car windshields, and the sunglasses of the tall, wiry man who stood at the top of the stairs, arms crossed, black robes rippling in the light wind. As Annie struggled to free herself from her seatbelt, Henry made his way up the walk to greet the robed man. The latter lifted his sunglasses and perched them on his forehead. He had cleaver-shaped sideburns and red lips offsetting his pale flesh. He appeared to suffer from a defect of the eye that rendered the irises nearly translucent, the small pupils a rich, dark black.

"Good sir," the man said at Henry's approach. "Am I to take it you are the father . . . of the bride?"

The man's accent took Henry aback. He couldn't place it, exactly—of the Balkans, maybe, but with touches of the short, sharpened vowels characteristic of spoken German.

"I am," he said.

"And this lovely lady is the mother?"

"Who?" said Henry as Annie, huffing and puffing and sighing, reached his side. "Oh. Yes. Her."

The man placed a pale, long-fingered hand over his belt buckle—scuffed silver, an image of a ram with elaborately curled horns—and bowed. "I do have to congratulate you," he said, "on having combined your obviously considerable forces to create such a marvelous daughter."

The Goat Priest

Annie reddened as Henry swelled so thoroughly with pride he trembled and stuttered, attempting, but failing, to muster a reply. Annie recovered first. "Are you Simon?" she said, pleased at the man's height, his posture, his sharp, angular good looks.

Henry elbowed her so hard she grunted. "Pet, this is the *priest*!" he said, contempt in his voice.

The man laughed—a sound like thick glass cracking. "You honor me, sir, but I am a mere magister in this particular, erm, *episcopate*. But your lovely wife was indeed correct—I am Simon."

"Oh, well, of course, I should have . . . " As Henry stuttered in his attempts at a gracious recovery, Annie introduced herself.

"I would love to meet your parents—are they here?"

"Sadly perished," Simon said, his face contorting into a semblance of crushing sorrow. "Some years ago."

"Oh, dear, I am truly sorry to hear it."

"Yes, terrible, terrible." He glanced at his watch—expensive looking, Annie noted!—and looked up at the pair, aghast. "Oh dear. We should hasten in. We held the ceremony for your arrival and look at me, chatting away the day as though a wedding isn't in the offing!"

"I hope we have a chance to catch up at the reception," Henry said. Annie nodded vehemently, fearful the couple would be in such demand they wouldn't be able to interrogate him. And, of course, congratulate the newlyweds, and to make plans for the future.

"Oh, indeed, of course, all the time . . . all the time there is in the world," said Simon gamely, grinning a sharkish grin, one eyebrow leaping upward. For a brief moment, Annie thought she detected suppressed laughter in his voice. It was, she reasoned, probably just joy.

Her instinct was to embrace her soon-to-be son-in-law in the spirit of the occasion, to squeeze his shoulder during the embrace in order to express familial sympathy. But something about him seemed to defy touching, to psychically ward off that degree of physical closeness. Feeling foolish, but having no idea what else to do, she held out her hand. He took it eagerly into his . . .

talons enfolding a mouse

. . . and squeezed. Her toes twitched and her left eyelid fluttered. An electric jolt thrummed in her hand, then it went numb. The numbness climbed up her arm and spread throughout her trunk, shook her stomach, shot down her other limbs to her extremities. A roaring, rushing sound filled her ears. Images assailed her, flashing strobe-like: a black altar crowded with candles sporting sickly blue flames, purple blood running down the waxen shafts; a cowl-clad goat like the one she'd seen outside, standing on its hind legs in a fire-ringed meadow, a sword held aloft in each human hand, infants impaled, cross-hatched, on the blades; a fire-swaddled Jesus Christ hopping up and down outside a hut of thatch and mud in a drought-dried village, trying haplessly to bat at the flames climbing his robes, his feet singed and swollen, the sandals melted into the smoking flesh.

She felt herself crumpling to the ground, but there was no ground to catch her, and she instead plummeted down a narrow, branch strewn, red-walled column with no end, faster and faster she fell and everything smelled like a freshly lit match and the feeling came back to her all at once as the branches scratched her skin and her organs climbed from her stomach into her chest cavity and then into her throat and she felt her throat swelling like a frog's throat and oh Lord she couldn't breathe . . . *I can't breathe, I can't breathe, I can't . . .*

" . . . I can't say enough about how happy we are that you found our little lost lamb," Henry was saying. His big red hands engulfed Simon's hands up to the wrist. Annie ducked into a crouch as though landing on her feet after a fall, then, suddenly self-conscious, realizing she had been standing there all along, straightened out again, grunting loudly. The two men ignored her. She could breathe, she was grateful to the Lord for the ability to breathe, and she took full advantage, she breathed in the sweet air, breathed it in deeply and, to her surprise, it burned from the outside of her nostrils down through her lungs. The smell of smoke suffused the air, as though someone nearby had a bonfire going. The sky, however, was a cloudless bright blue. She looked at her hand. It was smeared with ash.

⛧

She exited the washroom, drying her hands on her blouse. Something must be terribly wrong with her, to have had such thoughts and visions. She put it down to the leftover chicken she'd eaten the night before. Henry had warned her she should throw it out. She should have listened.

But Annie, the ash, the ash on your hands.

Annie hushed her inner voice. Simon had probably been lightning candles, or cleaning. He couldn't be a bad man—he was so handsome, so well built . . . so *dreamy*. Annie felt her ears get hot at the thought, and she scolded herself.

Then it hit her—she snapped her fingers at the simplicity of the explanation, the obviousness of it. Surely he'd had car trouble and it was just grease! She'd seen that happen when Henry tried to open the hood of the truck. Have a little faith, Annie.

But why does it smell like smoke out there . . . and, for that matter, in here?

The Goat Priest

Organ music meandered down the carpeted hall from the nave. This part of the church—an alcove adjacent to the hallway, a combination meeting and storage space with a chalkboard and comfortable seating and wheeled racks lined with folding chairs—was dark, the lights out, the windows tinted. She was walking past an arrangement of chairs and loveseats when someone coughed and she yelped, startled.

"Oh my gracious," came a thin, raspy voice from the shadows. She peered. Sitting there, leaning forward as though to regard her closely, was an ashen looking man clad in tweed and a bowler hat with a red feather. The man was grey and wizened, his eyes framed with sagging wrinkles. "I didn't mean to startle you."

"Do you smell smoke?" Annie said.

"My darling woman, I *am* smoke." And he gathered himself up into a cloud and billowed outward and upward, spreading across the ceiling, laughing ashy laughter. Annie hobbled away as quickly as she could as the smoke spread across the ceiling above her. The chicken, she thought. Bad chicken. Lucky I'm not sick to my darn stomach.

⛤

The nave flickered wildly with candlelight. Flames shimmied in the red hobnail glass cups that lined the windowsills and the balconies and the rafters all the way to the high, peaked ceiling. They crowded the altar. They lined the aisle on both sides and the walkways to the right and the left. At the top of the aisle, carpeted stairs led to a red velvet curtain whose hem puddled over the top step. On either side of the curtain, smaller staircases curved to upward into shadows, their terminuses obscured by the curtains. Above, a black-suited man with a tower of black hair sat at a curved pipe organ whose sides wrapped partway around him like some futuristic space pod. His hands flew up and down a staircase of keyboards with black and red keys. His body bounced at his feet worked the many pedals. Above the organ, a row of tall, polished, vertical pipes shone, purple smoke billowing from their tips and collecting at the arched ceiling. On either side of him, a silent chorus of women in black angel wings swayed, their lace-gloved hands tracing shapes above them.

Henry was in one of the frontmost pews—Annie could recognize the back of his head anywhere, mussed white hair surrounding a terminally red and peeling patch of flesh. She walked down, careful to keep the hem of her dress from touching the jumping flames. She glanced to the right and to the left, wishing to smile at the other guests, but they stared straight ahead. They all wore black, from their shoes to their elaborate hats; all had beaklike noses and sharp chins, like a congregation of malformed ravens. Annie resolved to look straight ahead until her hallucinations—for that's surely what they were—passed.

Annie put her hand on Henry's wrist and he beamed up at her and patted the pew next to him. Annie sat, and the two clasped hands. Henry looked around, confusion on his face. "You know," he said. "No one has talked to me about walking Maxine down the aisle to give her away."

Oh, yes—what an oversight! That tradition had to be upheld. "Well, Henry, quick, before the ceremony starts, talk to someone. That's not right!"

She let him up and he shuffled up the aisle, hand raised, calling out. She stayed standing so she could watch him. When he reached the narthex, two tall, robed officiants emerged from the shadows to consult with him. That was Henry. If it wasn't right, he'd take care of it. She slid back into the pew. After a few minutes of waiting, she found herself a bit bored. So she plucked a leather-bound prayer book from the holder behind the empty pew in front of her and opened it to a random page. What she saw there was so grotesquely obscene, so foul and perverted that she let out an involuntary squeal and jammed the book back from whence she'd pulled it. *Vandals*, she thought, though the illustration had looked to be printed directly onto the page. *Even in church, you can't escape them.*

Or, she thought, it was another hallucination. Clearly, they hadn't subsided, because just then, as the organ music swelled to a crescendo, from either side of the transept swept in a troupe of red-cloaked, silver-skinned, horned children—no, not children, but adults curiously short in stature, like imps. Some were obviously female, conically breasted and wide of hip. The males were sinewy but muscular. They gathered where the curtains met and pulled them apart, revealing a deep chancel. In the foreground stood a podium carved in bas relief with strange runic letters; a suggestively shaped microphone jutted from its top. Several yards behind the podium stood an altar of a deep black, the blackest black Annie had ever seen, as though it wasn't an object, but the hellish void that remained after an object's facade had been torn away from reality. On the great back wall behind that obscene altar, where Annie would have expected to see the crucified Christ, instead was a backlit carved wooden wheel, larger even than the Wheel of Fortune from the television program, within it a five-pointed star. It spun slowly, red sparks shooting from behind it.

Tall choir stalls of elaborately carved oak stood at the right and left of the chancel, facing the podium, and the imps, having tied off the curtains, gathered there, sitting atop one another's laps, frolicking and rough housing and hissing at one another like outraged cats. The organ blasted four dissonant, ear-crushing blasts, accompanied by bursts of red confetti

The Goat Priest

from cannons in a recessed trench that ran the length of the stage, and then fell silent as a chorus of demoniac voices took over, swooping and ululating and trilling and screeching in multifarious harmonies, at times dissonant, at times consonant, mostly deranged and cacophonous.

A tall and broad silhouette, swaddled in swirling smoke, emerged from the shadows behind the altar. When the lights hit it, Annie gasped. Even filtered through the profuse spiraling red rain of confetti she recognized it as the goat she had seen in the yard, and then in her hallucination, now striding unsteadily forward in on its hind legs, taller than three men standing foot-to-shoulder. Embroidered purple vestments and a brocaded veil adorned its torso; it was otherwise obscenely unclad. Its curled horns were painted in psychedelic colors, and its eyes glowed with mystic, knowing bioluminescence.

It spread its forelegs and the smoke billowed outward, engulfing the goat, the choir stands, and the whole stage. When it dissipated, Simon stood on the left side of the goat, and on the other stood Maxine. The crowd gasped and sighed as one, and Annie gasped as well, though hers was the gasp of shocked epiphany.

This wasn't the effects of bad chicken, it wasn't a hallucination—it was *real*. And Simon hadn't led Maxine to the lord; quite the opposite. This was majestic, ceremonial, ecstatic blasphemy. And yet, it could not be denied: Maxine was beautiful. No longer thin and stooped, she stood proud and straight; her shape that of the classic hourglass, accentuated by the clinging black gown. Black makeup circled her eyes and painted her nose, and a wide grin of painted-on teeth spread across the lower half of her face. She wore long earrings shaped like something between an inverted cross and a capital G. Her legs, long and shapely, were wrapped tightly in red and black fishnet. She was barefoot, her toenails red. Both Simon and the goat-priest looked at her with admiration and awe as she curtsied and smiled at the crowd, a red grin within a grin.

The chorus went silent, only their echo remaining like sonic mist ringing the rafters. The crowd, too, hushed.

Annie needed Henry. And then she realized he hadn't come back down the aisle. He hadn't come back at all.

In a hoarse and guttural voice, the goat spake, saying:

> *We gather here today in chaos and firelight to mark a great transition, not of two souls into one, but of two souls—untainted— cleaving together, each still one, unique, singular, and strong—in control of their lives and destinies, letting them intertwine loosely and lovingly, without restraint nor restriction. And in this union let there be joy and glorious gluttony, let there be lust and*

honeyed avarice and long, languorous stretches of sweet, untrammeled sloth. Let envy be constructive and let greed reign, not greed for the property of others nor for unearned wealth, but for life and for its richness. Let He Who Shall Not Be Named remain silent, not sullying this union with His trusses and tethers and His gold-gilded fetters. Let his name go unuttered at all human ceremonies that mark love and loss, and let the names of the humans ring.

And before we proceed to the avowals, Maxine, would you do the honor of cutting the tethers to your past so that you might freely embrace the future?

Maxine stepped up to the podium and adjusted the microphone. Annie clasped her hands together, caught in a complex of emotions: fear, love, bafflement, outrage, and exhaustion. "Mother," Maxine said. "This was supposed to be addressed to the both of you, but Father decided to interfere with the ceremony. I'm not too good at speeches, so I'll make it quick. You tried to form me into the perfect child, and in doing so, you sent me in the opposite direction. And strangely enough, as you'd wanted in the first place, I found religion. Just not the one you would have picked for me. But this one is so much better—there's no restrictions, living is not held in abeyance while you wait for joy in the afterlife. It's freed me to be my own person, in a relationship with an equal not an owner, not a supervisor. So, in a way, I have you to thank for my new life in Satan's accepting grace. My life moving forward is one in which you will have no part. In a strange way, I love you. You were doing what you thought best. If only you'd had the bravery to break free from the dogma that kept you and Father in fetters. If the ability was in me, surely the potential was in one or both of you. It's too late now, anyway. Shame."

A noise came then, a rushing of air, and the pew buckled as Henry crashed into it from above. His corpse was a heavy tangle, its eyes, red as cherries, bulging from their sockets, the pommels of daggers resting against his ears. Annie shrieked as the floor opened up in the aisle and the pew titled upward, spilling Henry onto her, and then the couple and the pew they were in upended and slid into the hungry maw. Down they fell, down and down and down, entangled. Annie clung to Henry as the pair fell, not knowing their fall would be eternal, unending,

Forever and into forever they fell.

The Goat Priest

The Gossineau house teemed with life. Squirrels chased each other under beds, around corners, up door jambs, avoiding the broken glass and shattered China. Birds twittered on the mantel, conversed chirpily atop the television, flew from room to room, knocking pictures off the wall. Jesus beamed upward at the ceiling through broken glass. Centipedes like peripatetic eyebrows crawled the walls. A grey and white goat, lithe and serene-eyed, stood by the easy chair, chewing mindlessly on Annie's abandoned needlepoint flag. Dogs snapped at each other's jaws, their claws scraping the kitchen floor tile as they circled one another. Dried leaves piled in corners; among them, sightless beetles swarmed. A deer stood in the hallway, its body a venue for a crowded party of bloodthirsty ticks. Bats roosted on curtain rods and cats loafed on cushions. Snakes slithered in the halls and rats feasted on detritus from the fallen refrigerator.

It was a better place now.

Figgy Pudding

VIVIAN KASLEY

Inspired by "Con Clavi Con Dio"

"Tonight, on *Chilling Cold Cases*, we'll re-visit a mystery that has intrigued and puzzled many around the globe for over thirty-five years. The Christmas Eve murders of Marcus and Greta McVerry, and presumably their unborn child, is as bizarre as it is horrific. Their story has been pieced together by the information uncovered about the young couple and by the evidence left behind at the crime scene. The portrayal of what you are about to see is not a news broadcast, but a dramatized re-creation of what may have occurred according to the authorities. Please be advised tonight's episode contains sensitive subject matter and may be too graphic for some viewers. Viewer discretion is advised. Join us, and perhaps you'll be able to help solve a *Chilling Cold Case!*"

"**Oh, just listen** to them Marcus, singing their hearts out in that bitter cold! I've always loved the idea of Christmas carolers, but I can't say I've ever actually seen any outside of the movies before. Those hooded black cloaks they're wearing are quite odd... I suppose I expected something different, more festive, red or green maybe, but black? And why're they standing in a circle like that?" Greta McVerry closed the curtains and stepped back from the large bay window.

Figgy Pudding

She stuck her hand into her robe and rubbed her bulbous belly through her flannel nightgown. The baby kicked.

The days and weeks had flown by so quickly, and at nine months, she was ready to pop. She'd even been doing her make-up at night, just in case. She wanted to look her best when she delivered their bundle of joy. They hadn't even decorated for Christmas because neither one of them felt like dealing with it, because *just in case*.

"Marcus, did you hear anything I just said?" She shook her head and smiled. Marcus had a habit of not hearing her. Selective hearing is what she called it.

Marcus put down his tumbler of bourbon, removed his glasses, and rubbed his temples. "Yes, yes, I heard you. But barely over the incessant warbling of those annoying mongrels. Who knows why they're in a circle, what I do know is, they've been out there singing the same damn song for nearly thirty minutes. They need to move on. We don't have any damn figgy pudding!"

"Oh, they're hardly mongrels, and I'm sure they'll be on their way soon. The sun's going down, and there's more snow on the way," Greta said. She patted her belly again, as the baby's kicks had become rowdier.

"I sure hope you're right, because I'm getting a splitting headache. What're they doing all the way out here anyway? I bought this house in the sticks for a reason. Whatever you do, don't acknowledge them, or it'll egg 'em on and they'll never leave. They're like stray cats, give 'em one tiny handout and they'll never leave!"

"Marcus, you're being terrible!" Greta chuckled.

"No love, I'm being honest. So, tell me my lamb, how's our little miracle doing this evening?"

"Oh, he's pretty squirmy, but other than that, good, I think," Greta smiled. "Although I did eat some olive loaf earlier, and I suspect he may not have liked it. It's as if he's practicing Kung Fu in here!"

Marcus made a face and said, "I'd squirm too . . . nobody likes olive loaf!"

Another thirty minutes passed, and the caroling outside continued. Marcus and Greta were unsure what to do. Should they open the door and ask them to leave or let them keep singing until they wore themselves out? It was frigid out there, and no one could stand those temps for long. What the couple agreed upon was it had begun to bother them, scare them even. They ignored the hairs standing on the back of their necks and turned on the television to try and drown out the singing, but it only grew more fervent, turning into what sounded more like a menacing chant. The louder the chant got, the more afraid the couple grew. They turned the tv volume as loud as it would go, and covered their ears with their trembling hands.

Marcus paced the living room, his blood pressure through the roof. He went to the window and tried to count how many of the singing bastards were out there. He could see at least six but wasn't sure if there were more hiding in the woods or around the property, waiting for him to open the door so they could do God knew what. He didn't want to call out the police unless necessary. He hated to make a fuss, especially when he knew that's what those little shits outside were hoping for. Marcus gritted his teeth and snarled.

He was sure it was a bunch of teenagers, playing some sort of cruel prank, wanting to get a rise out of him. Maybe it was even a few of the same ones he'd seen when he was in town a couple weeks ago. He hadn't gotten a good look at their faces, didn't think he had to. He figured they were a bunch of local yokels who'd never seen a fancy car like his around town. They were dressed in all black and leaning on his Mercedes, like restless crows. He'd rushed out of the hardware store and threatened to call the cops if they didn't scram. They'd sneered at him, lewdly fingering the famous hood ornament on his car before moving on.

But this, this was different. Whatever these kids were doing seemed menacing. Although, elaborate pranks were what bored teenagers did to entertain themselves. He did wonder where they came from though, since he didn't see any vehicles of any kind. It had to be a long cold walk on what were sure to be ice-slick roads and woods full of snow-laden trees. Even their steep driveway was a pain in the winter, especially with the black ice.

Marcus was still trying to work out what to do when the television exploded and the fire in the fireplace extinguished itself. Greta screamed and the lights flickered like a lightning storm inside the house. The walls around them began to vibrate, causing books to jangle from the bookcase and crash to the floor. Marcus rushed to Greta, encircling her into his arms as glass shattered in picture frames, sending their memories flitting to the floor below. The terrified couple ran to the window and nervously peeked out the curtains. They gasped at what they saw; two slaughtered deer swung from the branches of their maple tree and a pentagram painted in the bright, white snow beneath in what appeared to be the animals' blood and entrails.

One of the hooded figures looked in their direction; their eyes glowing like hot coals in the blue-black winter's night. The figure nodded at them, walked over to the mutilated animals, and lit their carcasses on fire. Greta cried out and gripped the curtain to keep from falling backward. Marcus

Figgy Pudding

raced to the phone, but there was no dial tone, only static. He slammed the phone into its cradle repeatedly, shouting curse words at the inanimate object as if it would cry uncle and begin to work.

Panic swam like icy eels through the couple's veins and they weren't sure what to do next. Greta cried hysterically as Marcus tried to formulate a plan. His heart broke as he looked at his pregnant wife, her beautiful face streaked with mascara-blackened tears. All of this stress couldn't be good for the baby. *Think, Marcus, think!* If he opened the door, one of them might try and get in, and while he was no coward, he wasn't prepared to fight off several people with his pregnant wife left vulnerable. He closed his eyes, trying to focus, but finding it almost impossible. His head and heart pounded in time with all of the noise—the chanting, Greta's cries, and the vibrating walls. His ears felt like they might burst from the pressure surrounding them on all sides. He snapped out of his stupor when a brick sailed through the bay window.

Marcus's face turned red, then to a shade of purple and he shouted, "All right, that's it! I'm gonna teach those little bastards a goddamn lesson if it's the last thing I do! They won't get away with this!"

Greta shrieked and ran after her husband, pulling the back of his sweater before he could reach the door. "Marcus, don't . . . please, it's not safe. I . . . I think I know what they want."

"W-What're you talking about, Greta?" Marcus panted and studied his wife's flushed face.

Greta's mouth twisted and her chin trembled as she looked at her belly. She handed her husband the brick. "Read it," she rasped.

Marcus's heart stopped as he read the message scrawled in blood: *WE WON'T GO UNTIL HE GETS SOME!*

"What the fuck is that supposed to mean?" Marcus asked, the brick still in his hand. "Greta, what does this mean?"

"I-I wanted to get pregnant. We'd tried everything and . . . I . . . I asked for help. I didn't think it'd really work . . . I—"

"Whose help, Greta?"

Greta bit her lip and squeezed her eyes shut as she shook her head.

"Goddamnit, I asked you a question! Whose help?" Marcus had never thought of putting his hands on a woman in his entire life, but in this moment, he wanted to rattle his wife's brains until she told him what the fuck was going on. He shouted again; his fists balled at his sides. "Greta, so help me God, if you don't answer me—"

"The Dark Lord! I asked the Dark Lord! No one else would help us—I had to do it!" Greta wailed and collapsed to her knees onto the carpet.

"The Dark Lord—as in, the Devil? Did I hear you right? Are you on something?" Marcus's anger boiled his blood and broiled his insides. His guts churned like a turbulent sea. He was drunk and dizzy with rage. Marcus dropped the brick, and knelt next to his wife. He gripped her forearm harder than he meant to. "Have you been taking drugs while our baby's in there? My little boy . . . do you know what that can do to an unborn child? For Christ's sake, Greta! What have you fucking done?!"

Greta pulled away from her husband and rolled around, clutching her abdomen. She screamed in agony and Marcus shelved his boiling anger and lifted his wife into his arms. He had to get her to the hospital. It didn't matter those lunatics were outside anymore, all that mattered was his little boy. *Oliver*, that was what he was going to be named. With Greta still in his arms, he went to the fireplace and grabbed the poker. If any of those hooded sickos tried anything, he'd have no choice but to gore them to death. He leaned the poker against the wall as he opened the front door.

Snow and ice blasted Marcus in the face like a frozen hurricane. There was no way he was getting to the hospital in this weather, so he shut and locked the front door. He laid Greta back onto the carpet as he tried to work out what to do next. He ran back to the phone, but it was still static in his ear. The walls and floor continued to shake as the earthquake of monotonous chanting echoed around the house. It was a chorus to chill the bones and curdle the blood, on and on it went, over and over, "*We won't go until He gets some! Until He gets some! Until He gets some! So, bring it right now!*"

Greta lay with her eyes closed, panting like a stressed dog. Her skin felt like it was baking from the inside out when Marcus touched her. He ran and soaked a washcloth with cool water, and placed it across her forehead in the hope it would cool her down. He was no doctor, just an accountant. The fleeting memory of his parents urging him to consider medical school caused him to let loose a strangled sardonic bark. He paced the living room, looking at Greta, before circling back to the window, straining to think through all the noise. He couldn't see what the hooded figures were doing through the blizzard, but he knew they were there because their glowing eyes pierced the blinding white. Marcus emitted a moan of frustration. He felt helpless and useless.

He looked at his wife again and noticed she'd finally opened her eyes. His breath caught when he noticed the whites of her eyes were peppered with red. She let loose a string of guttural shrieks that brought Marcus to his knees.

Marcus matched his wife's cries as blood sprayed from between her legs and saturated the cream-colored carpet beneath her. As she wailed, the front door blew off its hinges and every light bulb in the house shattered. Marcus scrambled to get to the poker, but before he could, someone tripped him and stepped onto his back with enough force to pin

Figgy Pudding

him to the ground. He struggled to breathe as the boot ground further into his back.

Marcus tried to turn his head to locate Greta. He couldn't hear her anymore. In fact, it was silent except for the whistling arctic wind from outside. He took the small breaths his pinned body allowed, and turned his head enough to see the hooded figures surrounding him. If they had faces, he couldn't make them out, but he saw their horrific glowing eyes staring back at him. He struggled beneath the heavy boots crushing him and begged for them to leave them alone.

"P-Please . . . I'll give you whatever you want. M-My c-car . . . you can have it! M-Money? I got some in the safe. Please. Anything. My wife . . . she's pregnant, please don't hurt her," Marcus said. He still couldn't see where Greta was, couldn't lift his head enough to look.

The figures grinned, but remained unmoved by his pleas.

One of the figures grabbed the poker and tossed it to the one that restrained Marcus. Marcus blubbered as he pleaded for his life, "Please! Pleeeease, don't do this! God, help me!"

The figures nodded at one another. The one who pinned Marcus crushed the heel of his boot harder into his back and said, "God is dead." He rammed the poker between Marcus's shoulder blades like they were made of butter, dragging it down his spine until it reached his bowels. One by one, the figures dipped their hands into the flayed meat of Marcus's back and used his guts and blood to paint various symbols all over the walls.

Greta didn't protest as the figures surrounded her and held her down. Her mouth opened into a dry, muted scream as they peeled her robe off and removed her nightgown. The cold air bit into her bare skin like needles. They held her arms away from her body and parted her legs wide. Blood poured like warm honey from between her legs. The figures began to chant again, this time in a different tongue, one Greta couldn't understand. The house started to shake once more, the popcorn ceiling falling like snowflakes around her and onto her face. The chanting seemed to quicken in rhythm but lower in volume. It would've been soothing, thought Greta, under different circumstances.

The chanting stopped and they released Greta. They stood around her, undulating and moaning as if in the throes of sexual pleasure. Greta shook like she was having a seizure, until she floated off the blood-soaked carpet. Her body was at level to the shadowy faces surrounding her. She gazed dreamily into their glowing eyes, feeling both wonder and fear. *Maybe they'll spare her, maybe they need me?* she thought. Then all her thoughts turned darker than the bottom of the ocean. She foamed at the mouth and her eyes rolled back in her head. The chanting started again, rising to a deafening level, getting louder and louder, until Greta's womb split open like an overripe melon, spewing forth steaming debris and fluids in every direction, painting the faces of the figures around her.

    A baby's furious cry rang and the figures quickly retrieved its small slippery body. Greta cried out, her full breasts aching with each cry her babe let loose, but she couldn't get to him. She was sinking into a warm, black sea, one where she would be carried away from everything. Oh, it felt so good, her limbs floating, floating, floating, but no, wait! Her baby! *My baby! Our baby! Marcus! Where's Marcus?* She tried to pry open her eyes, but they were glued shut. She tried to scream, but her voice wouldn't come. Her baby's cry became more distant as the figures carried him away from her, outside into the wintry night.

    She knew what she'd done. At the time it all seemed like fun, something to take her mind off the fact nothing they were trying was working. How could a silly book on Satanic rituals be serious? *They wouldn't put dangerous books in a library*, she'd thought. And so, she had checked it out, hid it in her underwear drawer, taking it out and reading it whenever Marcus left for work. She bought black candles and followed the ritual for a baby. She'd performed it for weeks. The blood sacrifices she'd made, the ritualistic daily prayers, all of it seemed like a farce. "Ave Satanas," she had chanted over and over, reveling in the way the words rolled off her tongue like tiny happy bubbles that tickled her barren womb.

    Again, it had all seemed like fun at the time, like a dirty little secret only she would ever have to know. Except, she didn't know it would work. If God hadn't answered her, why would He? And when she had gotten pregnant, she decided to forget about what she had done and chalk it up to a miracle. And it was a miracle, just not one given by the right God. She had forgotten, and now here she was, in mid-air, bleeding out while her baby was ushered off into the freezing Christmas Eve night.

    "They won't go until *He* gets some," Greta whispered, dangling in the air for only a moment more before her battered body landed with a sickening thud back to the carpet below and burst into flames.

Creation

BENJAMIN KANE ETHRIDGE

Inspired by "Genesis"

Her Uncle Carmine stood in the hallway, holding his side and grimacing under his pale blond hair that reached his chin.

"What's happened?" Lynn asked.

"Gall bladder surgery." He moved into the apartment with a wince. Black cassock coat unbuttoned, his red silk shirt hung precariously from his gaunt frame and his charcoal slacks pooled over his loafers. Notes of a sharp, metallic cologne drifted in his wake.

Another man in a dark hoodie pushed inside behind him.

"Who's your friend?"

"Victor's helping me out during my recovery," Carmine said and made for the couch.

The man, Victor, was a head shorter than her uncle. He tossed back his hoodie and nodded an indifferent greeting. His shaven skull had the blue memory of hair and a thin pink scar ran from his lip to his left earlobe. "Nice apartment," he said, looking around.

"Thanks." She joined her uncle on the sofa. "Are you going to tell me what this emergency is? Surgery complication?"

Victor deadbolted the door. Lynn glanced at him quizzically as he leaned against the wall. "Habit," he muttered. "Sorry."

Her uncle Carmine softly rubbed his ribcage. "I should be better by tomorrow. Meds haven't really kicked in. This isn't about that."

"Ok, so what's up?" She played idly with her long, bleached curls. "I've got studying today." A laptop rested askew on the glass coffee table. Prank videos on YouTube. A mosaic of goofy closeups with laughing lamb eyes. She snapped shut the screen and sat back, burying herself in the sofa cushions.

Uncle Carmine interlocked his fingers on his lap, his eyes sadness polished in turquoise. "You recall I am a Blood Cardinal in the clergy."

Lynn's eyes moved to Victor and then back. "That RPG you played with dad sometimes?"

A subdued snarl quivered at Victor's lips, perhaps a smile, perhaps not.

Carmine replied, "It's not a game, Lynn."

"Dad told me it was."

"Well, he lied often enough. It should come as no surprise—look, I need a serious drink. What do you have hard?"

"Should you be drinking?" she asked.

"Not really. But anyway."

Sighing, she tossed a pillow aside and stood. "I have Absolut. Does he want some?"

"No thanks," Victor replied.

Lynn went into the galley kitchen.

"You should have one too," Carmine called after her.

"I'm good." She filled a tumbler with two fingers of vodka. "Ice?"

"None."

She set the drink in front of him. He took it and sipped. Looking into the tumbler, he searched for words. "The conclave has made its choice. They will vote for me this Sunday . . . there will be a new pontiff."

"Congrats," she replied blandly. "Will you make more money?"

His hands shook as he rested the tumbler on the table. "This isn't about money."

"Yeah? I find that difficult to believe." Lynn folded her arms now, making angry ripples in her army green sweater. "Is this about my allowance? You're not paying my tuition anymore. That's what you're saying? I only have a media job on campus, I can't do all of this alone—"

"Be quiet, let me finish," her uncle said. "I'm here to discuss requirements for the ceremony. We need your help. Stop with that look—you can hear me out. I've not ever turned my back on you. I've been here ever since your mom passed, haven't I?"

"Yes," she answered, her posture deflating, "but I have to study. I'd like to be part of . . . whatever this is. I just have a lot of work to do, you know?"

A half-formed smile touched his pale lips. "You aren't busy, Evelyn."

Her eyes narrowed.

"There's no school," he remarked. "There hasn't been for years. You didn't even get an associate's degree."

"That's not true! Just because I didn't attend the ceremonies—"

"You didn't attend *anything*," he insisted. "You have no campus job, or any job for that matter. My money has been burned through and gambled away, for years. I've known for some time now."

Creation

She seethed. "If I have squandered everything, how do I live here?"

"This apartment belongs to your venture capitalist boyfriend, your *married* venture capitalist boyfriend. John Carlson, I think his name is."

She leaned forward, arms still locked to her chest, eyes smoldering. "Is this the morality police making house calls? From where I'm sitting, you're the one in some weird ass *blood cult*."

Uncle Carmine finished the vodka and set the glass down with a loud clatter. "My point should be taken—you aren't busy. You can be there for me, for a change."

She threw herself back into the couch. "What then? What're you asking?"

"Let's talk about your father again." Carmine rubbed softly once more at his side. "Where's he living now? Have you heard from him?"

The impact of the question dazed her. "Why?"

"As I said, there are ceremonial requirements for family."

Lynn canted her head. "Why *are* you here? Who's this guy you brought?"

Victor bristled and rolled his shoulders anxiously.

"Ever since you were a kid, what did I say?" Her uncle's eyes entranced her, two frozen, lifeless planets.

She looked away.

"Lynn," his voice raised, "what did I tell you? Every birthday? Every time I handed you another check. What did I say? Look at me, please."

Slowly, she did. Her own eyes, much like his, lonesome in their orbits, made him soften. "You remember, sweetheart. Say it."

For a moment she pressed together her lips, her love and hate for him battling it out. "You'll make my life meaningful someday."

"This is the moment, honey. It is now. We cannot do this without you. There's no way your father will leave his drugs to come with us. You have to convince him."

Her voice quivered. "Why do you need him?"

"He's part of the Marl family." Carmine swallowed his words, like broken glass. "It is the ever-holy Lightbringer who commands this. The genesis of a new clergy pontiff cannot be conducted without bloodlines present. My brother is all I have."

"You're serious?" She laughed. "This is too fuckin strange. Just forget my allowance. Forget the checks." She scooted back into the sofa but could go no farther. "And you both should go."

Victor did not move. A short grin broke on Carmine's face, a flicker of perfect ivory teeth, made for grinding through the fiber of moments such as these. "You've pushed all your chips over to the venture capitalist—he won't help you."

Lynn tapped her lip with her thumb, considering him. "What did you do?"

"As of this morning, your game here is over. Carlson's wife is not happy with her husband and his expensive toy who lives here rent free."

Lynn's mouth dropped open. "Who the fuck are you?"

"Your uncle," Carmine said with a heavy sigh. "Who has always taken care of you, unconditionally. Your uncle, who is just asking for your help."

"I'll find my own way." Her tone changed, each word forced and disingenuous. "I can make my own money."

"Better get cracking on that. Mrs. Carlson may be on her way as we speak." Carmine checked his silver wristwatch and stood with some effort. "I wouldn't waste a whole lot of time."

Victor unbolted the door and opened it.

"Shit!" Lynn slammed a pillow down and sprang up. "I can take you to where I saw dad once. But if we find him, you can't do anything . . . weird or hurtful to him at this ceremony thing. He *is* my father."

"Never. You have my word," Uncle Carmine replied with a slight smile.

"And since you ruined this, *you* will move my stuff out," she added as she slipped on her sneakers, "and find me a new place."

"Absolutely."

Lynn grabbed her purse from the table, shaking her head in disbelief. He brought a comforting arm around her shoulders and ushered her into the hall. She stabbed the key into the door and hissed in exasperation.

"Easy now," her uncle said. "New beginnings are difficult, but only at first."

※

The freeway overpass hung with death's perfume. They made quick search of the top ledge and the rows of sleeping bags, dusty chrysalises drained of color from years of sun. None of the residents were coherent enough to offer information on Axel Marl.

Lynn waited at the bottom, watching Carmine and Victor's short interviews.

"Nothing?" she asked.

Victor jogged down the rotting embankment. "A couple thought we were talking about Mister Serious. What's that mean?"

She shrugged. "Mister *Seriously* High. I don't think that's dad they're talking about."

Carmine made the trip down the embankment with slow measured steps. His hand shook as it hovered near his right flank. "There's a tent city past the tree line," he huffed.

Creation

"Maybe just send Victor there to check it out?" Lynn suggested.

Victor shot her a dirty look.

"No," said Carmine, "we're all searching together."

And search they did. Through the damp coastline oak trees. Through the shanty town of cardboard boxes. Deflated, sagging tents with miserable troll-faced inhabitants. Bedrolls swarming with insects. Aromas of vomit and cookfires. Overhead, in the baleful sky, the sun burned through any uprising of clouds. The ugliness of life prevailed over everything in this place and greeted the group with blends of delusion, rage, bewilderment, and stark terror, which was the prevailing flavor throughout.

"I want to find it!" shouted a toothless man, initially only a filthy head poking from a plaid sleeping bag.

Victor backed away, shaking his head in defeat. "These people are so—"

The man swung open the sleeping bag, revealing a thin, jaundiced body covered in sores. He grasped a pale thing between his legs. "Speak into the mic, love. Speak into it!"

As Victor recoiled, Lynn chuckled. "Did he know anything?"

Victor glared at her. "*No, he didn't.*"

"Does anyone need water from the cooler?" Carmine scrubbed his sweaty brow. His silk shirt's armpits crawled with the darkness of sweat.

Lynn stood there rigidly, tapping one foot. "Maybe we should go. Maybe dad moved on from this place."

Carmine pointed to a distant line of trees. "I see more tents over there."

"Wonderful, I can use that water now," she said.

They trekked back to Carmine's burgundy SUV. They sat half in the vehicle and half out, heads lowered in an exhaustion. Victor took a water bottle from a smaller cooler in the back seat, twisted off the cap and handed it to Lynn. She nodded and drank half the bottle in a single go. Victor took one for himself and dragged it several times across his forehead and the back of his neck. In the front passenger side, Carmine Marl drank from a flask.

Lynn raised her eyebrows. "What are you doing?"

He took another pull from the flask and let out a hiss of relief. "This has my nerves on end."

"You should be drinking water," she noted and took another sip from her bottle.

Carmine tossed his flask on the dash. "Let's go."

They investigated the next leg of the tent city. More sleeping, fallen angels. More filth. Despair. Their shoes, pants, and skin fused together with the swirling dust as they probed every red-eyed junky and unsettled spirit, all still locked inside their world-war brains. This area of the community had the benefit of being more spread out, giving them time to regain some composure before continuing to the next hopeless encounter. All the while, the sun did not relent in its mission to kill them with its life-giving rays.

Lynn held her water bottle to her temple. "Can we slow down? Getting a little dizzy."

"On second thought, Evelyn, maybe you should wait in the car," Carmine suggested.

"Hey!" Victor hollered. "Think we have something."

He stood over a massive woman in a moldy blue tank top that covered little, save her rolling breasts and a spool of fat. Most of her hair had fallen out and skin cancer had blasted her nose apart in disgusting divisions of rosy pink. She placed the twenty-dollar bill Victor gave her into a plastic Hello Kitty purse on her blanket.

"Tell them about Mister Serious," Victor instructed.

She sized Carmine and Lynn up for a moment. Her stunning green eyes belied the rest of her physical configuration, the last piece of beauty life hadn't taken from her. "He got black hair, handsome guy, wears a leather jacket—"

"That's Axel!" Carmine winced in pain at his excitement. "Where—is he out here?"

"Dying by the creek," the woman said, in a croaking voice. "Code 17, OD'ing. I think someone went for help but nobody gets help out here. Creek's back through those trees."

"*Fuck!* Run!" Carmine hurried around the woman and scrambled down a hill through thinning oak trees. Victor and Lynn followed but soon outpaced him, rushing down towards a mossy slash in the earth where water had once run. A dark-haired man in a leather jacket lay on a bedroll. His eyes were watery slits. Bubbles formed at his lips.

"That's not dad." Lynn stopped to catch her breath. "Feel like I'm gonna puke," she whispered and braced herself on her knees. "Should we call for someone?"

"We aren't here for this," Carmine replied, blue eyes transfixed on the man writhing on the bedroll. "That's Axel's jacket, for sure."

Lynn glimpsed the inverted cross symbol of the clergy on the jacket shoulder. As she leaned in to see better, she staggered and brought her hand to her mouth. "Having heatstroke or something."

Carmine caught her and took the water bottle before it fell. "Hold on," he instructed. She lazily brought her arms around his waist. "Victor—take her back to the car."

Victor slipped his arm around Lynn. Blinking for focus, she looked back through her dropping eyelids. "You're . . . bleeding, uncle," she murmured.

Creation

Carmine checked his right abdomen. A wet patch, darker than sweat, seeped through the red silk. He grunted in self-disgust and buttoned up his cassock to cover the wound.

When Victor and Lynn at last disappeared through the trees, he stepped around some skull-shaped rocks to approach the junkie. "Hey!" he called. "Can you hear me? Can you wake up?"

He snapped his fingers. The man's eyes were now shut tight. His lips, blue. "Hey! Who gave you this jacket?"

The man's eyes cracked. "Jacket?"

"Yes!" Carmine stepped closer. "The jacket."

His eyes widened as recognition set in through the haze. "You're a cardinal . . . right?"

The roar of a pickup truck came from the trees beyond and a calvary of dust clouds blanketed the creek area. Carmine stumbled away from the man, retching on hot dust. The blue Dodge halted with a noisy whine, the driver door immediately banging open. A figure with black hair emerged and went into a headlong sprint.

"Axel!" shouted Carmine.

His brother froze, nearing slipping on the rocks underfoot. "Carmine? What're you doing here?"

"Gotta talk."

Ignoring this, Axel hurried to the man on the bedroll. He rolled him on his back, lifted his head and started squirting Narcan into each nostril. Axel checked for a pulse on his neck and dropped his head to the man's chest. "Come on, Charlie."

A pitying cloud blocked the sun and grayed the scene. Axel placed his hands atop Charlie's chest and pushed rhythmically. Axel's dark eyes widened, a man twisting through an unsolvable labyrinth, more desperation at every fork. "Come on!" he whispered.

Charlie let out a rattling cough and turned sideways, absently pushing Axel away. Subdued, Carmine watched as his brother stood. For a change, Axel's skin had a healthy hue. His polo had a community services logo over the heart. He took a white band from his pocket and pulled back his black wash of hair. His handsome face was raw and without laugh lines.

The Marl brothers faced each other, antitheses in every way.

"Water?" Carmine held up Lynn's half-finished bottle.

Charlie scooted back into the dirt, crumpling his bedroll. A trail of blurry blue and red tattoos traveled from his hairline down behind his ear and across his throat.

Axel looked over. "Saint Tobias Hospital?"

Charlie peered through his own private fog. The sun returned and ignited the gloom. "Not going to the ER again."

"That's stupid," Axel scolded.

A couple of homeless men emerged from the trees. Both wore ratty backpacks and one carried a large thermos. Charlie clearly recognized them but said nothing. Axel picked up the Narcan spray and handed it to them. After a brief discussion, he left them. As he walked by, Carmine lifted the water bottle again. Axel considered it a moment and shook his head. "Thanks, I have something." He ducked inside his truck's cabin and pulled out a soda, which he directly gulped down.

Carmine watched over him with pained amusement. "Resurrecting junkies now? Instead of being one."

"Why're you here?" Axel tossed his empty soda bottle into the truck bed. "It's too late to be my brother, if that's what this is. I'm not being abandoned again, now that I have shit together."

"These aren't your people."

Axel stepped onto the truck's sidebar. "You need the clergy and Lynn . . . needs Lynn."

Carmine straightened. "She's why I'm here actually. She had to go rest in the car. I'm really hoping it doesn't have anything to do with these oncologist bills I keep getting."

Axel stared at him. "*Oncologist?*"

"She won't tell me much."

The tension in Axel's eyes diminished to suspicion. "This better not be about the clergy."

Carmine snorted. "She wanted to ask about Mary's diagnosis. Her mother's medical history and such, I assume, because of . . . what she's going through now, you see."

Axel jumped into his truck. "Get in. You parked far from here?"

"We're beneath the overpass."

They had been on the road for nearly an hour. The SUV's listing around the hillside roads brought Axel awake. He blinked in pain, coughing, trying to regain his whereabouts. The seatbelt held him fast, but he managed to twist around enough to see his zip-tied wrists.

"Sorry for the sleeper hold," said Victor, eyes keen on the snaking road.

Sitting in the passenger side, Carmine closed a book on his lap. The inverted cross blazed in silver on the black leather. "We still have water if you'd like to rest peacefully like Lynn."

Lynn had her head against the window. A thread of drool slid from her mouth to her chin. Her wrists had been zip-tied as well.

Creation

"Evelyn!" Axel shouted. "Baby! Wake up!"

"Depressants," Carmine explained. "Quiet down. Don't worry. She doesn't have cancer. At least, I don't think she has."

"Fuck you. Let us out!" Axel kicked Victor's seat and jarred him.

The SUV swerved and Victor fought to recover the wheel. "Knock that shit off!" He shot a quick glance to Carmine. "Can we ether him?"

Carmine Marl peered back in icy solemnity. "He doesn't want us to crash, and he's never seen a papal conclave. He'll behave."

Axel looked down wearily and shook his head. "So, Pope Raven must be gone." He rested his temple against the window, face flushed with subterranean rage. "And you'll finally get the credit you deserve."

"Our family will."

"Bullshit," Axel snapped. "You're living a fever dream—"

"This is more than dream!" Carmine jerked around in his seat. "I receive phone calls from *Him*. Did you ever have that? Ever? In the whole time you prayed to our Lord? You chose your pills over everything."

"I did. That's true." Axel looked at Lynn with searching eyes. "I missed a lot. The little girl who I always fought to get back to . . . she's a woman who ghosts me now."

Carmine turned his eyes back to the passing trees, gathering shadows. "Family is fate. If either of you understood that, this trip would've been easier."

"I found my higher power," said Axel, shutting his eyes. "Know what it is?"

"No."

He opened his eyes again. "The moon. It's always there for me in the dark."

"Quaint," said Victor.

"Sacrilege." Carmine folded his hands over his book.

"Thanks," Axel replied. "That's the thing though, isn't it? Higher powers could be just about anything. You only have to find one first."

Carmine remained unfazed. "What you seek finds you, not the other way around."

"There it is," said Victor, pointing to a diseased stretch of wilderness ahead. "The Garden."

"Carmine," said Axel, straightening in his seat. "Please don't do this."

His brother's cellphone rang.

"It's *Him*. Isn't it?"

Carmine answered the phone, calmly, with reverence and dread. The short conversation rendered him speechless after it ended. He stared at the phone's dead screen for several minutes. Any sparkle remaining in his blue eyes had extinguished.

Carmine demanded a few minutes alone outside with his whiskey. Victor and Axel waited in the quiet SUV, while Lynn mumbled in sleep.

Then, abruptly, Carmine tossed the flask into the dead trees and returned.

Victor got out and opened the passenger door. As he stripped off the seatbelt, Axel drove his forehead down. The cartilage in Victor's nose ruptured and he wheeled back. Axel threw him aside and waddled up the steep hill, hands still bound.

Carmine propped Lynn up on her feet. Her head hung and body swayed.

Victor retrieved a bowie knife from his pocket. He flung scarlet from his fingers and started up the hill, knife lifted, eyes blinking for purchase.

"Don't kill him," Carmine warned.

"Not gonna," Victor snapped. "Just come down—okay?"

Axel rushed into the half bald trees, ducking beneath a smoke tarnished sign: FORGE BOTANICAL GARDENS.

"Everything's burnt here," Lynn remarked with a drunken lilt.

"Arsonists, sweetheart, years ago." Carmine led her toward the mist and dead trees. "Let's go find your dad."

Far ahead, Axel clumsily wove through the cindery landscape. Fallen trunks aimed at him, spears hunting behind the gauzy cloaks of vapor. In the distance, trees poked up like thin charred hairs on a bleached skull. Axel tripped and stumbled forward. Below, the soft earth was urn powder under his shoes. The sky, overcast and heavy with ancient clouds, formed a cauldron-lid that kept the forest scents pure enough to be tasted: bubbling rot—catamenial blood—sulfur.

Axel twisted around the elbow of a sturdy, yet savaged tree. A gnarled branch stopped his momentum and forced him into a neighboring collection of fallen trunks. As he attempted to recover, figures advanced from the hills above. Four-legged with black robes hanging from strawman bodies, their movements were a dance of voids through the spectral mist. Flashes of their metallic masks revealed little, save for the muffled gasps of bloodthirsty anticipation. In the fading light of dusk, Axel was surrounded by imps, angels, demons, all wearing horns aplenty.

Axel charged through a path of stones and black dirt that opened suddenly to a vast clearing. He continued his awkward sprint until he reached the center. And stopped. A knowing look of dismay surfaced in his

Creation

face. All around him, dripping red candles dotted the perimeter of the ceremony grounds with dreary gray orbs of light.

The masked figures raised from four legs onto two, a slow evolution. They fanned out through the clearing. Approaching from beyond, the beats of unfathomable drums followed with the repetitive dirge of harmonizing lutes and lyres. Axel backed farther into the mist and bumped into an altar of burnt and blistering wood. A crude spear rested across the top. At the end of the weapon, a sharpened rib bone had been affixed with black wires.

The insistent notes of the clergy grew louder.

Axel fought to pull his hands free—but a banded arm caught his midsection and dragged him back. In breathless seconds, he was surrounded by more masked figures. He struggled while they gently cut through his clothing with rusty scissors and undressed him.

More robed members flooded through the candlelight galaxy like children coming home at long last. At knife point, a naked man and woman, fronted the group.

A large gash bled from the man's rib cage.

Carmine.

The woman let out a confused sound of desperation.

Lynn.

Axel thrashed as they dragged him away from the altar to an upright wooden box, like a wide, standing coffin. They shut him inside and snapped several padlocks shut. The top of the box opened to the overcast sky and another rectangular view port had been cut in the front with an old English heading, GENESIS. He would be able to watch the ceremony from inside the box.

Axel slammed into the box without budging it.

The unseen musicians softened their volume as Carmine and Lynn stood before the altar. Mist pulled away and revealed a bracketed wall of meat cleavers and rusted saws.

"Let her go!" Axel wailed. "Evelyn!"

Lynn glanced around with dream-heavy eyes. "Where's my dad?"

Carmine's swollen gaze beheld the robed congregation. In a dry, emotionless tone, he said, "New members. You were searching for a new beginning. It has found you. Life, Death, both are birth into something strange and exciting, gifts to not be squandered . . . are you ready to give your name to the Lord?"

"Take our names," an unmasked group uttered in unison.

They made a line before two clergy members, one with a knife and one with a black chalice. The first in the queue was Victor. He leaned forward and stuck out his tongue. The knife went through cleanly. He jerked in pain and blood rained into the cup. Then, he was fitted with a silver demon mask.

Benjamin Kane Ethridge

Axel recognized the next man in line. "Charlie!"

The man spied him inside the box. "I didn't tell them nothing. I swear. You shouldn't have ever saved me, Ax."

Charlie offered his tongue for the knife, bled into the cup, and took the mask of a screaming imp.

Several others followed the process.

Lynn gasped with recognition. "Johnny? What are *you* doing here? Help me!"

"Mr. and Mrs. Carlson," said Carmine, his naked body glistening with sweat, the gash under his ribs a fiery grin. "As promised. For your devotion. Approach please, return to a marriage of bliss."

John Carlson looked down while his wife stared daggers at Lynn. After they bled into the chalice and were masked, the ceremony continued.

The clergy poured blood into Lynn's forced-open mouth. She vomited. Carmine accepted the chalice willingly. He too vomited.

Dozens more clergy flooded down from the trees. Hundreds. The rib spear was lifted off the altar. Whispers on the hidden mouths, repeating, over and over: *sanguis et familia ad dominum.*

"Stop this!" Axel sobbed. "Someone, stop this!"

Carmine looked to him. "I didn't know He would ask this."

The ceremony progressed over Axel's screams.

They started with Lynn.

Taking turns. Each time, the rib piercing her flesh with surreal lethality. Stomach, breasts, legs hemorrhaging, Lynn fought them. She blubbered at the sound of her father's shrieks. She ran for the trees, knocked over candles, but they dragged her back. Taking her turn, Mrs. Carlson speared Lynn in the throat. She fell and bled out before many of the others had a chance. The spear was cast down to the earth beside her, as ceremony required.

Shock overtook Axel. He could only stare from the viewport, lips trembling and eyes peeled back in madness.

Carmine stood like a troubled statue that knew storms would one day pull it down to rubble. Chanting with fervor, the clergy tore him open with bare hands, starting at his gash. With an animated joy, they pulled his innards free, gleefully ripped away lungs, unearthed his heart with moaning exhilaration. Strangely, Carmine wept loudly even after they stomped the dense red organ underfoot.

With the cleavers and saws, the clergy dismembered Carmine and Evelyn Marl. Each clergy collected a body part and carefully dropped pieces into the top of the wooden box with Axel. Viscera showered down on him. He winced as Lynn's leg struck his face, and gasped as a Carmine's gaping mouth glanced his shoulder with bloody teeth. Piece by piece, the raw

Creation

human materials filled the emptiness of the box and embraced Axel's body like a womb.

After they finished, there was silence. He was left alone for several hours.

Time ceased.

Memories followed the rhythmic music.

Tears comingled with blood and tissues.

The faces of his only family stared with deceased, yet eager eyes.

"I'm sorry," he whimpered. "Nothing's left. Nothing anymore."

Then the pain and the horror ended, as it does, without formality. The padlocks unsnapped and the box opened on its wheezing hinges. The viscera tumbled out in perfect unison, old stock, refuse from a different life. Axel stumbled forward in bloody nakedness. In the clearing, thousands of clergy members now gathered.

With cloth rags, they cleaned him with freezing water flecked with bits of carbon and dirt. Axel watched with dull interest and made no attempt to run, even as they unbound his hands. They slid the robes of the pontiff over him. Painted his face bone white. On his head, he donned the miter hat.

A shrill voice announced Pope Renatus III.

The clouds parted and the moon bathed the clearing in skeletal, holy light. Among the crowd, the repetitive music fell away to a pair of acoustic guitars playing a series of flowering newborn notes. Every tree glistened with invigorated tar and pitch. Onyx leaves budded with new form and shadowy intentions. Ravens lit on branches.

A clergyman wearing a golden angel mask handed Axel a cellphone. It took him a moment to remember how to move. With shaking hands, he finally brought it to his ear.

The burning voice sounded relieved. Pleased.

Shining brighter, the moon gripped the entire garden in its light.

"*You are born new. Be content, my child, for I have never left you. And never will.*"

About the Editors and Introducer

A Nameless Editor was the sole mastermind behind this anthology. Their identity, whereabouts, or publishing history are currently unknown.

Mark C. Scioneaux is a Bram Stoker Award® nominated editor and author. He was allowed to help on this anthology by A Nameless Editor, though begrudgingly.

Ash Briscoe is a published photographer, makeup artist, and business owner, living in Southern California. Within the Ghost community she's known for photographing actors associated with Ghost's music videos, creating her own Ghost-inspired music videos and shoots, and running fun social media challenges for Ghost fans. You can find Ash on IG/TikTok as Fauxbias.Forge.

About the Authors

Robert Bagnall was born in Bedford, England, in 1970. He has written for the BBC, daily and Sunday newspapers, and government ministers. He is the author of the sci-fi thriller *2084—The Meschera Bandwidth*, and the anthology *24 0s & a 2*, which collects 24 of his sixty-odd published stories. Both are available from Amazon. He can be contacted via his blog at meschera.blogspot.com.

Michael Balletti lives in New Jersey. His work has appeared in *Full Moon Chronicles, Tall Tale TV, Novel Noctule, Lovecraftiana,* and *Theme of Absence*, among others. You can find him at www.michaelballetti.com.

Matthew M. Bartlett is the author of *Gateways to Abomination, Where Night Cowers*, and other books of supernatural horror. His short stories have appeared in a variety of anthologies and journals, including *Forbidden Futures, Vastarien, Year's Best Weird Fiction Vol. 3*, and *Ashes & Entropy*. He has recorded two full-length records and several 45s for Cadabra Records. His current ongoing project is a chapbook subscription service entitled the *WXXT Program Guide*. He lives in Western Massachusetts with his wife Katie Saulnier and their cats Peachpie and Larry.

Everett C. Baudean, Esq. makes his literary debut in *Tales from the Clergy*, published by October Nights Press. As an attorney and firearm instructor, Everett's publication history to date has been solely nonfiction articles for legal and gun training publications. However, as a lifelong nerd, fantasy enthusiast, and heavy metal fan, he is excited to be part of this collection with his first published work of fiction. He currently resides in Baton Rouge, Louisiana with his wife, Lauren.

Lauren Bolger lives in a suburb near Chicago with her spouse and two kids. She's a Horror writer and a drummer. Ghost is her favorite band. Her debut novel *Kill Radio* was published in April 2023 with Malarkey Books, and she has short fiction forthcoming in *The Magazine of Fantasy and Science Fiction*. Info on other past and forthcoming work or events can be found at www.laurenbolger.com.

M. Wesley Corie II makes his literary debut in *Tales from the Clergy*, published by October Nights Press. Wesley is a lifelong lover of horror and all things occult. He is a professional project manager and currently resides in Baton Rouge, Louisiana with his wife, Jennifer, and two children, Liesel and Emil.

David Costa was born in the beautiful city of Lisbon where he grew up daydreaming about knights and dragons. Throughout his life he kept nurturing his love for books, movies, and videogames, and after becoming a researcher in the field of health psychology he decided to pursue his dream of becoming a writer. When he is not working on his next novel, he can be found glued to a screen, working out, or playing electric guitar.

Benjamin Kane Ethridge is the multiple nominated and Bram Stoker Award® winning author of fantasy and horror novels since 2010. You can learn more about Benjamin on Wikipedia and at his website www.bkebooks.com.

Mackenzie Hurlbert is a New England horror writer with publications in *Coffin Bell, Not One of Us, Written Tales: Horror, The CT Literary Anthology*, and *Flash Fiction Magazine*. She enjoys getting lost in the woods and is an avid collector of Pez dispensers and cool-looking rocks.

To read more of her work, visit her website at www.mackenziehurlbert.com.

Pedro Iniguez is a speculative fiction writer and painter from Los Angeles, California. His fiction and poetry has appeared in *Nightmare Magazine, Shortwave Magazine, Worlds of Possibility, Speculative Fiction for Dreamers, Star*Line, Space & Time Magazine,* and *Tiny Nightmares,* among others. He can be found at www.pedroiniguezauthor.com.

Jo Kaplan is the author of *It Will Just Be Us* and *When the Night Bells Ring.* Her short stories have appeared in *Fireside Quarterly, Black Static, Nightmare Magazine, Vastarien, Horror Library, Nightscript,* and anthologies such as *Haunted Nights* edited by Ellen Datlow and Lisa Morton, *The Hideous Book of Hidden Horrors, Chromophobia,* and *Into the Forest: Tales of the Baba Yaga.* She is the co-chair of the HWA LA chapter and teaches English and creative writing at Glendale Community College. Find more at www.jo-kaplan.com.

Vivian Kasley hails from the land of the strange and unusual, Florida! She's a writer of short stories and poetry. Some of her street cred includes Brigids Gate Press, Vastarien, Ghost Orchid Press, Death's Head Press, and poetry in Black Spot Books inaugural women in horror poetry showcase: *Under Her Skin.* She definitely has more in the works, including her first collection. When not writing or subbing at the local middle school, she spends time reading in bubble baths, snuggling her rescue animals, going on adventures with her partner, and searching for seashells and treasure along the beach.

Michael Paige has been featured in literary magazines such as *The Furious Gazelle* and *The Scarlet Leaf Review* as well as anthologies for Savage Realms Press, Crimson Pinnacle Press, Ill-Advised Records (*The Dark Door Issue #2*), a charity anthology coming through the Great Lakes Horror Anthology (GLAHW), as well as Volume 1 of the *Chilling Tales for Dark Nights Anthology.* And now, the *Tales from the Clergy* anthology. Find more at www.michaelpaigeblog.wordpress.com.

Colt Skinner is a typical Canadian dad. He spends his days giving up his seat on the bus and holding open doors for strangers, but while he's being polite, he is also daydreaming about monsters, serial killers and what it would feel like to be drawn and quartered. Colt has been writing terrifying tales ever since he was a young boy growing up on a goat farm in Bastard Township, Ontario, and in Fall 2023 he will be publishing his first novel, *The God Damn Dead.*

Brian J. Smith has been featured in numerous anthologies, e-zines and magazines in both the mystery and horror genres. *Dark Avenues*, *The Tuckers*, and *Three O'Clock* can be found on Kindle and available in paperback. His second novel, *Consuming Darkness,* was published on Godless.com and published in paperback. His third book *Abbie's Wrath* was published by Alien Buddha Press. He resides in southeastern Ohio, has too many books and buys more, and doesn't drink enough coffee. He is an affiliate member of The Horror Authors Guild and can be found on Facebook, Twitter, and Instagram.

Doris V. Sutherland is a UK-based novelist, scriptwriter, and nonfiction author. Her personal work includes the creator-owned comic series *Midnight Widows*; she has also written licensed tie-in fiction for Doctor Who, Survivors, and The Omega Factor. Her nonfiction writing has been published by Liverpool University Press, Amazing Stories, 2000AD.com, Mind's Eye Publications, Belladonna Magazine and the multi-Eisner Award-winning Women Write About Comics, while her scriptwriting clients include BBC Sounds and Big Finish Productions. The horror genre is something of an obsession for her, and she was proud to take part in this melding of fictional fear and musical morbidity.

David D. West lives and teaches in the Pacific Northwest. The dark, gloomy atmosphere of the region makes its way into all of his writing, creating vivid worlds with rich descriptions that pull readers in. His work has previously been published through Black Hare Press, Sans Press, and October Nights Press. When he is not teaching or writing, he is exploring the gray beaches and dark forests of southwest Washington with his wife, son, and their dog, Buster. Find him on Twitter and Instagram, or his website, www.davidwestwrites.wixsite.com/home.

Printed in Great Britain
by Amazon